was born in Co. Kildar serious
Hunting and Fishing r little
education at the hands y came
from a Somerset family and her mother, a poetess, was the author of "The Songs of the Glens of Antrim". Molly Keane's interests when young were "hunting and horses and having a good time"; she began vriting only as a means of supplementing her dress allowance, and hose the pseudonym M. J. Farrell "to hide my literary side from my porting friends". She wrote her first novel, *The Knight of the Cheerful ountenance*, at the age of seventeen.

As M. J. Farrell, Molly Keane published ten novels between 1928 nd 1952: *Young Entry* (1928), *Taking Chances* (1929), *Mad Puppetstown* (1931), *Conversation Piece* (1932), *Devoted Ladies* (1934), *Full House* 1935), *The Rising Tide* (1937), *Two Days in Aragon* (1941), *Loving Vithout Tears* (1951) and *Treasure Hunt* (1952). All of these are now published by Virago. She was also a successful playwright, of whom James Agate said "I would back this impish writer to hold her own against Noel Coward himself." Her plays with John Perry, always directed by John Gielgud include *Spring Meeting* (1938), *Ducks and Drakes* (1942), *Treasure Hunt* (1949) and *Dazzling Prospect* (1961).

The tragic death of her husband at the age of thirty-six stopped her writing for many years. It was not until 1981 that another novel – *Good Behaviour* – was published, this time under her real name. *Time after Time* appeared in 1983, *Loving and Giving* was published in 1988. Her cookery book, *Nursery Cooking*, was published in 1985. Molly Keane has two daughters and lives in Co. Waterford.

0860 688 003 1 547 24

VIRAGO
MODERN
CLASSIC

NUMBER

356

Molly Keane

(M. J. Farrell)

TREASURE HUNT

WITH A NEW INTRODUCTION BY

DIRK BOGARDE

Published by VIRAGO PRESS Limited 1990
20–23 Mandela Street, Camden Town, London NW1 0HQ

Reprinted 1991

First published in Great Britain by William Collins 1952

A CIP catalogue record for this book is available from the British Library

Printed by Cox & Wyman Ltd, Reading, Berks

To

JOHN PERRY

with whom I wrote

the play

INTRODUCTION

IF YOU are presently holding your very first copy of a novel by Molly Keane, then you are indeed blessed. You are, of course, unaware at this moment that you are standing on the threshold of untold delights and splendours, quite apart from all the glorious fun that awaits you. Fun is one of Mrs Keane's greatest gifts; mixed in with the very gentlest of seasonings; malice smothered with charm. Oh! Indeed. There is malice here; but you'll hardly know it, it's like garlic in a properly cooked dish. Enhancing the flavour, never intruding brutally, sharpening your palate for what is to come.

You will also be entering into an almost lost, practically forgotten world from which, eventually, you will emerge satiated by its pleasures and, I can only imagine, astonished to think that there ever was such a dotty place, and that it could exist. But exist it did. Such a world there was and, to some extent (hanging on by mere threads almost) such a world yet exists, in small pockets only, among the bogs and fogs of that desperately sad and troubled Ireland.

Mrs Keane is well aware of this, she is a part of it, and always has been. She is well aware today of what once was, and is now lost, and she is adept indeed at total recall. For today's reader (you), she sets down the oddities of speech, of place, of behaviour and of a pattern of life which died almost completely in 1939. In her words the twenties and the thirties come back to life again—they are vibrant, brilliant, sparkling, filled with glorious eccentrics so soon doomed to perish, almost entirely, for the rest of time. There is elegance, cruelty, mischief, beauty and the most acute observation of her fellows: nothing is false. All is as it was and indeed, as I have said, as it very occasionally still remains. The world of Molly Keane. Her world is observed with a clear, shrewd, cool eye.

Presupposing that this *is* your first voyage of discovery, it is essential that I offer you a little of the author's background. So much has already been written about it that I shall merely give you the barest facts and content myself, and you, with those.

For many years Molly Keane wrote under the pseudonym of M. J. Farrell (a name she cheerfully took from a public house) for family reasons. Writing books, especially for a woman, was not considered to be "quite the thing" in those early days, especially in the "set" in which she spent her entire youth; the huntin' and shootin' (but above all the huntin') gentry of that exceptional race—the Anglo-Irish. They were a peculiar lot: arrogant, idle, rich, impoverished, horse-mad, snobs, inbred, wild and uninhibited, almost entirely isolated in their class and their soggy green land. Europe and, for that matter, England were vaguely "over there", and that meant a beastly, if not dangerous, voyage across the sea. That voyage was not a welcome idea and was taken only under great pressure.

The Anglo-Irish preferred to remain in their

crumbling mansions in the mists, living for the next "meet", the next cry of a horn, the next sound of baying hounds. Their lives were ruled almost entirely by the "bullfinches", spinneys, copses, and plough, the dreaded wire in the hedges, and the stink of wet dogs, the smell of Proparts Leather Polish, the cut of a pair of breeches, the shine on a boot. Their reading matter, if they ever read anything, was *The Field, Country Life* and, of course, *Horse and Hound*. Occasionally they had a look at *Surtees*.

That was all Above Stairs. They were a little more odd below. Molly Keane wrote her very first book to augment her slim dress allowance at the age of seventeen. It was called, *The Knight of the Cheerful Countenance*. It was a success. She went on to write ten more novels and a few plays between 1928 and 1952, all of them greatly appreciated by an unknowing readership who thought that Farrell was a regular huntin' fella. Then tragedy struck. Her beloved husband died, she put aside her pen, and only picked it up again in 1981 to write what was to become her masterpiece *Good Behaviour*. This caused such a clamour of delight and awe, particularly in a whole new generation of readers who had missed out on her work before, that she was instantly back, as she might say, "in the saddle again". And in full command.

A chat show host who spent time with Molly Keane told me that, as far as he was concerned, people were "either drains, sapping your energy, or else radiators warming you to the centre of your being". Mrs Keane, he reckoned, was the most glorious radiator he had ever encountered. I reckon he was right. However, beneath the brilliant and laughing surface lies a shrewd, wise and clever mind. A mind perfectly capable of intense and emotional feeling, aware of frailties and faults, and which all the time is tirelessly, almost relentlessly, assessing and analysing character. She sets everything she finds on the page before you; should you miss one little subtlety, do not worry. You will discover a hundred others to delight you.

Treasure Hunt is, perhaps, not Molly Keane's greatest book. It started life as a play, and as a play it worked prodigiously well. She adapted it into a novel, rather than the other way around, as is usually the case. In spite of her clever mending, the shape of the play remains and is an added pleasure in a way, because it was, according to one of the best newspapers "the most diverting treasure hunt the stage has shown us for a very long time". I saw it myself, all those years ago (1949 to be exact), and have never forgotten the sheer hysteria of that audience before a cast of dotty, beguiling grotesques. The play was as full of stars as the heavens, and a British audience, exhausted, despondent, rationed, taxed and still recovering from a savage war with all its terrors and deprivations, welcomed it with roars of delight. It ran for a year, a record now and a greater record then. Alas! Almost all of that rollicking cast have fallen from the bough: Sybil Thorndike as the amazing Aunt Anna Rose; Irene Brown as the splendid Mrs Cleghorn-Thomas; Alan Webb as Hercules; Milo O'Shea as the houseboy . . . These, and many others who glittered and gave life to *Treasure Hunt* are no more.

Anne Leon, who played the original "Veronica" is, mercifully, still with us, and when I asked her about the show she cried out in delight:

"Oh! What joy it was, every single performance, and what a dear little darling Molly was. So sweet, so funny, so gentle with us all, but, and it's a *big* but, she was on the ball all the time and very much in evidence. Golly! How we all loved her. *How* we laughed."

"Dear little darling Molly" is as sharp as a box of knives, and her work is here to prove it.

Has the work changed, you may ask, since her first effort at seventeen? No, frankly. Hardly at all. The lustre and detail are all there, only the caution of experience, the wisdom of age, the understanding of writing, of prose, of comedy-timing, and, above all, of tragedy and sadness, have given the works an added force. But the born writer who is Molly Keane has been altered relatively little by personal sadness and the rearing of a family. The long silence which she had to endure seems to have made her stronger, and she is restored to us quite intact, as if, in fact, she had never been away.

Now to the story of *Treasure Hunt*. All Mrs Keane's ingredients are to hand: the below-stairs staff, who open the book/play, all barking mad as apparently befits an Anglo-Irish household; the house itself, a great looming mansion spared from fire during the Troubles and now slowly crumbling into ruin; the owners, now impoverished by war and the almost Civil War they have had to endure, and almost as deranged as their staff. Consider ageing relatives living on, behaving just as they always have, that is to say, as children. And pretty naughty children at that. The chief character really is as mad as could be—beloved, funny, absolutely barmy Aunt Anna Rose who spends most of her time in a sedan chair, happily convinced that she is on the Orient Express and that she is on her way to glorious places. She also has a "terrible secret", which she doesn't reveal until Mrs Keane thinks it wise for her to do so. And there is a lost cache of jewels, the subject of the treasure hunt, of course, and English Paying Guests which the family are forced to entertain in order to make ends meet in the crumbling and almost unplumbed great house.

And so we have the cast and the setting. What Mrs Keane does with them is nothing short of miraculous. As I have said earlier, she kept a packed theatre crying with joy and laughter for a year. I see no reason why she should be less entertaining and wickedly funny for you for years to come. You have in your hands, at a reasonable price, the work of a Master Writer, although I am pretty sure that she'd scoff at such a high falutin' description of herself. But go ahead: step into wonderland and you'll see that I am right.

Dirk Bogarde, London, 1990

1

The armoured cat's face of the house withheld itself entirely from the afternoon—the house was high and square, built of stone blocks, rough cut like fish scales, but the cut stone round all the windows fine as skin. The windows stared hollow-paned, stony-browed, into afternoon. They had stared into about two hundred September afternoons, so what was there different about this one?

The sun struck into the cold face of the house, compelling from it an unwilling beneficence; it poured over the great flat width of limestone that bridged the area opposite the hall door; five cut stone steps, steps shallow and unostentatious, with a pretty low curve of wall, led up to this kind space; children and drunks protected from the drop to the area below by elegant iron railings, tidy as hairpins in a box. Over the narrow door the family arms, Leda and her Swan, were warmed by the sun in their stone embraces. The hall door was open. The sun poured through, spreading inwards. There was no movement anywhere at all. The house was empty. In the absolute quietness a robin, sheltering somewhere in the box hedges that buttressed the front of the area, sung and stopped. Empty glasses were set down on the low stone wall of the steps, and any quantity of freshly drawn champagne corks lay about on the gravel among the wheel tracks of cars that had come and turned and gone away to-day.

Within the hall a fire burned in its high, basket grate, fighting for its life against the sunlight. In its heat and that of the sun a tremendous smell of flowers filled the air. It plunged down to the hollow of the house and, warming itself there, floated upwards again in oily drifts —chrysanthemums were the base of the smell, but stephanotis and lilies and roses defeated this country, turpentine breath. For all the feel of being within a great tent or bell of scent, there was not a flower to be seen except, lying on a table, one bridesmaid's sheaf of red carnations, dozens and dozens of carnations sinking against one another and into one another like feathers on a great bird, and stretched out vibrant on florist's wire. It lay in shadow on the table, the air coloured red near it and the sun lying down like a dog on the steps of the stairs behind it.

* * * * *

From the back of the house the silence was broken by the sound of running steps, loud and insistent in their haste—someone in a ferment of hurrying—something to be done against time. One of the mahogany doors on either side of the stairs burst open and a little man ran in, seized the sheaf of flowers in his arms and turned to hurry out again. He was a little, elfish creature, very slight, prettily sunburnt, with grey hair that curled like a drake's tail at the back of his neck. He was as well made as a grey wagtail and looked as neat and clean. He was exquisitely dressed for royal Ascot or a wedding, and when he took up the great bunch of flowers the air of the grand gala about him was quite irresistible. The sheaf lay across his arm and as he looked down to make sure he was not crushing any of the flowers, pleasure and satisfaction suffused his whole attitude and shone from his great big (slightly blood-shot) blue eyes. He might have been just off to any romantic assignment. Even his age—he was spryly, skippingly sixty-eight—did not forbid the idea, for there was something healthy and living and sweet about him in his wedding suit which had so obviously been composed for him by the hand of a great master. The only original notes, which clashed so resoundingly as to be almost pleasing, worn by this neat and well-to-do piece of perfection, were a pair of black, rubber gumboots pulled on over his striped trousers. They were honestly needed, too, for they shone with wet above the ankles.

" Master Hercules—Master Hercules, weren't you well, Master Hercules? " a voice came calling up the passage behind him.

" Yes. Coming, Beebee, coming." He turned to meet her—a mouse-like, wispy devotee, anxious and loving, dressed in a black coat with monkey fur and a very jaunty dot of a black hat sitting far away from her long, worried face on the awful top of a permanent wave.

" Oh, Master Hercules, you've run yourself into a perfect fever," she said reproachfully. " What happened to you at all? I thought you were sick when I saw you leave the church."

" Couldn't see my flowers anywhere," he explained, " nearly dotty looking for them and a crick in my neck peering round—a bit awkward to turn right round in church, isn't it? Then it just flashed into my mind I'd put 'em down here so everyone could see them, and I hopped it back by the short cut, 'fraid they'd miss the finale."

" Sir Rockerick'll wait for us," she said, and holding the door open, she followed him out.

A staircase mounted strictly in a wide, single flight of steps which floated apart underneath a window, dividing itself into two exactly similar flights that climbed separately, flight beside flight, to the top of the house, gracious and superbly unnecessary.

On either side of the stair foot mahogany doors opened into the back part of the house. On the right and left of the hall door two immensely high windows looked south-west. Six panes in each half window, their narrow, white slats marking a definite distance between room and outdoors. Through these windows everything was exquisitely, justly, far; not floating near and oppressive as through plate-glass.

Nature's lush hand was curiously absent in the outlook. Beyond the gravel sweep groups of trees grew in a field of particularly dark grass. The trees did not enclose the house, but had been planted at a distance which made their size and spread in relation to the house as right and exact as the relation of house to house in a street. Even the sheep fed in undisturbed, formal wreaths on the black-green grass. A slight, bluish mist, lolling distantly, suggested water, and in the later afternoon, movement and sound of water birds suggested quite a lot of water, so did two narrowly flowing stone bridges over which the avenue (in Ireland always the avenue) approached the house and disappeared towards unseen gates. There was not too much beauty to apprehend, to swallow all at once. The house, for the sake of its south-western aspect, had turned its back on mountains as well as water; only a certain sharpness reminded one of mountain airs. Looking over the dark, park-like demesne, fields, only the round, bright cheeks of empty cornfields showed between the beech trees and the oaks.

The hall was by no means a room to sit in—all its furniture was strictly that of an entrance hall—Sheraton half-hoop tables, a glass-fronted mahogany cabinet thin as a knife blade against the wall, rigid Empire sofas, their long bolsters rocks of good style and proportion. On the walls a flock paper had turned from peony to a warm tomato red, and all the portraits of ancestors and race horses hung still in their proper places; there was no peony square to show where a sale had been made; indeed, nowhere was there any sign of picturesque Irish poverty.

Half an hour after the little gentleman and his follower had left the hall the house still kept its strange, soundless holiday. Not even a dog stirred or spoke. The two baskets on each side of the fire were empty. No draught lifted the smell of flowers or moved the day's light dust that edged the tables nearest to the fire. The late September sun poured in with the priggish benignity of a fine afternoon succeeding a terrible morning. The four closed doors waited for the people of the house to return.

They came back quietly yet hurriedly, entering the hall from the back part as the two first comers had done —three servants, dressed in their best. The anxious one with the tiny hat, then another who swam into the room with authority and splendour, a well kept silver fox fur on her dark grey coat, double-strapped shoes on her feet

—she was the best cook in the countryside and knew it well. Then there was a young manservant of the kind which never quite outgrows being a boy. However much responsibility he may achieve he never achieves stateliness, or that kindly, worldly helpfulness of the good butler. Still in his belted mackintosh, he whistled now as he hurried across the room to the fire.

"Willy!" The anxious one reproached him, a suggestion of untold ceremony in her voice. "Hurry up, hurry on till we straighten the drawing-room before the cars get back from the church."

They moved across the hall, all three in a body, and paused before the door of the drawing-room. The only possible gesture was to fling it open, disclosing God knows what of bridal flowers, tables covered in presents of glass, china, leather; one felt silver cardboard bells were swinging silently, and great September arrangements of pink Belladonna lilies and rusty purple leaves matched against each other; across the room there would be lesser affairs of dahlias, rich michaelmas daisies, lavish and without prudery. But it was before the lilies that a bride must stand, with her groom of course, and her train wound flat about her feet like a water lily leaf or a python's head on the floor. . . .

The pause outside the door developed into a hesitation before the confident woman in the fox fur threw it open. The scent of flowers met them in a warm rush like the room of the nursing home's spoiled darling at visiting hour. But again there were no flowers to be seen, only this evaporating ghost of them. Like the hall, the drawing-room was as truly designed as any other eighteenth century room, the circle within the square, height the fair reply to width, windows uninspiringly right, decorations light and brief, fireplace plain, plaqueless marble, but pretty in size as a bare birch tree is.

Within this shell four generations had struggled to obliterate each other's efforts at furnishings and decorations, and to-day the outstanding features were Edward VII and George V. The good, red carpet, clear as an apple in colour and as thick and unworn still as the day it arrived from Waring & Gillow, belonged without doubt to the early 1900's. So did the solid, white chintzes with their garlands of red and grey leaves, so did the muslin cushion covers with their fresh, fluted frills and embroidered shamrocks. Some aunt of the date had started the idea of lavender in long, thin bolsters sewn to the backs of the cushions. No doubt the hammered copper half-copula over the basket grate had been a gentleman's contribution together with a good representative of the fender known as clubhammered; copper flowers on its black ironwork supports went very nicely with the copula. There were no pelmets on the windows —the curtains belonged to the nineteen-twenties. They were net and rep and silk and as sea a blue as baby blue is blue. Happily nowhere else in the room was this brave note of colour followed up. But the gay gramophone-playing twenties was again manifest in a large piece of Lalique glass, its opalescent glamour pathetic as an unfashionable tart, or the record of a tune called "Whispering."

The wallpaper was white moiré and closely covered in pictures all hung very high and practically no two at the same level. Here and there between the pictures, large and small plates from what was left of a blue, fish-scale Worcester dinner service hung on wires that looked as fine as cotton. Almost all the pieces of furniture in the room were collector's pieces, in beautiful order, deeply polished, their glass doors bright and clear as water—thin, green water faintly altering the colours of the china and glass massed within. Through a Victorian glass-topped table one looked down into a perfect pudding of Battersea enamel boxes, little hearts and lozenges and oblongs, puce and white and apple green.

The whole countenance of the room was warm with the affection of years; nothing had been entirely changed though changes had been made. Quite certainly it was not a party room or a room for the ladies of the house. Their men have always sat here with them. Here in the deep chairs, their backs faintly stained with hair oil. Piles of Racing Calendars and copies of the *Field* almost outnumbered the *Tatler* and the *Queen*; surgical instruments for pipes and a piece of wool embroidery lay side by side on a spinet. This was the room for the largest radio and the best fire. The men and women who lived here obviously liked to be together in a room facing south-west. Here they had quarrelled and made love, argued and made up, scolded and petted their children—beloved generations intolerable each to each.

The servants who now disturbed the quietness went busily round shutting the open windows, mending the fire, setting urgently to rights everything except the two mahogany hall chairs (Leda and the Swan, tangled in the family crest, going on nohow on their backs) which faced each other six feet nine (a coffin's length) apart in the middle of the room. The chairs were obviously out of their normal places and studiously ignored for lesser duties.

The cook in the fox fur still stood by herself. This was not her province, and only a day of extraordinary exception brought her into it. She stood as one who knows her own power, strong and slightly contemptuous of the other two, as though she waited for some comedy or drama to unfold itself for her grim amusement. The anxious woman, on her knees before the fire, spoke first: "Hurry up now, hurry up with them two chairs, Willy."

The young man gave the chairs a distracted, ignoring look: "I must bring up my tea tray first, Bridgid—it'll be no time till they are back from the church."

"And don't forget an extra place for Mr. Walsh. He'll be in to read the Will, I suppose," the cook put in succulently, turning the business side of grief about in her mouth.

Bridgid blew at the fire with little, whistling breaths. "It's not draughting right at all," she complained. "Oh, merciful God, wouldn't a fire go against you above all times on a smart occasion like a County funeral? Move back your two chairs, Willy, between the two windows of *your* hall where they come from."

"I'll not meddle them chairs and well you know the why."

She lost patience: "Ah, what ails you? Shift them quick now, boy, or I'll tell it out what I saw you at on this sad and holy day, with our dear friend lying in his last bed, heaped high in flowers, drenched down in tears."

He ignored the first part of her speech. Tears indeed! He took her up—"The champagne flowed to-day and champagne and tears never flew together."

"Indeed," said the cook sourly, "they drank the place dry."

"What matter?" Bridgid gave an indulgent laugh.

" There's always more where that came from. There's always plenty in this place."

" Plenty of everything," Willy conceded, " only petrol."

" Petrol, did you say? Petrol indeed "—the opening was irresistible—" 'twas petrol for your motor cycle I seen you pinching from the holy hearse to-day."

" Well "—he did not deny the charge but admitted it with slight pomposity, mechanical male to witless female—" motor propelled vehicles won't go on wind and water as you may have heard, Bridgid, and my cycle is the only reliable mechanical messenger in Ballyroden."

" Oh, listen to the big talk out of him and he wouldn't put the two chairs even back in their places." The cook paused as though waiting to put the final touch to a dish before she added: " Although it seems to me if fair's fair the two chairs is in Bridgid's drawing-room and by rights herself should shift them."

" Oh," Bridgid turned, stung, " put them back yourself so, since you're so nosy into other people's business."

" I would too," Mrs. Guidera remained standing like a rock, " if I'd met civility. I'm not so cowardly as some, listens to every old fairy tale and bad luck story."

" Oh, God between us and harm," Bridgid and Willy were both shocked. " Some things," he suggested bleakly, " are best left unspoken."

" Well "—she retained her crisp, queen pudding air—" thank God it's not my place to lay a hand on them. All I came out of my own nice clean kitchen to say was —lay an eggcup and spoon for my Mrs. Howard's tea. A fresh boiled egg never yet showed disrespect for a dear, dead brother and nothing goes to your heart like a lightly boiled egg in trouble."

"And what about my Master Hercules," Bridgid struck in with nervous insistence, "who always fancies a scrambled egg in trouble?"

Mrs. Guidera's voice was like something coming out of a mountain, something quite small coming out of something monumentally significant. "If them two hundred hens laid two eggs a day between the lot of them the shock of it would finish them."

They accepted this without comment. Only Willy added plaintively: "What about Miss Anna Rose—my pet—she'll need something very extra for her tea. Give her some nice little nicety."

"Chocolate cake is her favourite"—Mrs. Guidera ruminated, one saw the cake in her mind—"and I haven't a crumb of chocolate with all the new English residents clearing the delicacies out of our grocers' shops."

"Well, if that's all's troubling you," Willy said, "I'll give you a private little piece I have for myself—God love her, she'd want some little treat sometimes."

"Very well so, I must run." Mrs. Guidera spun round with the horrid speed of a bull, and as she left the room she suggested coldly: "Sir Philip and Miss Veronica won't want anything extra, I suppose?"

"Ah, no, they're hardy," Bridgid passed them over in a tolerant, materialistic way. They were Bores and Strong Bores, too. It was in her voice.

"Listen!" Willy held them all taut for a moment. "There's a car."

They listened:

"Are they back from the church?" they said. "Never

so soon? " they said. " And we in our best hats." They ran for it.

" Girls, girls." Willy tried to stay the panic. " Help me in with Miss Anna Rose's nest first. She'll have to get into her nest whatever "—but they left him, flying away to dress themselves in the correct garments in which to succour their Loves.

Alone, Willy whipped off his mackintosh, folding it into a kind of parcel as he walked across the hall. He opened the door of a cloakroom, a darling little room where the sun poured in; it was warm as a hot-air cupboard or a nursery fender. Lovely tweed coats hung here, mature and delicate with age, their colours pale as barley stacks or foxy as bracken. Some were over-checked faint green, and in some there was a continuous frail note of blue in coat after coat—as though such eyes were to be flattered. There must have been fifty years of coats hanging here, well-brushed and cared for. And then the hats—there were three ironwork Victorian hatstands crowned by them—great, brandishing, iron arms hung like a winter tree with birds—supple, thin felts and velours, soft as birds' breasts, and shallow, Lovat-coloured deer-stalkers and brown and white checked caps; and high on a shelf quite one hundred white boxes held more hats, hunting hats and town hats. Besides hats and coats and binoculars and shooting sticks and umbrellas there stood awkwardly and stupidly with the afternoon sun glaring in through its windows on the olive green leather buttoned with ivory buttons—a sedan chair. Its outside carriage work was perfect, its silver handles were bright, Leda and her Swan sprawled delicately on the doors. On the seat within lay folded neatly a very soft, very expensive, very modern green cashmere rug, neatly monogrammed.

Willy gave the sedan chair a hopeless look before he stuffed his mackintosh underneath a round, frilled ottoman and ran in his neat blue suit to open the hall door. He seemed surprised to see only a thin, elderly man in an overcoat and muffler with a leather dispatch case in his hand. He looked ill and melancholy, but the melancholy seemed appropriate to an occasion rather than to an illness.

"Good evening, Willy"—he spoke through an epoch-making cold in the head—"a sad day, boy, a sad day."

"'Tis. 'Tis a fright, sir. 'Tis a holy fright. Were you not in the church?"

"No, Willy, as a matter of fact I'm only just out of my bed." His voice was luxuriously plaintive, and as Willy helped him off with his overcoat, he bowed forward and sneezed disastrously.

"Oh, Mr. Walsh, sir"—Bridgid came back into the hall, neat and decorous in her little afternoon apron and sprig of a white bird on her grey hair. She stood galvanised by the terrible sneeze, a basket of turf in one hand, a pair of gentle, jaeger slippers in the other. "Oh sir, what a dreadful cold." She spoke as though it was a dreadful leprosy.

"Yes, it's quite nasty," Mr. Walsh agreed proudly. "As a matter of fact I've been in bed with it but I felt," he found his handkerchief at last and blew his nose, "under the circumstances, as the family solicitor, I should be here to read Sir Roderick's Will to-day—so I defied my doctor and here I am."

"Of course," Bridgid accepted the tremendous necessity, "it will be a powerful Will. But, oh sir, I wonder are you wise? Please don't breathe near Master Hercules, will you? "

" I shouldn't dream of it, Bridgid," he answered seriously. " And how have you been keeping through this sad time? "

" Thank you, sir, not too bad. We eat all right—thank God. We got into our winter woollies this month—wasn't that wise? for death's a chilly thing—but as for our gumboots, we were as *naughty* about them, wouldn't put them on till the coffin was leaving the house—that's how we forgot our flowers "—she used the royal nursery ' we.'

" Well," he spoke with charming sympathy, " I expect you've had the worst of it, keeping him going."

" Oh," she was delighted, " only for my heart and the tricks it plays on my legs, I wouldn't mind."

" It's weights kills her." Willy spoke. " And that reminds me, sir—would you ever give me a hand in with Miss Anna Rose's nest? " He opened the cloak-room door again, displaying the sedan chair in all its beautiful awkwardness.

" Certainly, certainly," Mr. Walsh was pleased to be of any help. He and Willy fitted the shafts into the chair and carried it between them across the hall to the drawing-room, Bridgid clucking gratefully along beside them, pleased by the proper importance shown towards her bad heart.

Mr. Walsh seemed to know as well as Willy where in the drawing-room the chair should stand. They placed it one window towards the sun and one towards the fire, on a small square of unfaded carpet into which it fitted exactly. But for this rather more purple square the carpet might have been laid down the week before.

Now Willy fussed cosily; he ran off and came back with a bow and arrows in one hand and a telephone, the tall kind, with two separate earpieces and an enormous quantity of wire flex, in the other. He worked away busily installing the instrument in the sedan, occasionally giving something to Bridgid to hold. Between them they led the flex under chairs and sofas until they had connected it with a similar telephone to the one in the chair, which stood on a small table near the fireplace.

The bow, a beautiful one made for grown up archery, and its quiverful were hung on a hook in the wall conveniently near to the chair.

Mr. Walsh went to the fire, where he sneezed and shuddered and watched the work without comment or, indeed, much interest, until with a sudden jerk of memory he opened his brief case and took out a bunch of highly coloured folders on foreign travel—bunches of bananas and blazing blue skies. " I thought these might interest Miss Anna Rose," he said.

" Oh, thank you, sir—they will." Willy accepted them with pleasure. " She hasn't been abroad for a long time now and these look very nice with winter coming on, don't they, Bridgid? "

" Right enough, they'd liven a person up on a day like a funeral," Bridgid agreed, looking them over with pleasure.

" A great crowd at the church, I suppose? " Mr. Walsh questioned drearily.

" Well, such a bedding "—Bridgid capped the pretty word with another as gay—" 'twas only like a wedding, that's all about it."

" That's the wholely all about it," Willy echoed reverently before he went 'Ping' on the telephone;

Bridgid at the fireplace end, lifted her receiver and spoke into it, while she addressed Mr. Walsh.

" In spite of the petrol ration there was a line of cars after him like a race meeting. All the new English residents in their V.8 Fords, and his own old friends from Lords to beggar men——"

" Receiving you," Willy hooked up his end of the instrument.

" Well," Mr. Walsh accepted the Lords, the new English and the beggar men, " when a man has lived so long and so hospitably as Sir Roderick Ryall, his friends should muster to say good-bye."

" 'Twas royal," Willy amended, " a real impressive funeral. And a *very* nice Bentley in it, too."

" What about the Bentley—the Bereaved," Bridgid took it up, " looked beautiful—Master Hercules in his tail coat, bless him—Mrs. Howard, her black, of course, and the sables, she really looked very well."

" And my Miss Pidgie," Willy struck a jealous note—" Quite the toff. All in black too, and her bird in her hat. Oh, she was in her elements and the right word for everybody."

" And the heir? " Mr. Walsh put in with a certain sly intention. " The new Sir Phillip."

" Drab and untidy," Bridgid answered without hesitation, " and he looked very old. Not at all spry and stylish like Master Hercules."

" And Miss Veronica? " he insisted gently.

" Indeed, I never remarked her, did you, Willy? "

" Indeed, it's easy to miss her—poor Miss Veronica." An extraordinary lack of importance was apparent.

" Poor Miss Veronica," Mr. Walsh echoed with

amusement, " except when she's on a horse, then our poor little lady becomes a queen."

" Well, we can't be always on a horse, and she hasn't been out hunting since the war "—Bridgid was ready for that—" and no one should use the word ' Queen ' to Miss Veronica while her mother is still going. Oh, Mrs. Howard is magnificent in looks and words and deeds. I suppose," she indicated the brief case, " there's a lovely little independence willed her in there. Sir Roderick was mad about his darling sister."

" What would you consider a lovely little independence, Bridgid? " Mr. Walsh asked interestedly.

" Oh, some little dower house on the place where she could live cosy if poor Sir Phillip ever gathers a wife, and my Master Hercules along with her—you couldn't part herself and the baby brother."

Mr. Walsh looked at the brief case and said nothing.

" Of course, changes must come, I've known that." Bridgid accepted the thought with toleration.

" And what will happen to *my* pet if changes come? " Willy protested. " My pet doesn't care for changes. Look, Bridgid, I can't find her snail shells any place—you never threw out her *snails*? "

" Oh, I had to, Willy," she confessed it bravely, " they had Master Hercules' stomach turned."

" Oh, Bridgid, it was our little all-in-all, our little museum. Some of them snails is very rare specimens, did you not know that? "

" Oh, they smelt rare, all right."

" Well, I call that," Willy spoke with considerable feeling, " a very *common* thing to say."

Mr. Walsh, leaning forward, hands clasped behind his back, camel-like, hollow-chested, relieved the situation.

" I may be wrong, I'm deafened with this cold of mine, but I think I hear a car, am I right? "

He was right. They rushed to the door, both glad to be relieved of the weight of argument. Before she went Bridgid spun back on her heel:

" That boy is gone again on me—oh, young boys are fearful—Mr. Walsh, pardon the liberty, sir, but while I get a log for my fire would you ever have the goodness to put the two chairs back in the hall for me? "

" Certainly, certainly, I know you're busy." Before her grateful eyes he laid a hand on the back of each funeral chair and carried them out to the hall. " I know it's unlucky," he smiled at her as he returned: he was not tricked. " But Sir Roderick would have the laugh of you, wouldn't he? "

" Oh, God rest him, he would."

She left him alone in the drawing-room with his back to the fire. He stood there looking regretfully about him as if he saw the smooth comfort of the room drowning before his eyes. As though he looked over a quayside and down into water and saw a new car underneath the water. He did not go out into the hall to meet the returning mourners—he stayed where he was quietly waiting and listening to the voices he knew very well.

He heard the fluting, creamy boom of a woman's voice like an amorous blackbird on a wet mid-may afternoon: " Oh, it all went beautifully, beautifully, such flowers, oh, such beauty and colour. . . ." And the charming, clear voice of a man whose ear would never hear a wrong sound. He would never have known which words could go wrong: " The Parson should have had the grass cut in the churchyard—mend him for a fool! Very wet, very wet. I'm so glad I wore my gummers. Idle chaps, these parsons. . . ." Then a light anxious young voice: "Aunt Anna Rose, you must change your shoes, come upstairs. . . ." This was answered by a voice as round and young as though it came out of a great, healthy baby: "*Must* I? Find Willy, my dear, find Willy. Ah, there you are, Willy. Now I'll go. . . ." A strong, grave voice asked: "Is that Mr. Walsh's car, Willy?"

"Yes, sir. He's within." Willy sounded quite preoccupied. . . . "And how did you enjoy it, Miss?" His inquiry was tenderness itself.

"Oh lovely, lovely." The baby voice floated out in happy recollection. "Such fun. Lots of old friends. . . ."

They poured into the drawing-room with the same sort of eagerness for bodily comfort with which one gets into a hot bath. The first through the door was the lady with the fluting blackbird's voice—she had a tiny bird's head, too, carried as prettily as a girl's; it seemed to float in air like a fragment of a tune above her really vast body—she was enormously tall and fat—too fat—but she moved every part of herself with elegance, rough, not refined, elegance. All the assurance of a beauty was still here and unconsidered by a woman of sixty. When she took off her gloves she did it with enchantment. They were fine, expensive, pale chamois gloves of a very old-fashioned kind. They were as narrow as ribbons and immensely long wristed. The black hat on her little head fitted her as securely and as becomingly as if it had been nailed to her skull. She had enormous blue eyes like the little gentleman who had hurried in and out with his sheaf of carnations. He followed her now as she advanced, peeling off her gloves, on Mr. Walsh. Her voice caressed him as though of all men he alone could comfort her now.

"Mr. Walsh, how kind of you to come. But how is your influenza?"

"Better thank you, Mrs. Howard."

"Better? I'm so glad. Tots," she turned to include the little man, "wasn't it wonderful of Mr. Walsh, for Roddy's sake and our sake to get out of bed to-day? People *will* risk their lives for us—so very kind."

"Not at all, Mrs. Howard," Mr. Walsh disclaimed any high sacrificial motive, "it's my business after all."

"How de do, Walsh? Very kind"—Mr. Hercules Ryall looked anxiously at Mr. Walsh and longingly at the fire. "But risky, though. I dread 'flu—dreadful thing—you don't mind if I keep a little distance, do you? Fearfully cold, isn't it?"

A solid purposeful looking young man in a dark blue suit (no tail coat or other glamour) came into the room. There was something terribly direct about him. Although in features he was a blunt edition of his elders, he did not have that air of cosseted glamour which they wore with their clothes, without their clothes and under their skins. There was a commoner colour about him, about the strong way his hair grew, about his bigger bone (with all the flesh she carried, the tall woman's bone was light as twigs on a wintry tree). The way he walked across the room was different, there was no grace, inherited, studied, or forgotten. There was no leisure or dalliance with amusing thoughts by the way—no anticipation of pretty thoughts, no time for anything but the direct approach. No tolerance of any halfway measures. It was as if he had missed some young easiness and joy. There was something useless yet valuable which had been cut out of his life. He was twenty-five. He had gone from school to war and from that to this inheritance. Now he shook hands warmly with the solicitor. " How are you, Gerald? You shouldn't have come to-day really, old boy—rather rash." The whole address was different from the previous royal approach. It was echoed by a little girl who followed on like a shadow. She, too, wore a blue suit and the grim, entirely joyless expression of an errand boy on a bicycle or a lady companion with a grievance. She carried a dark blue beret in her hand and her soft, mouse blonde hair was badly cut in the style before the style before last. " Your wreath was beautiful," she said as she shook hands. " Uncle Roddy would have loved it."

" Oh yes—very, very lovely—our brother would have been so pleased—wouldn't he, Tots? " Consuelo Howard spoke in an affectionately reminding voice to the little man. She was glad that someone besides herself had forgotten to mention Mr. Walsh's sumptuous offering.

" Oh, what? Oh, yes. Very cold. Very bad corner. I thought the horses were goin' to be awkward, didn't you? " He wasn't attending. All he really wanted at the moment was to mesmerise Mr. Walsh away from the fire, so that he could warm himself up without catching Mr. Walsh's cold.

" No. Flowers, dear—wreaths."

" Oh yes—yes, Consuelo. Red carnations, I thought of—magnificent, weren't they? Many a good dinner the dear old boy stood me and he always wore a carnation. My brother was out and away the best dressed man I've ever known."

Consuelo said with dark, joyous meaning: " I hope my orchids gave him wonderful memories too."

The young girl said with a quaver: " Mine was just

a bit of white heather, made up into a horseshoe—just for luck."

"Quite unnecessary, my dear." The mother's rebuke was light but sure, "your Uncle Roddy will have the best in every sphere—I'm sure of it—aren't you, Tots?"

"I'm quite sure Roddy's in the members' stand now as always"—he spoke seriously—the pretty blue eyes clouding—"Royal Enclosure, most likely."

"Don't make me cry. I see Roddy at Ascot when you say Royal Enclosure." Consuelo smiled bravely. "Wonderful horses—wonderful weather—wonderful fun—wonderful—now *there's* an idea——" Her voice left the classical summer poem as she stepped briskly towards the bell, a painted china knob in a gilt half circle—"wonderful champagne. Champagne, of course—the very thing for Mr. Walsh's influenza."

"*Please*, no," Mr. Walsh deprecated the idea, almost pleading against it.

"Roddy would have wished it," Consuelo insisted. "Wouldn't he have wished it, Tots?"

"He certainly would," Hercules agreed emphatically, "specially if he was in range of these pernicious 'flu germs."

"We'll drink a bottle to his memory before Mr. Walsh reads his Will and wishes for us all." Consuelo turned the bell again most decisively. Almost before it had slipped back its little circle Bridgid was in the room with an armful of really dry sticks.

"Bridgid, my dear, how thoughtful. We're all chilled to the bone." Consuelo glared at the huge fire burning like a tiger in the basket grate behind Mr. Walsh. "However, we mustn't go near the 'flu germs, must we?"

"Oh, God forbid!" She flung on the sticks. "Now,

Master Hercules, let me take the boots." She was down on her knees. He might have been a four-year-old child that one sits on a table and strips of its gummers and pull-ups.

"And I'm very hungry, too," Hercules said as he yielded up his boots. "Any Biccys left, Bridgid? I'd like a Biccy with my glass of wine."

"No more till Monday," she told him. "I gave you the last three to take to church."

"Now, darling, champagne's one thing but you really can't eat biscuits at this solemn moment." Consuelo's reproof was sweetly done—"and I *did* think it was a little unnecessary to scrunch them quite so loudly during the Bishop's beautiful address."

"My dear girl, I was so busy not scrunchin' I almost choked myself."

"Oh Master Hercules," Bridgid saw the whole picture, "and you in your lovely tail coat."

"Bridgid," Consuelo said, "tell William a bottle of Clicquot '29 and"—she counted—"one, two, three, four, five, five glasses."

"Champagne again?" The young man, Phillip Ryall, looked up. "Not just before tea for me, thanks."

The girl spoke in prim agreement. "Not for me, either, thank you, Mother."

"And quite honestly," Mr. Walsh said, "I'd rather have a cup of tea." He sounded dismally honest about it.

"Well," Consuelo spoke in a voice of sacrificial righteousness. "Well, you and I will drink it, Tots. We owe it to darling Roddy's memory. It's a debt we never can repay." The room round them warmed in approval. The fire sprang through Bridgid's extra sticks. The pictures glowed in their frames. Tiny landscapes lit, cold, pale engravings suddenly showed peachy red mouths, dust furred wintry white on the grotto blue of the monster plates. It was simply that the sun shone directly in at the windows, but it did it at the moment which agreed most perfectly with Consuelo's resolution. Thoughts of tea seemed distinctly shabby and middle-class and disrespectful to the dead in contrast with the gold of sun and wine. "Let William know at once please, Bridgid. The Clicquot '29 and two glasses. After that," her pause despised them, "tea for all."

Unashamed and still standing in front of the fire, Mr. Walsh spoke to the young man: "Shall we get on with reading the Will, Phillip?"

"Well, yes," the boy agreed without fervour or sentiment of any kind apparent in his voice, "I suppose we'd better."

"My dear, why this undue haste?" his aunt asked gently, subsiding with that odd, rough grace she had, into a corner of the sofa.

"Yes, yes," Hercules agreed, "give William time to bring up a bottle—order, dear Boy, decorum: you modern chaps have no real sense of the occasion—*most* important."

"And another thing"—Mr. Walsh looked up from his papers—"Miss Anna Rose—I'm right, aren't I, always *Miss* Anna Rose?"

"Well, of course," they said, "don't dream of calling her anything else. . . . Surely you know her well enough. . . . She'd be off for an evening flight. . . . Good gracious, the idea. . . ."

He went through their protests like someone swimming out to sea, his eyes at a distance. "Miss Anna Rose ought to be with us, I think. She is a Beneficiary, too—under her married name, of course. The Baroness——"

"Hush, don't say it."

"All right, all right, I wasn't going to. But would somebody ask her to come in."

"One more thing," Consuelo raised a staying hand. "You do know her favourite subject now?—travel, foreign travel."

"It's just this new Peace that's got her." Hercules brushed the whole thing off with affectionate understanding. "During the war she felt terribly cooped up here; but she's off to Moscow on Thursday—hopes to get a real peep behind the Iron Curtain, bless her."

"Berlin, Vienna, Constantinople, Petersburg, always Petersburg"—Phillip spoke more sweetly than he had done. "They're all one to her. Veronica, be an angel and ask Willie to bring her down."

"Get her yourself, my dear: Willie's busy with the bottle of wine." Hercules was worried.

"I'll try," she said sadly, "but it may be difficult and she *did* want to go and be a nesting swan before tea."

"Nesting in *September*!" Hercules' little worried look became very upset. "She'll be shooting pheasants in August next."

"Poor darling, she's had almost too much fun and excitement for one day. A *real* funeral. Not just a bird in a matchbox," Consuelo spoke with quiet understanding.

"It's just her age, Uncle Hercules," Phillip comforted clumsily.

"Her age, my dear boy, you don't know what you're talkin' about. She's not *old*. Never heard such a dreadfully silly remark." He bounced a little on the sofa cushions. "I do wish William would bring up that bottle, I need it. Besides, it's *September*. She shouldn't be nesting now, it's almost gaga. In March it's perfectly reasonable, but if she does it now people may think her a bit odd. Ah," he said, "ah, *now*," screwing round his head as William came into the room with a trayful of glasses. "But the wine, the wine, boy, the wine."

Willy put down the tray and stood slightly stupefied in the doorway. "I thought you had the last bottle up here, sir. Three dozen left the cellar to-day and the cellar is dry to-night. Two dozen and eleven bottles they drank on the gravel sweep to-day. 'Tis paved in their corks." He went out. There was something else on his mind.

"But"—Consuelo spoke in a stunned voice—"I simply fail to understand. There's *always* more in the cellar."

"Roddy really hasn't been himself lately," Hercules reminded her. "We must restock the cellar at once, Phillip. I'll look into the matter for you. No trouble, dear boy. Really not. Lucky you have your old uncle to advise you."

"Awfully lucky, Uncle Hercules." Phillip gave him an unexpectedly charming look. "I'm *so* sorry about the champagne." And, as Willie returned with a little silver vase of flowers (the kind that once held gloriously common malmaisons and clipped into a Rolls). "Has anyone got a cigarette they could spare me?"

There was a silence. Not a helpful kind of silence, and William spoke from the sedan chair where he had been hooking up the vase—generosity was a disease with him. "I could manage one, sir—if you're desperate."

"Oh, thank you, William." He was so pleased.

" That makes ten you're owing me now, sir." William spoke gently and with every respect.

" Remind me. Remind me. *Please* remind me. Got a match? "

" Since there is no champagne "—Consuelo spoke with melodious chagrin, deploring the lack as another might deplore the need of bread, a practical necessity non-existent. " As there *appears*," she amended, " to be no champagne, let's get this business over and have tea —I'm quite faint—what are we waiting for? "

" For Aunt Anna Rose," Phillip reminded her. " Where is she, William? Not really nesting in November, is she? "

" No, no, sir," William smiled, " only waiting for a great big Poacher in the turn of the back staircase. She wants to dot him one over the head as he comes up."

" Only catchin' poachers! That's *much* better "— Hercules was delighted. " Well, go and *be* a poacher and get dotted, William. Anything to please her."

They sat around patiently and expectantly, a kind of subsidence calming them—she was all right . . . only poachers. . . . She would be here in a moment. Only Aunt Consuelo showed the slightest nervous tension. A sort of mild snapping feeling was going on inside her head. All this delay. *Really*, sometimes a little trying. However, bedtime for Aunt Anna Rose was not far off, that was one blessing. She glanced at her watch. Four-fifteen. Ah, not long till six o'clock—not long now.

The door was opened by Willy as if for royalty, and as quietly and simply as royalty Aunt Anna Rose came in. She stood for a moment looking round at them and her eyes matched the voice that had floated out so buoyantly in the hall—they were huge, untroubled eyes like pools behind rocks. One always felt they were going to smile, to break out into some vital, turbulent expression; because although they were nearly as big, they were not really like a cow's eyes. There was nothing out of the way about her except her prettiness. She was not teeny wee, she was not tall, she was a comfortable size—a comfortable size with grandeur. Her clothes added a romantic quality to her appearance. They were the clothes of nineteen hundred and seven without exaggeration. The skirt of her orchid coloured coat and skirt was long, but not to the ground. The coat was gently sloping down the shoulders and faintly egg-boilered at the waist. Naturally there was a certain amount of soft lace at her throat, but not a shred at her wrists. She wore little doeskin gloves with a wrist button—her pink palm bulged like a peardrop through the gap. She leaned on a thin duck's headed umbrella with bright eyes. On her head she wore a particularly soft and becoming hat with a bird in it, a cross between a dove and a seagull, curiously complete throughout graceful wing-spread and soft breast, it was a bird, not just feathers in a hat.

" All sitting there condemning me to bed, I suppose." She surveyed the group of her relations with tolerant humour. " I haven't even had my tea yet. Have I, William? " she appealed, suddenly a little bit uncertain.

" Not yet, miss. Where will you have it to-day? " Willy seemed to lean about her.

" In the Orient Express." She walked towards the sedan chair. It was the station walk, head high, looking anxiously for the platform number, for the right carriage, the empty one, the reserved corner seat with its face to the engine. One could almost smell the lovely smell of trains in the room. The romantic height of foreign trains was visible as she lifted her pointed shoe and held her skirt at her bent knee. She paused to say: " How do you do? " to Mr. Walsh, head over her shoulder. He might have been a friend at the barrier.. " How do you do, Miss Anna Rose." He waved. She smiled back and climbed up and settled in to her corner seat, put the papers that were on it beside her with her jewel case, too, and looked out from her window in the moment before departure to say as a last thought: " And if any-one wants to talk to me they can call me up on the long-distance in Budapest—eleven o'clock we should get in. Thank you so much, Porter." She extracted air from the hole in her glove and tipped William. " Bed, indeed! " She wound up her window finally and pulled down the blind. Indeed, she was lost to them.

" You see what I mean "—said Hercules triumphantly to the room at large—" same as you or me really. She *knows* it's not the right thing to nest in November."

" That's right, sir," William agreed. " She's off the notion altogether, God bless her."

Consuelo dismissed him: " William "—a little nod—" you may . . . Yes—tea in half an hour, please."

" Very good, madam."

" Make it 15 minutes, William," Hercules pleaded.

" Never fear. I'll hurry them, sir."

" I'm afraid, Mr. Ryall, this business may take longer than fifteen minutes," Mr. Walsh hinted sourly. " Now, if I may have your attention "—he bent over the long paper and began to read in a stifling monotone: " ' This is the last Will and Testament of me, Roderick Philip Ryall in the County of——' "

Veronica came in very gently, to be hushed by all except Phillip, who gave her quite a natural smile and said in an ordinary voice: "We've started." She sat down again in her little beady chair, looking very grave and apologetic.

" '——I hereby revoke all wills and testamentary dispositions heretofore made by me' "—Mr. Walsh subdued a sneeze heroically.

" ' (1) I appoint Gerald Walsh of Marysfield, Knockanore and John Lestrange of Dangerfort, Knockanore to be the executors and trustees of this my will, and I declare that if either of them shall die in my lifetime,' " he coughed sacrificially and went on in a fainter voice, " ' or renounce probate of my will——' "

"Speak up, please." Hercules didn't want to miss a word—he was like a child at a lantern lecture.

" 'And I give to such of my executors and trustees who shall prove my will and accept the trust thereof a legacy of two hundred and fifty pounds each——' "

"Very proper, very nice," Hercules agreed heartily. This largesse—he liked to be in every bit of everything.

"Hush, Tots, hush." Consuelo put her hand in his. She wanted it all kept on rather a deeper note.

"Now we come to the bequests. 'I bequeath one hundred and fifty pounds to Bridgid O'Keefe and Mary Guidera if they are in my employ when I die and a sum of fifty pounds to William Burke.' "

"Just what I should have expected." Hercules joined in again.

"Please, Mr. Ryall——"

"Sorry, sorry. Dear old Roddy, so generous."

"I won't keep you much longer—'To my Aunt' "—he raised his voice and his head towards the sedan chair across the room—" 'the Baroness—' "

"*Please.*" Consuelo raised a protesting hand.

" Mend him for a fool," Hercules muttered.

Even the silent boy said quietly: " Skip it, Gerald, shall we? "

" ' To my Aunt '—oh, very well," he retreated, to speak differently, " ' Miss Anna Rose, I bequeath two thousand pounds—to my dear sister Consuelo Howard ——' " He fumbled maddeningly.

" Gallop on. Gallop on," Hercules muttered again.

" ' Ten thousand pounds and the dower house at Ballynadyne. To my brother, Hercules Ryall, seven thousand pounds and my thumb stick. And to my niece, Veronica Howard, I bequeath three thousand pounds. The residue of my estate I leave to my very dear Son, Phillip Peter Ryall.' "

There was a stirring and a sighing in the warm, rich room, the inheritors turning their comfortable portions over in their minds as happily as turning over in a big bed. Consuelo spoke first, she was truly moved as well as materially comforted: " Darling Roddy! Blessed Heart! Each of us provided for so perfectly."

Hercules spoke softly and gratefully: " I'm terribly pleased about that thumb stick. I always wanted it. It's a lovely stick." Then, anxiously: " Phillip, dear boy, you're not hurt at his leaving it to me, are you? You shall have it next, you know."

" Thanks awfully, Uncle Hercules. You'll need it for another twenty years, I hope "—one saw Phillip's years stretching forwards limitlessly and Hercules' suddenly a strict, small span.

" Oh I hope so too, *at least*," he said ruefully.

Consuelo was ready again: " And as soon as you want to get rid of your old aunt and housekeeper, Phillip, I'll be off to Ballynadyne. I shall put in four bathrooms and electric power everywhere for my old age. What fun! "

There was a pause before Phillip said: " That's all right, Aunt Consuelo. I'll never want to get rid of you, I promise. Just as well perhaps——" He stopped. " Oh, you tell her, Gerald. I'm not very good at explaining things."

" Actually, Mrs. Howard," Mr. Walsh said with entire satisfaction; this was the moment he had been righteously awaiting. For this he had got out of his bed of 'flu. " Actually, do you follow me?—the Bank owns Ballynadyne."

" The Bank? " Consuelo repeated the word as vaguely and prettily as though it meant the bank whereon the wild thyme blows, oxslips and the nodding violet grows, or the one the moonlight sleeps along, none of the hard anxiety usually so emphatic in the word—" The Bank? Oh, just a little mortgage, I expect." She was practical now, quite the business head. " That's nothing. That's rather the thing to have, I understand. Just take no notice—that's what Roddy always said."

" I'm afraid," Mr. Walsh proceeded, still with satisfaction, " the time has unfortunately come when the Bank is taking every notice."

That, too, she took magnificently in her stride: " Banks have *such* bad taste and display it at such unnecessary moments. Well, if they are really going to be unpleasant, we'll have to sell out something and pay up, I suppose."

" A very reasonable point of view, very," he agreed gently. " But the trouble is, dear Mrs. Howard, that you can't pay up. You haven't got the money."

She looked at him with complete, absolute, candid

disbelief: " I haven't got the money? Don't be perfectly ridiculous."

" Most unfortunately," he persevered happily, " you have not."

" What do you think you mean, Mr. Walsh? " The very faintest flutter of panic was noticeable.

Hercules, aware of her in everything, patted her hand reassuringly: " Don't fuss, darling girl, I'll settle, I'll settle. Rely on me, Pets."

" Tots, dearest boy." They looked momentarily into each other's identical eyes. Fortified, she went on: " But, Mr. Walsh, you must be quite entirely mistaken. My brother's Will leaves me Ballynadyne and ten thousand pounds. Not much, I know, but every little helps and he knew I'd be quite happy living quietly and economically. At my age one doesn't want to spend."

" Mrs. Howard," Mr. Walsh's head was raised again after a long calculation. " I'm terribly sorry to tell you that your own investments as they stand at present bring you in just eighty pounds a year. Net, mind you. And the investments mentioned in Sir Roderick's will have been "—he sneezed aggressively six times and Hercules shuddered six times—" have been sold out years ago."

" Good heavens." She sat up at last, her comfortable lounging grace abandoned. " I *fail* to understand this muddle you've made."

" Never mind, Pets. Don't let it bother you for a moment. I've got a bit. We'll manage."

Mr. Walsh fixed Hercules, too, with his eye: " Possibly you remember certain deeds of gift you made to your brother at different times. Both of you? "

" Yes, yes," Consuelo agreed trippingly, " just little temporary measures."

"Occasionally the old boy was in need of a bit of ready. I was delighted, *delighted* to be of any use. Just a flea-bite though, my contributions." Hercules deplored the necessity for any such confession of generosity. "Don't think of it again, dear boy," he said to Phillip in an agonised little voice.

Mr. Walsh bore onwards: "You, Mr. Ryall, have, I think, an income of fifty pounds left you out of the considerable fortune inherited from your mother, Lady Jane Ryall."

"Well, Mr. Walsh," the answer came grandly and gratefully, "I've had considerable fun and I don't grudge one farthing of the money. Fifty pounds will keep me in cigarettes, anyway." He sat back smiling.

Mr. Walsh's temper and hands flew up together. He was at the end of his patience with these spoilt, doting old aristos. "Cigarettes—my God. And who will keep you in clothes, food and drink?"

"In what did you say? Speak up, old man." Hercules, between his own slight deafness and Mr. Walsh's cold and crossness, had not quite got the idea.

Mr. Walsh gathered up his papers and pushed them across to Phillip. "I'm through," he said. "You explain the situation to them."

"Right." Phillip became suddenly desperately alive. He seemed obstinately strong and young, sure of his strength, certain in his convictions, immovable in intention. "Right." His voice had a much stronger, commoner timbre than that of his uncle or, one could be sure, of his father. "Darlings, we're pretty well sunk and broke. Dear old Dad just spent it all—his own and yours, too, I'm afraid."

Consuelo said hotly: " He spent it on us as much as on himself."

" Yes," Hercules clamoured, " he gave us a royal time always."

" I'm so glad of that," Phillip said heartily, " because I can't pay up his legacies to you. After death duties and overdraft and debts are settled up, there's nothing left except the house and the home farm."

" And two miles of a good salmon river—and the Lake, best mayfly fishing in Ireland—and a couple of thousand acres of rough shooting—my dear boy, it all adds up." Uncle Hercules was going to make people see sense.

" And my advice is," Mr. Walsh's weight came down again, " sell out. The market for these Irish places is at its peak now."

" Sell," Consuelo breathed, " sell Ballyroden. It wouldn't mean anything to you of course, Mr. Walsh, but there's been a Ryall at Ballyroden ever since——"

" Mrs. Howard, the family histories in this part of the world have long been my hobby. Ever since your ancestor Harford Ryall did the dirty in the Star Chamber on his great friend and patron, Sir Walter Raleigh."

" *Poor* Sir Walter," the whole incident might have happened yesterday, " always the fool of the party."

" Of course, I've considered selling," Phillip went on with cold sense, ignoring yesterday's stink with the Star Chamber, " but who's going to buy an enormous house without electric light or telephone and with the roof in a very doubtful state—dash of dry rot thrown in."

" My dear," Hercules stated placidly, " these English will buy anything."

Suddenly Veronica spoke, with a great struggle: " It's ten miles from the nearest Catholic church or cinema.

No servants except Mrs. Guidera, Bridgid or William would ever stay."

" The prospective buyers won't know that." Consuelo, to put her daughter in her place, put herself almost in favour of selling the estate. If Veronica had spoken another word out of her turn she would have done a temporary swivel to Mr. Walsh's side of the argument.

" Oh," Phillip said roughly, " we've got to live on here somehow. Even if we sold it we'd have to find somewhere else to live. Besides," he gave a hidden look round the room, " I don't really want to sell Ballyroden."

" Oh, I'm with you there, dear boy, all the way. All the way. Much better live on here." Hercules snuggled down.

" At least," said Consuelo in a really self-sacrificing voice, " we can live on lamb and chickens and salmon and grouse and woodcock without paying for them—that's what I say. In any case all I ever want for dinner is a jack-snipe, *lightly* cooked, and a glass of Burgundy. What would that cost you in a London restaurant? Here—nothing."

" But we are paying for them," Phillip was quite patient—" over and over again."

" Oh nonsense, my dear! " She was patient too. " Here they are—they've always been here."

" Oh, Lord! " he said. He looked sick with worry.

Veronica, very moved, said angrily: " Oh, how hopeless we are. Can't anybody think of anything."

" I know, I know," Uncle Hercules answered gaily to the spur. " Can't we touch a few of Aunt Anna Rose's nest eggs. She has quite a bit from her marriage settlement."

" If that had been possible," Mr. Walsh said smartly,

" there wouldn't have been much of it left this afternoon."

At this moment a telephone bell rang as determinedly and as insultingly as telephone bells always do ring. Phillip leaned behind him and took up the receiver. " What? Yes—yes." He held it towards Consuelo. " Aunt Anna Rose wants you on the long distance."

Consuelo hurried across from her sofa to the fire where the telephone sat on an oval, tray-edged Sheraton table. It would have been much nearer to go to the sedan chair.

" Yes, Aunt Anna Rose, yes—Consuelo here. You heard every word? You have wonderful hearing. I said —*You have wonderful hearing*. No. I wasn't shouting. . . . *What* do you want to do? Aunt *Anna Rose* "—she put her hand over the mouthpiece, whose faint quacking vibrated still, and raised her great eyes despairingly to the ceiling —" She wants to live in a villa in Anne Street, Knockanore, and go to the pictures every Thursday." She added in lightest comment as one talks of a really sane person's preposterous idea: " She's crazy," then put back the telephone.

" It's the sanest remark I've heard this afternoon," Mr. Walsh said approvingly.

" Anne Street? Why, what about the dogs' walkies? Has she thought about that? " Hercules chattered in horror.

Even Phillip looked disturbed: " If Aunt Anna Rose stays on with us our joint income soars up towards a thousand pounds. If she goes," he wrinkled his forehead like an old foxhound, " she can't—I'll ask her." He picked up the telephone: " Hallo! Hotel Continentale."

Consuelo, faintly accurate, added: " Buda nine seven hundred."

"Buda nine seven hundred—Oh! Reception? Give me Aunt Anna Rose, will you? Aunt Anna Rose. . . . Phil. You can't walk out on us, dear, really. , . . Yes, of course I can give you an excellent reason—we want your money." He paused. "Good. I knew you'd see my point."

"Ring off, dear boy, ring off." Hercules suddenly felt tired and peevish; he wasn't getting called up from Buda like everyone else. "It's long past teatime."

"Can't hear, darling," Phillip said, "it's a bad line. I'll ring you later." He put the telephone back on its hooks and wound the awful little handle decidedly. "It's quite all right," he said with satisfaction. "Thank God she was only kidding about Knockanore."

Mr. Walsh gave Phillip the look which said: I expected better things of you, and got himself on to his feet. "I think perhaps, as I can be of no further use, I'll go back to bed before pneumonia sets in."

"Now, dear Gerald," Phillip took him by the arm and put him back in his chair, "don't be the man of law—we do want your help awfully. Of course we could let the fishing and shooting." He held his chin over it, considering further.

"Yes, what about a little syndicate, dear boy?" Hercules struck in helpfully. "Me and you and you and me, you know. Perhaps we could knock fifty pounds out of that rich English immigrant at Galtee Castle. Fifty pounds is ridiculous though—say a hundred and fifty or two hundred and fifty."

Now they were on to Economy like hounds settling to a line: "Of course, Tots, you and I can't drink champagne except on very special occasions." Consuelo volunteered the sacrifice.

" Of course not, Pets." He gave a tiny sigh. " And I really think whisky suits me better—Jameson's." He thought what else he could give up and said with a deeper sigh than the champagne had called up: " I must say good-bye to English race meetings, I suppose. Anyway, I hear they are most uncomfortable since the war. Yes, English meetings OUT. O-U-T. What else can we cut down? "

" Apart from champagne and English race meetings, I don't see why we shouldn't jog along much as usual "—Consuelo was large-minded. " Whatever these two bogey men," she smiled at Phillip and Mr. Walsh, " may say. Why, it isn't even as if we were still hunting."

Hercules gave that little bark of derision so often heard from the fox-hunting man for to-day's conduct of the chase, for the hounds of to-day, for the country they hunt over, even for the foxes so faintly pursued in comparison to the fire and drive and delight of hunting twenty-five years ago: " Who'd want to ride over this country now, place is like a birdcage." He leaned over to tap Phillip's knee with a finger like a parrot's beak. " There should be no wire on a gentleman's estate, old boy, old boy, except on a champagne bottle, and that ought to be ready to come off at a moment's notice."

" Darlings," Phillip put both hands desperately in his hair (so much less pretty than Hercules'), " you must try and begin to understand. It's drinking all the cream and eating all the salmon and peaches and game and giving the rest away. . . ."

" My dear boy—you can't sell game. What an extraordinary idea! I hope they didn't teach him that sort of thing in the Army," Hercules was distressed.

" Can't you, Uncle Hercules? When you're broke

you can, and must." Phillip very nearly brought his fist down on the table, so near are we to our grandfathers.

" Oh, Phil . . ." Veronica swallowed three times. " You are terrific."

Hercules looked really dazed: " But there's no end to that sort of economy."

" Perhaps not—but there's going to be a beginning." Phillip had got under way; he was like a little boy who runs before the wind holding on to a rug with both hands, almost flying, out of control. " For instance, killing a sheep a week for the household must stop."

Consuelo spoke reasonably in a calm tone of voice: " Killing your own sheep keeps the butcher's bill down to nothing."

" They don't understand the principle of the thing, Pets. They simply don't understand. Poor children." Hercules was lamentable.

" Cutting down a tree every week must stop," Phillip went on.

" Try buying coal," Consuelo said with the expression of one who puts the last piece in a difficult puzzle. " After all," she said with sober conviction, " you must heat the bath water."

" Very well," Phillip said, " six raging hot baths every night before dinner must stop."

" Oh, oh, we'll all be ill. And what about the doctor's bills? " Hercules looked very frail indeed at the thought.

" I'm on Phil's side absolutely," Veronica said with unattractive zeal. " Never mind my chilblains, I'll have a cold one every morning myself."

" My *darling*," her mother looked her over, " a good idea. Very calming and beneficial, I believe, at your age."

" Oh," she cried out in schoolgirl tongue, " give us a chance, Mother."

" Yes, Aunt Consuelo," Phillip spoke more heatedly than before, " the situation is pretty desperate."

" My dears," she answered with the gentlest wisdom and understanding, " I remember darling Roddy being just as upset about finance when Father died. But things went on. Things do go on."

Mr. Walsh, who had been listening in silence and approval to Phillip's efforts, lifted his voice again: " Mrs. Howard, have you ever heard of bankruptcy? "

" Well, of course, who hasn't? It's a way of stopping paying bills."

" And *not* a very nice way either. It also makes it difficult to buy a cutlet or a bag of biscuits."

" Oh dear! . . ." Hercules couldn't face bankruptcy.

" Unless," Mr. Walsh conceded, " you pay for them in ready cash."

" Bankruptcy "—Consuelo showed pardonable amusement—" a trump card! But it won't happen."

" No, it won't happen," Mr. Walsh promised quietly, " because Phillip is selling out all he has to pay his father's and your debts, overdrafts and mortgages. When it's all settled he'll be lucky if there's a thousand pounds left."

" Is this true really, dear boy? " Hercules appealed to Phillip at last, as to the other man in the family.

" Yes." Phillip looked confused.

Consuelo said anxiously: " Shan't we have enough to eat? "

" When you've lost a stone, Consuelo, me dear, I'll pop the rubies." Aunt Anna Rose's head appeared suddenly and dramatically in the romantic hat out of the window of the train. She had been so far away it was almost frightening. She held on to her hat with both hands and shouted against the rushing air: "Not till you've lost a stone, remember." She gave a little cackle of delight—very sweet.

"Don't make fun of me, Aunt Anna Rose," Consuelo pleaded. "We can't all have your figure."

"Just my little joke, dear," she called comfortingly. "And it cost me five pounds to make it."

"What d'you mean you extravagant old puss, don't you know we're broke?" Hercules asked anxiously.

"I pulled the communication cord. Just once—and a million kronen, but such fun——"

"Oh, I see, you're back in the Express"—he understood now.

"Of course, of course. I'm on my way to Moscow. I can't keep my hat on in this wind—off the Steppes, you know. My poor Tito will be blown away." She looked up towards her bird like a star to the gallery. "Oo, La Bise, La Bise! Cheer up. Good-bye, don't forget the rubies—they'll come in so useful." She snapped up the window and was carried out of sight.

"If we knew where she'd put that clutch of rubies we'd be home and dry," Hercules sighed.

"Thank God for her eight hundred pounds a year—never mind about the rubies." Phil did not deal in dreams past or present.

"Rubies, indeed," Mr. Walsh really was not going into that question. "Well, all I can say now is—good-bye."

Consuelo put out a hand; it was extraordinary how well she conveyed the impression that she was being good like a little girl who has been told to say good-bye, a little girl who really can't bear to touch the stranger, but noblesse oblige and all that. " Won't you stay for tea? " she said very coldly, " please, please, do."

" Thank you very much—no. I feel my temperature rising every moment."

" Bed's the place, bed's the place, don't delay," Hercules implored him.

" Rising higher every moment." Mr. Walsh was off and away. " I'm sorry. But I feel angry. On Phil's account. He's young and the four best years of his youth have gone fighting rather creditably in a hideous war. And now, when he should come into a tidy inheritance and a peaceful life, what does he get? Nothing! Nothing but hard work and heartbreak, owing to the ghastly extravagance, waste and fritter of your generation." He looked round him at the bland, shocked faces, shocked at such plain, rude words, not at all at their implication. " I've said too much I expect. I usually do. But before I go, may I suggest one hope of solvency to you, one lifeline—one thread I should say—by which you may hang on here at Ballyroden. What would you think of Paying Guests? "

Consuelo burst out laughing, her beautiful, round, shattering, brainless laugh, the success of so many parties. Her full shaped teeth came into it and her eyes and her throat. The sound itself was a distillation of purity and strength. " Now," she said, really amused and relieved that they were out of the serious mood, " you *have* said too much! Good-bye." She shook hands, more kindly far than she had intended.

" Ha-ha—lodgers—ha-ha! Jolly funny," Hercules echoed. " Well, I won't shake hands—Bridgid gets so cross if I catch colds—you understand."

" Good-bye," Veronica came across to him. When she tilted up her chin there was a flow of prettiness, but an undependable little stream easily turned off its course, no strong, unquestionable beauty but a certain wandering, small enchantment, as in little streams smelling, of bruised mint and faint, clear water flowers. " You were such a help," she said determinedly, " explaining everything."

" Good-bye, Veronica—you and Phillip are two clear-sighted children. The heirs of muddle, God help them, often are. Will someone please say good-bye to Miss Anna Rose for me when her train gets in."

" Well," Consuelo drew an ambrosial breath of relief. " Thank God. At last. What a damn boring man he is."

" I don't think he's really very sane—imagine thinking you could live in Anne Street, Knockanore. Poor chap's rather out of his depths." Hercules excused him.

" Anne Street." Consuelo looked up to the high ceiling and round the grave room. " I can't live in a small room, I must have space. I must be able to strike out. He made me feel like a salmon in a goldfish bowl."

" Mother—he couldn't because a salmon couldn't get into a goldfish bowl. It isn't possible," Veronica contradicted solemnly.

" Yes, it is. I'm a very supple sort of fish."

" But it just isn't possible."

" Why not? I only weigh five pounds. As a matter of fact, I'm a grilse—I only weigh three pounds."

" All the same, you couldn't get into a goldfish bowl."

" *All right.* My whole point is I don't want to get into a goldfish bowl. But what about the other idea—paying guests! That's the final, the crowning insult."

Hercules was at last warming his bottom at the fire:

" Never thought old Walsh had such a dry wit. Pee-Hee "—he giggled—" lodgers! What a joke."

" He didn't mean it as a joke at all, I don't think," Veronica suggested timidly. She didn't know how far to go in the subject without a lead from Phillip.

" My darling girl, when you start thinkin' start on reasonable lines. How could we have paying guests here? " Consuelo might have been thinking of putting lions in the conservatory.

" They'd never stay," Hercules stated comfortably, " why, we can't even have tea when we ask for it."

Phillip came back into the room rather brisk and purposeful. He towered over Hercules by the fire. " I thought that was a very bright suggestion of dear old Gerald's, didn't you, Aunt Consuelo? "

" Which one? " she asked the question drearily—a little tired of it all, perhaps—it had been a trying day, after all.

" The last one," he answered firmly. " About the P.G.s. As he says, it's the only way of getting hold of some ready money until I can knock the farm into shape."

Veronica dashed into the opening again. " Now's the moment of course," she said, " when everyone in England, even the richest people, can't have servants and food and drink and comfort over there. They can have them here."

" But good gracious, dear children, why should they be allowed to buy our comfort over here? The greatest war in history is hardly over. We can scarcely keep ourselves in biscuits and sugar and chocolate with this terrible rationing. We don't want any more people coming over here. Only the other day I ordered a dozen bottles of my '02 Port from the Wine Vaults, and do you know what they said? "

" What did they say, Uncle Hercules? " Veronica had more gentleness for him than for her mother.

" They said that little brute of a fellow at Galtee Castle had bought the lot. It's disgraceful, that's what it is. Ought to be stopped."

" I know, Uncle Hercules—it is a shame. It's awfully trying. All the same it shows you how the English do spend money."

" My dear, it shows you nothing. Why, I *owe* the Vaults, I'm sure I must owe them two hundred and fifty pounds this moment."

With a hopeless glance at each other, Phillip and Veronica gave up the subject. She went on: " All the same, there are lots of rich, tired people who would find it heaven here. We can supply eggs and butter and cream and game and red meat ad lib—whisky, too." She considered it further. " But that would be an extra, of course."

" Extra! My dear, the language of a fifth-rate boarding house," Consuelo corrected patiently. " Where *have* you learnt it? "

" Not from you, Mother dear, you always stayed at the Ritz."

" It's *always* cheapest in the end to stay at the Ritz. And no one could possibly call me extravagant—look at my meanness over pins—common pins or safety-pins. See a pin and pick it up—that's me. Never bought a pin in my life—it's my *favourite* economy."

" You've a very saving nature—bless you," Phillip gave in and so concluded the argument. " Now," he leaned towards them, " will you help us face this idea fairly and squarely? " He looked both fair and square.

" Certainly," Consuelo gave him her most adorable smile, " let's, as you say, face it. It's impossible."

" Where would they sleep, dear boy, for instance? " Hercules rolled his eyes towards the ceiling and the two storeys over their heads. He called up a vision of empty garrets and leaking roofs and broken window-panes and very dissatisfied lodgers. " You've got to face things," he repeated soberly: " You've got to face things."

" We sleep in the best bedrooms "—again it was Veronica doing her comfort strip—" they must have them."

" Oh please, I've slept in that little room for fifty years. Don't believe I could close an eye anywhere else," Hercules said pitifully. " Why not ' Blue Beard ' or ' North Spare ' or ' Iceland '? " he ran rapidly over the names of the guest rooms.

" All charming rooms," Consuelo insisted.

" All miles from the bathrooms," Phillip pointed out.

" And the papers are falling off the walls," Veronica added.

" That's quite an advantage," Consuelo spoke with cool certainty, " they were always all of them quite hideous and revolting wallpapers. I don't think they'd like my room, Veronica—you can hear the hot water pipes gobbling at you all night in my room."

" It's very warm," Veronica said firmly.

" You young people are so wholesale. Throwing us to the lions." She laughed with a tinge of anxiety.

" You can't be serious," Hercules took up the matter again and this time with rather a saintly inflection in his voice: " Think of the servants—poor Bridgid has quite enough to do to look after me."

" And Mrs. Guidera would certainly leave if she had any more people to cook for—so!——"

"——Now!" Hercules ended the matter.

" My dears, please!" Phillip was really enormously forbearing. " Don't think I want P.G.s any more than you do. But you know how things are——"

" All right for me." Hercules moved away from the fire and sat down quickly on his nicely toasted trousers with a quiet look of enjoyment. " Don't worry about me."

" But you know we can't even afford a car."

This was laughable: " Dear boy, there's a Rolls in the garage."

" Yes," Phillip agreed, " there is. But only one of its gears works."

" Quite enough, too," Consuelo commented with a sort of Edward VII grandeur. " Most modern cars have far too many."

" Perhaps they have," Phillip gave Veronica a desperate look—" but the fact remains that Willy's motor bicycle is at the moment our only means of communication with the outside world. "

" It didn't worry us during the war," Hercules remembered bravely, " we took it in our stride. We hired cars when necessary."

" *And* we owe the garage three hundred and forty pounds in consequence."

" Robbers!" Consuelo condemned them.

" All right, robbers. But it brings us back to the money problem."

" We aren't buying, or thinking of buying a new car, dear boy, so I don't see what it's got to do with it."

" Uncle Hercules, we've got to raise some money somehow."

" I wish we could raise a cup of tea." Hercules evaded the unpleasant issue with a touch of genius. " My tummy has that dangerous, sinking feeling. Twenty minutes to six and no tea. Really, the world is rocking! Ah "—he leaned towards the door, raised his hand for silence and listened. He heard the approach of the tea-tray. It was like the first faint suggestion of a scent to an old foxhound. A quiver went through Hercules. He should have had a stern to feather. He should have been able to whimper. The sound of tea was not yet quite in the hall. But he was right. He was as great an authority for the approach of tea as any trusted third season hound for the line of a fox.

The delicious rattle came nearer. They were all on to it now—Aunt Consuelo arranging herself more commodiously on the sofa. One saw the Tea-Tray attitude of years once more taking shape. Before its appearance, the silver teapot's presence was manifest, its exact position, most convenient to her hand. The afternoon moon circle of the silver tray was printed on the drawing-room air as clearly as the smell of violets in christening mugs; they were not here to-day, but they would not fail to be here again as blessedly certain as the tray, as consoling, as innocently exciting.

" *Ah!* " Uncle Hercules went on holding the silence, his ear cocked, his hand raised. He was right—tea—tea for a million. The laden steps were heavy across the hall now. There was the gently bumping pause, Willy outside the door, and the rather splendid, flashy entrance. One felt it was the right completion to previous efforts in pantry and kitchen. He came slipping across the carpet—he was very light and gay on his feet—and stood a moment in front of Aunt Consuelo while the tea table which he carried underneath the silver tray did its daily miracle. Willy pressed something secret, and one after the other four legs shot downwards into space with four precise snaps. In fifteen years it had never failed to happen.

"Ah-ha," Hercules finished his 'ahs,' letting everything go on a great breath of relief. "Thank God. Tea at last."

"Excuse the delay." Willy was wafting busily between door and table. There was the low affair with the brass top to set ready and a stool to be stripped of its newspapers. Last, he brought a china bowl of steaming water in which two brown eggs looked as comfortable as only eggs can look. "Mrs. Guidera was down on her knees before that hen."

"Oh!"—Consuelo looked as pleased as a child—"boiled eggs—golly!"

"Only two," Willy said regretfully as he picked up a tiny cake covered in chocolate with a crystallised violet on the top and removed it from the reach of temptation: Hercules' eye had rolled approvingly towards it across the top of the egg he was tapping so neatly. "And the baby cake is for Miss Anna Rose. I gave my own little only bit of chocolate to put on it."

"No eggs for you and me, Veronica," Phillip smiled, including her in their own comfortable little understanding, conspiracy almost. "We *are* out of the picture."

"Eggs are dreadful scarce," Willy said sadly.

"Very small, too." Consuelo was eating hers as prettily as a bird.

"Jolly lucky they laid two to-day." Hercules put some salt on his strip of buttered toast.

Phillip sighed: "Three hundred hens and two eggs. Well, let's have some toast."

Veronica handed him the dish rather as though she was snatching food for her starving baby. She put it as near to Phillip and as far from the egg eaters as she could. The action was too petty for either of them to notice.

"My tea, thank you, William." Hercules stopped eating for a moment to take a whisky and soda and a plate, on which lay three little slices of brown bread and butter, from William. "When the day comes that I can't have a whisky and soda and three slices of brown bread and butter for tea, I shall know things are hopeless."

"Your eyes may be opened to-morrow, Uncle Hercules," Veronica said.

"But not to-day, dear Uncle Hercules, not to-day," Phillip amended.

"Cheer up, dear boy," Hercules smiled and drank. He jumped and frowned as the telephone bell rang again. "Never know when that thing's going to go off, bless her. William"—William was coming back from the hall carrying, on a little separate tray, tea, bread and butter and the chocolate cake. "——telephone."

William took up the receiver: "Willy here! Yes, I have it for you, miss. . . . Yes, that's lovely. . . . Yes. One minute now." He replaced the receiver. "She'll stop in the Pullman for her tea," he announced. "She says there's a slap-up attendant in a white coat and scented hair swaying around her this minute." He was at her carriage door in a flash: again the station smell as Aunt Anna Rose held an end of the tray with him:

" Thank you, thank you. Dear me, how this train sways." Before she had said it Willy was swaying with her. " Reminds me of the Orient Express," she added with her little toot of laughter, and sat down again, tray on knees. Willy closed the door and turned to the others: " Have you all now, madam? "

Phillip answered as Consuelo and Hercules were too busy eating to attend: " Yes, thank you. Oh—William, just ask Mrs. Guidera and Bridgid to come along, I want to speak to you all together."

" Very good, sir." He went off, enchanted with the new drama.

Consuelo and Hercules turned their empty eggshells upside down in their eggcups and whacked the bottoms as they had done since they were children.

" Bit odd, sending for the whole lot like this. What do you want them for? " Consuelo asked.

" They must be told about their legacies sometime, I suppose."

" As they can't have their legacies, why mention the matter at all? " Hercules suggested easily.

" Well, I don't know," Phillip was easy, too. " Seems fairer somehow. Also, they must be told about these paying guests."

" My darling boy "—Consuelo really sat up, fortified by tea. She was going to catch hold of things once and for all—" this idea of paying guests is complete and utter moonshine."

Hercules was pretty anxious, too: " You're rushin' your fences, old boy—really, really, it'll be Bustle over hairpins into the next field—do go slow, do go slow. Never gallop into banks."

Veronica wore that look of diffident importance children

wear when they know that disaster for once is known to them and not to the grown-ups. It is the most unattractive look one can see even upon the dearest child.

" All right, child, all right," Consuelo swung round on her unexpectedly, " it's *too* common and awful to sit there looking like the cat that's swallowed the canary."

Phillip said quietly, averting disaster: " Cats are my favourite thing and I hate canaries." So Veronica only glowed towards her mother, an almost more irritating attitude of face.

" Children," Consuelo went on, deeply serious now, " you don't know what a dreadful chance you're taking. We shall lose all the servants. It's touch and go, anyway, with our English friends offering double wages and endless outings all round us. It takes infinite tact, *all* my tact, to run this house as it is."

" I can only tell you," Hercules warned them, " that if the new fella at Galtee Castle entices my Bridgid away, it'd kill me. My blood is on your head."

" Uncle Hercules, I'll have to risk it." Phillip was looking beyond him to the door and the servants, three of them: Mrs. Guidera, assured, definite; Mrs. Guidera, who liked killing lobsters with a knife to ensure their tenderness, or a pig, if need be; there was such force about her, such a succulent brutality as belongs to all true gourmandisers. Mrs. Guidera's hair was black as a raven still, although she was past fifty years of age. She laughed at men, she had never had a lover. She was not even deeply religious. She loved racing and followed form closely. Her temper was fierce but contained. She cared for nobody, nobody except Mrs. Howard, and her affection for her was almost independent of the fact that Mrs. Howard never locked anything up, thus emphasising Mrs. Guidera's indisputable position as head of the household. Although she could, if she liked, give things away grandly to her friends, she really disposed of very little except the grand right of giving. If anything, she was a useful brake and check on Mrs. Howard's unthinking, uncalculating charity. The really undeserving poor cursed Mrs. Guidera from full hearts and empty stomachs.

Bridgid, dear Bridgid. She was another cup of tea, a warm, strong, sweet cup of tea. Religious to madness, her life was one long genuflexion, one long series of prayers against every kind of disaster. She was a beautiful housemaid of the old school; the kind to put hot water in your bedroom before lunch, and button every jersey before folding it away; the kind to iron your nightdress daily; the kind to comment freely and unkindly if the visitor's underclothes did not reach the proper standard. She, too, had never had a lover, but all the concentration of her womanly service had gone into her care of Master Hercules. She was a great amateur of medicine and he did adore a good doctoring. Besides all the patent medicines, yeast pills in every disguise and pomades and cough cures, Bridgid would knock up lots of wise little cures for this and that, brewing them with prayers and secrecy on Mrs. Guidera's day out. Master Hercules gave them all a run and found himself greatly benefited by most—especially the prune conserve with senna. Master Hercules, who had always been the child of Ballyroden, had in Bridgid, ten years his junior, the Nannie of all time. Her care and devotion for him made the joy in her busy days. She liked looking after him as much as she liked polishing brasses till they were primrose colour; the contact was as determined and as sexless as that, and left her in just such a glow.

William, who closed the door behind the females of the staff, was a different job again. He had come from an orphanage in the village, the child of a glamorous and ill-living horse-breaker and a sweet and foolish cook. Well, said her friends, as the state of affairs before William's birth became too obvious for hope or denial—when a thing like that happened to *Alice*, it could happen to the Reverend Mother herself. William's gay heart he got from his father. His frivolity, his determined intention he should enjoy himself and Miss Anna Rose should share in his fun was evident in the long process of paying by instalments for his motor bicycle; and not for the bicycle only but for a sidecar in which she and others might ride by his side. His devotion to Miss Anna Rose had that inexplicable sweetness that the Irish show to the children of the house they work in. Miss Anna Rose was his child to be minded and his little joke. He got real amusement and interest out of keeping her happy. His gentleness and industry came partly from his foolish mother (who had made a very nice marriage in spite of the horse-breaker *contretemps*) and partly from his early training as scullery boy in a monastery of Trappist monks on the mountainside. It was from there that he had come to Ballyroden ten years previously, to work under a beloved butler slowly dying of cancer and brandy, or brandy and cancer. The butler had endured for long enough to develop in William a real feeling for his work and skill in its execution, but he had never quite extinguished that zest for living which no true butler should have.

" Come in, come in. I want to talk to you." Phillip

was nervous and hearty, rather the big business man to his staff, or the young officer to the troops, He meant to be modern and sensible in his methods. " Sit down, Bridgid, William, Mrs. Guidera," he gave her a chair. Mrs. Guidera drew herself up a mile beyond her own height and gave him a pitying look. " Thank you, I much prefer to stand, Master—*Sir* Phillip."

" Well," William was murmuring, the human element on top as usual, " my feet, as I said before, is paralytic." He was just going to sit down when Bridgid made a sort of galvanised snatch at him. " William, are you *out* of your living mind? "

Mrs. Guidera said with cool propriety, " We want no modern ways and manners here. We like our proper place."

Phillip said with desperate jollity: " That's most helpful and encouraging to the new order."

Bridgid said, developing the theme: " There's distance and dignity in all things. . . ." Here Hercules gave a convulsive bounce on the sofa and began a sneezing fit, innumerable, tidy little sneezes like caps in a pistol. . . . " *Master* Hercules," she reproved him, " *use* your handkerchief! I hope you haven't caught that common cold of Mr. Walsh's. Eucalyptus on a lump of sugar tonight."

" Oh, must I? " Hercules pleaded. " Hot whisky and lemon does far more good."

" That's what you think, sir. Not what I think."

" I agree with Bridgid, I'm afraid." Phillip took the opening. " One thing that must go down in this house is the whisky consumption."

" Try an aspirin, Uncle Hercules," Veronica was brisk and suggestive.

" Never taken drugs in my life." He looked at her out of the inside corners of his big eyes like a shocked bloodhound.

" And we won't start now," Bridgid ended it. The nanny ' we ' to the foolish mother.

" Come out of the nursery, Bridgid," Phillip was uncowed, " and attend to me. Now, would you all listen carefully. . . ."

" Don't mind him, my dear," Consuelo looked backwards and upwards at Mrs. Guidera, who had taken up a position like a big guardsman on duty behind the sofa. " The poor boy's worried to death."

" It'll be all right." Hercules set everybody guessing the worst. " Just sit down in your saddles and pull your hardest for the shore."

" Oh Holy Hour "—Bridgid was at prayer immediately.

" Are we all fired? " Willy asked lightly.

" It takes two to fire me," Mrs. Guidera was militant.

" Steady yourselves." Philip got up and faced them, his back to the fire. " Just take it easy. Now—I only want to tell you frankly that I'm broke. You hardly believe me, do you? Yes, I see you don't. But I *do* assure you that it's not just an excuse for the nasty economies I intend to make." He looked round at the respectful, unbelieving masks about him; if an eyelid flickered it was towards Hercules and Consuelo—all questioning went that way, it could be felt like an arc in the air.

" All right," he spoke up, suddenly harsh. " Have it that way if you like it better that way. But perhaps you'll realise that there's some truth in what I say when I tell you the legacies my father jolly nicely left you in his will—one hundred and fifty pounds to Mrs. Guidera, the same to Bridgid, and fifty pounds to William—well, the money simply isn't there. I'm sorry, but that's actually how it is."

They had their drama. Together they cried: "Ah, what matter. . . . Don't think of it, Master Phillip. . . . Don't fret yourself. . . ." They knew absolutely that their legacies would not be the first economy.

Consuelo, seeing things going rather the wrong way, spoke up almost with tears: "You shall have your legacies if I sell my rings for you——" She spread her hands and took a last look at the collection (all old paste) that sparkled so charmingly. "The rings on my fingers." Her voice reached a beautiful note of sacrifice. She certainly had something there. A quiver of appreciation passed through everybody, everybody except the young.

"You've done that years ago, Aunt Consuelo." Phillip had an unfortunate and not very witty inspiration. "Try the bells on your toes, now."

"Oh, Master Phillip," Bridgid was deeply shocked, "you're a bold, unruly boy."

Hercules reached out his hand to pat Bridgid's lightly: "When I touch, you touch too, Beebee, I promise you."

"But oh! What a saucy answer he made his lovely auntie!" Mrs. Guidera spoke in a level voice. "There's a smile for her at every crossroads and I'd carry her on my back from the foundation stone up."

Everyone knew exactly what she meant and groans of assent went up all round, the loudest coming from Consuelo and Hercules.

"I'm delighted to hear you say so, Mrs. Guidera," Phillip tried to capitalise his mistake, "because if you really feel like that, three or four P.G.s in the house won't worry you."

There was a pause.

"You know what P.G. stands for, don't you, Mrs. Guidera?" Phillip persisted obstinately.

"I do, sir. It's a nasty name for a nasty thing. Well," she closed her mouth till her face looked like the back view of an ass with its tail tucked in, "Mrs. Howard and I can always start a nice little home together."

"But," Phillip met her eyes steadily, "Mrs. Howard's obliged to stay here. You see, Mrs. Guidera, she's got no money."

"Oh, what a *common* thing to say about your auntie," Bridgid squealed. "Master Hercules and me can have Mrs. Howard and Mrs. Guidera to stop with us in whatever home we go to when you let in the P.G.s, sir."

"When I let in the gipsies, Bridgid, Mr. Hercules will make his home here, for the same reason as Mrs. Howard. He's got no money, either."

"All right, old boy," Hercules reassured him gently, "I've got the hang of the thing now."

"Aha!" William gave a delighted snigger of laughter. "Yee're bewitched, bothered and bewildered now, gerrls. Oh, pardon me"—he put a hand to his mouth—"but yees is all rightly hobbled up now. Well," he made one forward step, he spoke to the young alone: "I'm here while I have my health and it's time I washed my tea things." He swept up the tray and was off, waiting neither for acceptance nor thanks.

"Well, Bridgid, well, Mrs. Guidera," Phillip spoke softly, "what do you say?"

"*I* say it's a disgrace, that's all about it." Bridgid was tearfully non-committal.

" What do you say, madam? " Mrs. Guidera ignored the children and addressed herself to her mistress. " *You'll* never order meals for lodgers, whatever name they go by."

Before she could answer, Phillip cut in: " You're quite right, she never will." He took a deep breath. " Miss Veronica and I will do the housekeeping."

Hercules it was who rose in agony. " What? My dears . . . this is FINIS! My God! You two would lunch on a hard-boiled egg. You like tinned sauces. I believe you'd even drink bottled coffee."

" Is it take my orders from the children," Mrs. Guidera went as near interrupting as she could get.

Bridgid tore at her heels—" I pushed out in their prams, and dried their tears and nappies——"

"——and made little cakes when they were good——"

"——and slapped their little bottoms when they were bold. We couldn't let ourselves down that far."

" The whole thing," Mrs. Guidera summed it up, " is a bit too derogatory."

" All right! " Phillip wound the matter up. " Make your choice tonight. Perhaps, Aunt Consuelo, you'd advise Mrs. Guidera, and Uncle Hercules, you talk it over with Bridgid."

Consuelo rose to her feet. Quiet, dignified, doomed great lady to the guillotine and *that* for the howling mob: " Have you a good fire in your kitchen, Mrs. Guidera? "

" Roasting, madam," Mrs. Guidera assured her reverentially, " there's the half an ash tree in the range. Six snipe for the dinner and snipe need a quick oven."

" We'll have our last little talk in there," she insisted,

gracious lady to the last, " where we've planned so many beautiful meals together."

" Madam." Mrs. Guidera followed her out.

Hercules got up too in a sad trickling little way. " I might take the dogs for a little stroll," he brightened slightly at the thought of giving them pleasure, " they've had an awful day, what with the funeral and everything. Besides," he brightened further, " I'd like to try my legacy—Roddy's thumb stick. Poor old boy, I'm glad he's out of all this. . . ."

Bridgid clacked after him: " We must take off our best suit, remember. We can't go out paddling in our best suit, can we. . . ."

Veronica and Phillip were left alone. Alone except for Aunt Anna Rose, nodding her great hat in her first-class carriage, sleeping her way across the Steppes, Karinina grown old.

" Oh, Phil, wasn't it ghastly? "

" It was like scolding two children for eating up an open box of chocolates at one go."

" You didn't scold them anything like hard enough," she said.

A natural force of life sprang up like a flame out of a sulky fire. Phillip looked his age, twenty-five, an ordinary, natural young man, not an anxious boy with responsibilities beyond his powers. Without Hercules, that exquisite of another date, with his razor blade nose and strangely set eyes, his enchanting hair smelling as fresh as if he had just popped out of his Bond Street hairdresser, his hands and feet like shadows, Phillip's coarser build looked tough and handsome enough. His out-of-the-Army blue suit did not seem unduly vulgar when Hercules had taken his own Beau's body, flattered by the world's best tailor, away. There was a faintly bear-like Father Christmas sort of quality in Phillip which now took its right and kindly proportion.

He lit a cigarette and gave one to Veronica. It seemed almost surprising that she should take it and smoke quite as if she had smoked before, quite like any other young girl. Without her mother it was as if the shadow of an elegant and important tree had moved and the afternoon sun shone with reasonable warmth for the child. There was a fusion between what she was and what she should have been. She was no longer a cross, uneasy schoolgirl, old for her age. She rounded out into a person of the proper unaffected mixture of childishness and adult discernment. She was real, she was someone worth talking to.

" Oh, my dear," he said, " were we too awful to them? "

" Yes, we were. Oh, Phil, why am I always so awful to Mummy? I can't help myself—my mouth seems full of plates and my teeth are covered in wires and my chin is covered in spots, and she can hardly bear to look at me, *and* I'm riding my pony slower and slower into a fence hoping he'll refuse."

" I'd feel exactly the same about Uncle Hercules if I hadn't had the war. I saw so many attractive old buffers mucking things up, I've got a different sense about him."

" They are both so idiotically attractive," she said, " it's *not fair*."

For she was vain of them. When they weren't there she had made people rock with laughter describing some ghastly misdemeanour of her mother's—some graceful derring-do, some other-worldly spendthrift madness. Now she said: " Phil, things are as bad as you told them, aren't they? "

" Worse. Quite frankly, Veronica, I'm going to put them both on an allowance—ten shillings a week, and they'll have to get on with it, God helping them."

" But you know Mummy—she must have her shopping. If she has no money she'll use her credit, and when she has no credit she'll use your credit, and when we find out the bills she's run up she'll buy us presents—*huge* presents to put us in a good temper. More bills for us. Why, if she even goes to the post office she buys three pounds' worth of stamps. She has an idea it helps their trade."

" She can't do that on ten shillings a week. Uncle Hercules is a naughty old thing too. We've got to stop that account with his bookmaker, and those little flutters on the stock exchange."

" But he won't have a note to flutter."

" He can always lose fifty pounds for a trusting friend. We must warn the P.G.s not to believe one word he says."

" Poor lamb—Mummy's much the most dangerous. Oh, Phil "—she put out her cigarette and looked at him despairingly—" I wouldn't let her guess it for the world, but how I dread these P.G.s. It's going to be awful, awful, awful. The bath water, the food, the fires. . . . How am I to persuade Mrs. Guidera or Bridgid to do any work for me. They think of me as a young twelve, not an old twenty-two."

" My dear girl, if they won't work for you they'll have to get out."

She gave him the first really adult look he had had from her. The pitying look of the housekeeper to the young organiser. The human side of the battle, the side that is wearily conscious of the dust on polished furniture; of the grimy rim in baths; of brasses going sadly green; of trays of unwashed morning tea things lurking in the pantry at three in the afternoon; of tired faces and sullen back views; of pieces of meat gone bad from negligence and pieces of meat cooked too soon from a lazy sense of convenience; of the week's washing that was never ironed by the end of the week but lapped and overlapped into the next week and the week after that until there was not a clean sheet left in the house or a pillowcase or a towel and Bridgid came grimly and accusingly to state that Master Hercules' bed was a disgrace.

She sighed unconstructively and changed the subject: "Do you think Uncle Hercules will spread sedition among the men? They do love him so and they'll tell him what a cad you are, cutting down and sacking people."

"Probably. No harm if they do. It's an outlet. Poor old boy, he *does* think I'm such an ass, too."

"Well, actually the war can't have taught you a lot about farming or running an estate."

"Anyway, it was a cad's war. *Not* like the '14-'18 business."

"They both think we're both quite hopeless. But I'd sooner be you than me."

"Poor dears—they'll soon find out they're pretty powerless. Money really does talk; it's very common of it, but extremely useful."

She laughed—"Oh, that pocket money—how much do I get?"

"You're my housekeeper," he considered the matter—

" you get a percentage on profits and tips perhaps, if the P.G.s are generous P.G.s."

" Well——" she accepted that. " I hope they don't think I'm too grand to tip."

" Seriously, I mean the percentage. We must work it out."

" Phil. . . ." It wasn't easy to say what she meant. She looked slightly paler and slightly less attractive, like a child when it is uncertain and anxious, all her looks flowing away. . . . " Phil, please, I really don't want any money out of it. . . . You know how it is, we both love Ballyroden. After all, I've lived here since I was born, haven't I? Things are tough enough for you, don't let's be silly about the money part."

" Don't let's be silly about anything," he said. " No. We must keep everything on a business footing."

" Strictly business? " She asked it a little faintly.

" Yes. If my father and your mother had done the same, I wouldn't be owing you about seven hundred pounds a year now."

" I wish you owed all the debts to me. I wish I was a good, kind bank. I'd wait—you know." She laughed it off. The laugh came out rather a silly giggle.

" You're wonderful," he said enthusiastically. " You *are* going to be such a help to me, pulling the place round. You're so—so capable and so sensible and so everything, and so quiet compared to Aunt Consuelo."

" Yes. I'm capable and sensible and generally as quiet as a mouse, but oh dear, dear, we have got a job in front of us. You know, Phil, Aunt Anna Rose has more sense than Mummy, Uncle Hercules and poor, darling Uncle Roddy all put together."

It was then that there began a tapping at the window

of the sedan; a bustling, a gathering up of belongings—the bustle and shuffle that precedes the drama of arrival at the grand terminus, went on inside. At last the window was lowered and the head and hat came gracefully forth. "Ah," she said, "*there* you are—splendid, splendid. Now call a porter! Let me out! Help me down!"

"That's right, Aunt Anna Fairy Rose." Phillip was at the door. "You get out of your coach drawn by twelve white rats."

She paused, very solidly regarding him as rather a fool—"White rats?" she repeated, then in extenuation, "you've been drinking, I suppose."

"Oh," said Phillip, "you know I haven't."

"There's only one reason for white rats—you're seeing things. Here"—she handed out myriads of invisible objects—"take my hatbox, my gladstone bag, my portmanteau. No, no, I'll manage the dressing case, thank you. And there are two heavy pieces in the van—black domed ones with the coronet and the initials." She had gone too far. Her face fell, growing obstinate and pinched: "They can stop worrying me," she said, "I won't say them. I won't say anything."

"That's all right. I expect they've just got 'Miss Anna Rose, pass to Moscow' on them."

"*That's* it, dear," she said on a warm, enormous breath of relief. "Nice of you to meet me," she went on in the voice of a guest confident of her welcome, "and isn't it cold? Now, let's put everything down on this bench. Are they all here? Portmanteau? Gladstone bag? Hat box? Umbrella? Ah, that's right. Now, I tell you wot, we'll have a little drink in the bar and a nice talk. The stuff'll be all right." She gave nothing a look across her shoulder and they all sat down on the sofa, tucking the rug round her feet. " I heard all you said, y'know. Got it on my long distance—marvellous reception! "

" Well," Phillip asked her, " what do you think about the P.G.s ? "

" *Great fun!* " The breath of strength and sense were in her emphatic acceptance of this new possibility in life. " I do wish you'd have some Americans," she went on practically, " always rich and not so inclined to hot you over the money as our own sort of people. Besides, I believe I'd get on like wildfire. I've been longing to meet one ever since Willy took me to that beautiful Western with the man who sings in it. What's 'is name? "

" I hardly think Bing Crosby would come as a paying guest," Veronica was dismally down to earth.

" Nonsense, why not? " Aunt Anna Rose picked her up on it smartly—" make a nice change for him from all these little dogies runnin' along and whackin' great blondes in saloons. Anyway," she went on in her most broadminded voice, " I'm with you, body and soul, but on one condition."

" What's that? " They knew this was going to be the great old tumbledown mountain of the position.

" I want to sit up late every night," she said. " I don't want to go to bed till the candles are burned down. Right down."

" Oh, darling," they sighed. " It's not wise—you'd be ill."

" Tell you wot—make it six-thirty," she said, the ' I'm giving it away ' tone of an expert bargainer in her voice.

" *That's* all right," Phillip yielded with relief. " Yes, yes, Aunt Anna Rose, of course you may."

" Gracious," Veronica said, " I thought you meant midnight."

" Six-thirty'll do for a start. It will be a treat. Consuelo's sent me to bed at six o'clock for the last twenty-five years. Besides, she's so rude. Does it in front of visitors: ' Long past bedtime, Aunt Anna Rose—off you pop, Aunt Anna Rose.' And the water's never hot at six o'clock."

" Poor Aunt Anna Rose. Why didn't you tell us? " They were charged with zeal.

" Oh, I'm a cagey old birdie," she said it in a wonderful dodging voice full of unspeakable secrets. " But do you know—only last Thursday she stopped me going for a nice little drive to Arigan in Willy's combination. Yes, *before* tea, too."

" Oh, how disappointing——" Veronica picked up her hand consolingly. But Aunt Anna Rose took her hand away with precision and straightened her hat.

" Now, if it had been pillion, or *after* tea, I could have seen the point. But, after all—je ne suis pas vierge—why shouldn't I go to the pictures in Arigan now and then? "

" Frankly," Phillip said, " I don't see why you shouldn't if Willy is able to take you *and* you wrap up warmly."

" A right and left—six thirty *and* the pictures—sickening for her. Now, tell me, tell me—is it true she's got *no* money left? "

" Quite true," Phillip assured her.

" Ahha," Aunt Anna Rose ahha-ed with great satisfaction. " Well, we won't pop the rubies for her, shall we? " She gáve Veronica a confidential poke. " They're going to be for little what's-your-name."

"Thank you, Aunt Anna Rose. In confidence, Aunt Anna Rose, where *are* the rubies?"

"My dear," she spoke very frankly and reasonably, "I don't know. But I put them somewhere very safe—very safe indeed."

"With these P.G.s to rob," Phillip showed awful cheeriness, "we shan't need them yet, shall we?"

"That's sensible," Aunt Anna Rose commended him. "And the paying guests are a very sensible idea, too. I like to see a bit of sanity in this house. Now," she went on without a change of voice, "talk of sensible ideas, why don't we have a drink? Champagne of course."

"Because," Phillip said with a tinge of bitterness, "Aunt Consuelo's hospitality did in the last bottle today."

"Sssh," Aunt Anna Rose put a long, gloved finger to her nose, "not *quite* the last. I snooped one while they were all carryin' dear Roddy out. I knew he'd like me to cheer myself up tomorrow morning. Nothing like a sip before lunch, is there? Unless it's after tea."

"Where is the bottle, Aunt Anna Rose? Is it a *real* bottle?" Phillip asked gently.

"Not one in your head, darling?" Veronica suggested.

"Oh, it's as real as real!" she said heartily, reassuring their doubtfulness, silly little things. "Lovely gold paper—long neck like a swan—knobbly gold cork and everything. But, do you know, I forget where I hid it. It'll come back to me in a moment—somewhere in this room, very safe. Very safe indeed—I can see it now."

"Do you believe in the champagne, Veronica?" he asked her sadly.

"Not really, it's like the rubies to me. But it doesn't

matter, Aunt Anna Rose darling, it's lovely to think about it."

"Think about it? I want to hear it go pop and sizzle-sizzle. It's quite safe, I promise you." She was not at all worried.

"Would Willy know where?" It was Veronica's suggestion.

"Oh, no," she waved Willy out of the matter. "I hid it by my own self."

All pomposity and economy gone, Phillip, his own age, burst out: "It's just what we need. Try to remember, Aunt Anna Rose. Veronica, think of something. Don't just sit there looking stuffed. Let's get stinking and be pleasant to people——"

It came to her, the inspiration: "I know," she said in her mouse's voice, "'Hunt the Thimble,' that might suggest it to you, Aunt Anna Rose."

"It's psychology," he was on his feet. "Now then, Aunt Anna Rose—hunt the thimble—you sit there." He put her down again on the sofa. "Relax and just tell us when you think we're getting warmer. It's not," he hovered near a lovely Regency black boy, "under Black Sambo's hat, is it?"

"No," Anna Rose said, dulled and sad, "I don't feel any warmer."

"In the Lion's mouth?" Veronica was investigating a great, pale pelt that swam on a dark stained sea of floor. It was a place the dogs were only too fond of on wet days.

"Cold," she said firmly.

"In the piano?" Phillip suggested brilliantly, "colder?" It was all rather gay: they chased about foolishly from object to object.

" The turf basket? "

" The wood basket? "

" Icy, icy cold."

" Icy cold," Phillip laughed, " oh, how good, and our last bottle for years." He laid his hand on a royal bust beside a healthy palm. " Queen Victoria? "

" I feel a tingle, a kind of a tingle. We're warmer, we're warmer." She looked all alive-o on her sofa.

" Help me, Veronica "—it was rather a business turning Queen Victoria upside down, and while they struggled with her Consuelo came sweeping back. She had got herself into a lovely chiffon head scarf, wildly becoming and suggestive of an Indian widow at a suttee benefit.

" What *are* you doing, you ghastly children? "

" Playing hunt the thimble, Mummy." Veronica said it. Phillip was laughing hopelessly.

" A delightful start to your new responsibilities "—Consuelo was enchanted at the discovery of such childish behaviour—" Idiotic and irresponsible as my generation is, we never played Hunt the Thimble on the day of our fathers' funerals."

" Don't pretend." Phillip was melted back into her favourite little boy. The little boy whose half-terms and exeats she had always attended with so much more pleasure than those of her own dim daughter. " You would if the stakes had been high enough. I don't care how many funerals your father had."

" Oh dear, perhaps we would." She accepted any implication that brought back her glorious youth.

" I remember my own father's funeral, Consuelo," Anna Rose piped up. " Poor Bowen the butler was so upset he went mad and came in here stark naked with the silver tea tray—very gay—very gay."

Consuelo ignored this little message from the past: "Did he? I didn't notice. Anyhow," she was firmly in to-day again, "it's Aunt Anna Rose's bedtime and here you are exciting her with Hunt the Thimble."

"And why shouldn't I have a game of Hunt the Thimble?" Anna Rose asked firmly. "Je ne suis pas vierge, am I? And in any case, it's not yet my bedtime."

Consuelo pointed to a tiny, thin walnut clock: its black openwork, iron hand, like a hand in a lace mitten, was on the stroke of six. "Aunt Anna Rose, what does that clock say? That clock says——"

"The clock," Aunt Anna Rose rose like a swan off its nest, with a clattering and beating of wings. "The clock—Oo—*burning*, BURNING. It's in the clock, of course."

They opened the clock and snatched it out, indeed as real as real, and with an added buried treasure glamour attached to it. The moment seemed almost miraculous, even the tray of glasses William had brought earlier and fruitlessly were waiting for the pop and the sizzle and the bubbles flying up their stems.

"Aunt Anna Rose"—Consuelo maintained her shocked voice although she was edging into position for a glass to be handed to her—"what are you doing with this bottle of wine? It's very bad for the clock and it's not at all good for you."

"Much better for Hercules and you, I suppose, than for the clock and me." She was as blithe as possible.

"Well"—the word that covers all loss of all words—"Really!"

"I'm havin' a glass just the same, my dear." She

stretched out an arm and a hand as steady as a rock and took one from Veronica.

"You too, darling," Phillip, always for a quiet life, gave one to Consuelo.

"Now," Aunt Anna Rose waited till they were all ready—"I'm going to drink success to these two children and their paying guests."

"Aunt Anna Rose"—it was a real cry against revolution, let the aristos hang together at all costs—"don't you encourage them in their crazy schemes."

"Yes, I will." All the flow of ideas in Anna Rose, all the ruminations and conclusions come to on her journeys were breaking surface like the bubbles shooting up the hollow stem of her glass. She had more words than she could use for this moment. "Changes are due here," she said firmly. "Oh, the years fly by, so quick, so quick. Twenty-five years have gone since you came back to Ballyroden as a widow, Consuelo—God!" She kissed her fingertips, "you were a peach, too—oh, a fine gal—can't *think* why you never got another man—anyway, you didn't—and I've watched you and Hercules encourage darling Roddy in every naughty thing he did. Where he spent a shilling you pushed him on to spend a pound." She paused to cackle. "I'm talkin' in riddles —*one* Pound, *Thousands*." The thousands rolled round the room. "If I hadn't kept a keen eye on the milkin' cows and the layin' hens, if I hadn't spent my days catchin' poachers and timber stealers, things would be past saving now." She took a great draught, as though she was drinking beer, paused, and hiccupped neatly. "But there's something for these two, something from the wreck—and I'll help them to keep it." She hiccupped again. "More, please."

" Aunt Anna Rose, you're wonderful." Phillip refilled her glass to the brim.

" This is real madness," Consuelo accused the children. She would not have dared to speak so to Aunt Anna Rose.

" It won't hurt her for once, Mummy," Veronica suggested weakly.

" Won't hurt her ? "—at last Consuelo had found a suitable victim—" What about her blood pressure? Do you want to murder her? Champagne gives her dangerous hiccups, and it's past six o'clock—bedtime! "

Aunt Anna Rose spoke in a clear, microscopic thread of a voice, spoke to Consuelo alone: " Bedtime," she said, " is now six-thirty. And I shall hiccup myself to *death* if I please." She turned to Consuelo, raised the brimming glass and smiled across a gold mist into the children's eyes.

* 2 *

OUTSIDE THE house it was wet and black with rain. Brilliant leaves were pasted to the gravel. The air was warmer than it is inside a cat's ear—it purred with warmth. There was sunshine in great strength and sweetness. There were odd roses, glowing brightly, and shrubs, azalea and rhus and berberis, flaming away. Under dripping garden walls, sugar pink and red nerines flowered more waxen than stephanotis, more beautiful, but scentless. Only when pinched out of their bruises came a smell as strong as blood or resin—there must be some splendid alacrity in them to sustain such beauty in winter time. Kaffir lilies, crimson and flannel pink, flowered more dismally among their grassy leaves. Birds sang wildly, vilely, variously: A November morning.

That was out of doors. Indoors, walls streamed with water, a condensation of damp almost impossible to believe took place. The walls pretended to be fungus, they grew fur like rabbits. If you touched them your thumb would sink in. A hot-water bottle in mattresses produced not clouds of steam but streams of water. All polished surfaces of furniture and the edges of floors were misted, grape blue. Masks of foxes and heads and horns smelt like elementals, and windows looked as if a sea fog was struggling to get out through them—out of the house at any cost. Velvet curtains had gone through a mangle but no further damp could be dried out of them. Within the house, cold seized on one like an animal, it was so strong and positive compared with the delicious warmth outside—the same kind temperature as hot manure, a gentle simmering day.

Two strangers stood in the drawing-room of Ballyroden—cold strangers, and their foreign breaths blew in visible, lingering puffs on the air. They had just and only just arrived. The taxi which had brought them over sixteen miles of mountain roads had disgorged a mountain of expensive baggage on the granite steps. Its driver had gently pocketed his enormous fare and a prodigious tip and driven away at high speed.

Appearing after a long interval, a sour and perturbed Bridgid had shown three strangers into the house. One of them, a woman, shuddered inside her mink coat before the unlighted fire. She had been a beautiful woman, a spoilt woman, a successful woman. Although she was thin as a lathe her good looks showed none of the quality so luminous through Aunt Consuelo's mountainous body. This woman's movements had a trained, fashion-plate kind of elegance. The jaw bone was weighty though fleshless in contrast to that tilt of light bone that cannot be lost. She had beautiful dark eyes, big and brown and emphasised with shadow and solid, strong lashes stiff with mascara. Her expensively cut hair curled pretty as a child's. It had been red. It was undyed. She held her tiny hat against her chest with an ungloved hand. In the other hand she held her dressing case in its canvas cover. Her exquisite legs lost themselves in enormous fur and leather boots. She scolded and complained into the cold air. Her voice was loud, but correct and easy. At every turn of meaning she repeated the same word or phrase.

" I'm completely exhausted. I'm colder than I've ever been in my life, and *now* you tell me "—she turned to Bridgid who was lighting the fire without much zeal—" that our wire didn't arrive and our hosts don't expect us till to-morrow." She paused, but not long enough for an answer. " Really. What a country! What a train service! What a telephone service! And, what a fire! "

" That fire don't like this wind, madam," Bridgid explained slowly and as though the fire had some variable human quality far more lovable and important than the chilled stranger. She looked at it indulgently as it flickered its way to extinction, and changed the subject brightly. " I'm sorry to read in my English Sunday papers that the telephone service on your own side is not what it was."

When Bridgid went out of the room a tall, old man who had been coasting round peering happily at pictures and furniture and china gave up his obvious pleasures and came across to the unhappy woman. He was good looking, too, and almost as like the woman as Hercules was to Consuelo, except for the eyes. His were small and intelligent. His voice was not quite so good as hers, but it was human and warm and had within it the amused quality which is only evident in the voices of those with a vast inner store of resource.

" Anyhow, Dorothy," he said, " it's awkward for them having us a day too soon. Sit down, my dear child, and keep cool."

" Oh, I shall remain infinitely cool beside this fire, dear. But "—she continued to the air where so much grievance is directed—" would somebody be good enough to break the news to our hosts that their *paying* guests"—she was suddenly aware that Bridgid had disappeared—"where is she?"

"Madam?" Bridgid returned with some very wet, unpromising-looking logs.

The tale was taken up in a masterly fashion—"Mrs. Cleghorne Thomas, her daughter and her brother, Mr. Eustace Mills, have arrived. After tossing on the Irish Sea for six hours, all I need is a hot bath, my bed, two hot-water bottles and a tray with something warm, light and refreshing." She spoke with a precise vision of the comforts she envisaged.

Bridgid answered, also with grim precision: "The bath water's not lit, madam—the beds is stripped off, and they're all out.

"Out?" It was too much.

Eustace, seeing the situation developing into something ugly, tried a more friendly line of approach: "Begorrah and begabers, now, find them like a clever colleen and tell them we wish them the top of the morning."

Bridgid stared at him: "Pardon me, sir—I don't understand *one* word you're saying."

His sister was almost appeased by this miniature disaster: "My dear boy, when *will* you learn that the natives never understand their own ghastly language?"

Unperturbed by the interruption, he proceeded: "What's your name, my dear?"

"Bridgid, sir, if you don't mind," she was distinctly more approachable.

"Well, now, Bridgid, just tell them we're really here on the wrong day, we are very sorry about it, very. But we are longing for a little something to eat and drink."

"It's too bad, sir"—she softened a further degree.

" Sir Phillip and Miss Veronica are shooting the Long Bog, Mrs. Howard and Master Hercules are gone for a walk with the dogs and Willy have taken Miss Anna Rose for a little joy-ride down the back avenue on his motor-cycle."

" Motor-cycle! " Mrs. Cleghorne Thomas disgustedly pinned down the one immaterial circumstance. " How ghastly! And what "—she was into the air again—" is Yvonne doing all this time? "

" The young lady is carrying up the small luggage. I think, if you don't mind, I'll go and give her a hand."

Alone again, the desperate woman took up the position of one who has missed the last train and huddles in a fireless waiting-room indefinitely. She spoke from somewhere far inside her mink coat: " So this is Ireland —and *what* a warm welcome." The man could have the responsibility of Ireland and its welcome.

But he didn't care. He was back at his prowling among the pieces. " What an exquisite pair of figurines." He stopped enchanted before two wreathed creatures embracing with that poised ardour and dislike most clearly felt in Shakespeare's cruel love sonnets. He hardly breathed his appreciation, he was so delighted. " Early, very early," he murmured.

" I'm shivering," she cuddled angrily into her huge coat, ignoring his pleasure.

His eyes changed their direction: " And I've never seen anything nicer than these sconces. Look, Dorothy, they're right—absolutely right, I think."

She would not look. " You're not buying for a museum now, Eustace. Do stop prowling. It's getting on my nerves. Let's try to revive this fire before I die of exposure."

He sighed. But he was beyond her peevishness. Coasting delightedly, unbelievingly from little picture to little picture, he gave her only the minimum amount of attention. " At the equator or at Claridges, you'd still complain of over exposure," he spoke with indulgence, as if her idiocies were old friends. " Please remember, it was entirely your idea to visit a damp Irish mansion in the middle of November."

" As a mother," her handsome eyes swept upwards, " I think I took the brave and right decision."

He was not quite so big about it: " Let's say, dear, you took a decision."

In her mind were recreated all the difficulties and horrors of that decision and departure: reading advertisements, answering advertisements, refusals, acceptances, half measures, arguments, letters, agony of decision, agony of indecision, discussion, sleeplessness, arguments: the burden that precedes change, the lack of necessity for change, the absolute necessity for change, the friends who advised for it—creating doubt—against it, creating resolution, advice only sought to strengthen her in resolution.

Standing here, now, in the strange house, her heart felt like a pebble, enclosed in pounds of cold, white fat. She had no feeling at all except a nervous greed for warmth and food and approval. She thought with agony of mind of that comfortable flat in Cadogan Gardens in which she had so creditably and honourably survived the war years. There she had stayed and worked—except for school holidays in safe areas. There Eustace had lived and worked too, putting his business into less astute minds and hands than his own, without a grudging thought. She had been happy, busy, frightened and important nearly all the time. She had had attractive men to flatter her and need her and take her out. She had forgotten her age. She had been a desirable and desired woman. She had done her job well and looked after her delicate brother with a nervous, dedicated devotion—the devotion a husband should have had. But she and her husband had been separated for too long. She was too sincere and catholic for remarriage. This was the first reason in her coming to Ireland—a change of life and scene for the child, Yvonne, who must be protected from the early, irretrievable marriage. Yvonne, who had known nothing but school and the W.R.N.S. and the success of always being the prettiest and the most popular with boy and girl. Now, with the war over and leisure and glamour and food and clothes becoming a possibility once more, and a beautiful daughter of eighteen, a mother's interest and reason for extravagance, here was Yvonne sullenly and unprettily determined to marry a young man lately returned from the Navy to a very subordinate position in Eustace's textile works.

It was not so much money snobbishness or social snobbishness as a wild refusal to see her own early, irretrievable mistake in life repeated. She knew the child's character, it was like her own. She had been in love before. She would be in love again. She was wildly attractive to men. At eighteen, what had she seen, what did she know? If a trip to Kilimanjairo could have lifted her mind from this obsession, to Kilimanjairo they would have gone. But in the years succeeding the Second World War of the century, it was considerably simpler to come to Ireland—considerably easier to persuade Yvonne to cross the Irish Channel for a month, and the change would in a way be as immense.

She saw again that advertisement in *Country Life* which had put the idea into her mind. After she had seen it, several of her friends had shown it to her and it seemed everything that was charming and suitable and the very thing for Eustace, who was badly in need of a rest and good food and hot fires. For Yvonne there was even a young man. Burke's Landed Gentry and Debrett had yielded up their authentic information on that subject. Everything had been put to Eustace and he had agreed with reservations. There was no harm in it, one way or other; tension was relieved and he didn't mind testing out Yvonne's stability of feeling towards the young lover in his works whom Dorothy fled. . . .

Shivering and looking for a quarrel, she repeated: " And you did agree with me it was quite an idea to get Yvonne away from that hopeless affair in your works."

" I don't look on Harry Holt as hopeless, you know. I'm quite sure of his stability, but I don't mind testing out Yvonne's."

" She's been madly in love with every attractive American she's met for the last three years."

" She's a shocking little flirt, but I think Harry will get her, myself."

This large outlook enflamed her: " I can't have it. Just a good-looking plumber's mate—*too* boring. After all I've done for the child. Now I wonder if this Sir Phillip Ryall mightn't be the answer."

" My dear Dorothy—you appal me. You really do. You don't know the first thing about him."

" Oh, yes I do. I've looked him up in everything. Aged thirty. Educated Winchester and Trinity College, Cambridge. Served Irish Guards and Commandos during war, attaining the rank of major. Interests—fishing, shooting and——"

"Don't say it."

"I won't. As a matter of fact it's farming."

"Well, that's better. But do Yvonne's interests coincide in any way. What *are* Yvonne's interests?"

"Men."

"I mean her mental interests."

"I told you—men. Oh, I follow you now—well, her hair, her nail polish, the pictures, men—yes, and cookery. She really likes cooking. It's her thing at the moment—and the chief reason I got her to come to Ireland. She's never cooked with new eggs and she wants to try."

"She knows nothing about Sir Phillip?"

"No, no. Sir Phillip will be quite a surprise. And as this house must be twenty miles from the nearest Odeon, she's bound to take an interest." She plunged at her handbag, finished with the subject. "Oh dear, I *am* so cold and hungry. I thought Ireland was roaring with log fires and rolling in fresh eggs and whipped cream."

"And eager, unmarried baronets." He said it without turning round.

She ignored that. "I've had nothing to eat except a mess in a basket since we left London." She yawned a hungry and exhausted yawn. "Do you think that bell rings? Try and see what happens."

He considered the bells—painted china knobs on half circles of fluted brass; there was one on each side of the fireplace—in a pleased absent sort of way. Then he shook his head. "Bellringing is a very antagonistic proceeding," he said. "Anyhow," he cocked his head sideways, good ear towards the door, "I think I hear somebody coming. But it sounds rather like a child—it's running. Listen——"

" Oh, my God—not a child——" Dorothy Cleghorne Thomas genuinely turned a little faint at the idea.

But it was Aunt Anna Rose who came hurrying in. Aunt Anna Rose, flushed from the open air, and about her an indefinable air of arrival and departure—a look of absolute virility and concentration, enchanting in one so old. Besides, she was dressed for something rather special, a drive in a Rolls with all the windows down, perhaps, for a pearl coloured motoring veil half hid the white bird in her hat, shaded her pretty eyes and bunched charmingly under her chin. She wore the softest, most important overcoat in pale wool with big pockets and a velvet collar slightly reminiscent of Oscar Wilde. Heavy suède gloves went wrinkling and wrinkling up her wrists.

" Ah." Her sweetest most triumphant voice—" only just made it—sixty m.p.h. up the back avenue! You've been travelling too? " Sympathy was in the question, also the indication that they could not expect too much of her time.

" Yes," Dorothy agreed, eager for the bliss of enlarging on the hideous journey.

" Yes "—for once Eustace was first—" we've been travelling all night." Who was this old enchantress and whither did she go? Obviously she was off somewhere. She was leaving, one felt it. The nicest people are always lost to us.

" And now we're praying for some food and some sleep," Dorothy went on.

" Oh, my poor people, you haven't an earthly hope." Aunt Anna Rose had sometimes a wonderful, round lisp.

She said ' earsly ' for ' earthly.' " Vese places are terribly full."

" Are they? " Dorothy looked round the room rather more keenly, peopling it with a four of bridge, perhaps.

" Many more guests in the house besides ourselves? " Eustace asked anxiously.

" Oh, one never knows." Aunt Anna Rose disclaimed responsibility. She wouldn't answer for anything. " They come and go, you know—they come and go."

" Really? " Eustace was intrigued. " Do you live here? "

" Yes, yes. On and off," Aunt Anna Rose admitted gaily. " Actually, I'm on my way to Honolulu." She sat down on the sofa and began to go through her handbag in a deft business-like way. " I can't face a whole winter in Ireland."

Dorothy sat down beside her. Thank God, a woman of leisure and luxury; a woman who knew her hotels; a woman of elegance and intelligence; perhaps even a bridge player. In this awful fireless room of this unwelcoming house it was like meeting a fellow spirit in a waiting room at Cologne, or a desolate mid-France terminus, or Manchester.

" How wise." Dorothy spoke in a comfortable, sound commonsense sort of voice, the prelude to a good talk. She sat down beside the smart old lady and wrapped the mink stole she had been hugging round her feet.

Aunt Anna Rose took a rainbow bundle of coloured leaflets (Mr. Walsh's present) from an outside pocket of her handbag and handed them carelessly to her companion on the sofa. " This is the sort of thing I'm lookin' forward to." She spoke in a throw-away voice—no enthusiasm at all.

Dorothy held them like a bright fan of warmth in her hand, looking avidly from one to another. The impression of two worldly travellers getting together in a pullman or on the deck of a luxury liner was startling.

" Oh, I think you're so right. Look at that, Eustace—sun-browned bodies—blue skies. If a little old Irish lady can fix up the money side of it and get out there, why can't you? "

" Largely because I'm not a little old Irish lady, I suppose." He took the leaflet she handed him and looked at it quietly, and from it to Aunt Anna Rose, who was snapping elastic bands round her passport. " Are you really going on a banana boat? " he asked respectfully.

" Oh no," she said, " B.O.A.C. always."

" Perhaps you're right." Dorothy considered the possibilities. " Personally, I always say Pan-American, don't I, Eustace? "

" You do, my dear," he agreed. " You always do."

Aunt Anna Rose looked at her watch and then popped a tablet in her mouth. " Do you get about the world much? It's my greatest pleasure."

" It was mine too," Dorothy spoke with real feeling, " ah, Paris before the war——"

" Mind you," Aunt Anna Rose interrupted in the most down to earth voice, " Paris can still be very gay. Very nice and gay—if you can afford it. D'you remember Vienna before the last war? " Here she really did permit a little nostalgia.

" No," the answer flashed back sharply, " I *don't.*"

" Ah, what you missed," Aunt Anna Rose sighed; but immediately put regrets behind her and looked brightly to the present and the future: " These wonderful airlines have opened up such vistas for our old age, haven't they? We should all get out of Ireland from November to March. Pourin' rain, leakin' roofs, cold beds and colder baths." She surveyed the prospect already as though from a splendid, warm distance. Such things happened, of course, but not in her kind of life.

" Oh dear, is that a universal picture? " Eustace asked rather miserably.

" Candidly, I've always found it so here." Then she looked at him and a light of kindness came into her child's eyes, fairy's eyes—eyes no more human than violets in a chilly April wood.

" Things may look up after tomorrow," she told them. " My nephew's got some paying guests coming—English. Not quite in the stud-book, I gather—but very rich."

Dorothy grew perceptibly chill and stiff inside her beautiful, warm, well-chosen clothes. But Eustace giggled delightedly.

" Rich—well, that's a help."

" I don't know," Aunt Anna Rose shook her head wisely, " I tell the children these people may expect a lot."

" P'raps they will." Dorothy spoke with icy certainty. " If they pay a lot."

" Well—they won't get much. Consuelo and Hercules are on the war-path. Out for BLOOD. I wouldn't be a P.G. in this house for something." She wrote the P.G.s off—quite a joke—and got up from the sofa as effortlessly as a girl. " Now," she said, " 'fraid I really must be off. I don't know why we talk to strangers travellin', do you? I always do it—one of my stable vices." In their surprised silence she stood listening. " I think my flight's about due—999, such an easy one to remember."

Dorothy retreated into the farthest corner of the sofa;

quite a little thing she looked when frightened. Eustace was rather upset too, but he was also enthralled: " Did you say you were leaving for Honolulu to-day? " he insisted—he had to know.

" Right now," she assured him briskly. " I hear my plane warming up. We'll be roaring down the runway in a couple of minutes." She walked across the room to her sedan chair with the very definite air of one crossing an airport. One foot poised above the little height of the step up to her sedan chair, she looked back: " Just think of me waking up in the Azores when the rain is slashing in at your windows tomorrow. Good-bye." She got in, leaned back, plugged her ears, put a piece of chewing gum in her mouth, opened a new, glossy illustrated paper and relaxed.

The room was as empty of her presence as though she had melted off into the damp air. Eustace and his sister faced each other. She was shocked and shaken, he was shocked and delighted. She made a grab for her dressing case and faced him, ready for the road, her mink stole bunched in her hands. " Eustace—let's get out of here quick. She may be violent."

" Nonsense," he reassured her maddeningly, " I expect she's as sane as anyone else in this house. It's the thought of Consuelo and Hercules that frightens me."

" Let's find Yvonne," her eyes were jumping, she was out of her depths—" don't let's unpack a thing. We can leave at once."

" Don't you know I've paid a fortune in advance for our lodging? " He could not quite keep the enjoyment out of his voice.

" Why on earth did you do that? "

" I can only suppose," he considered her, mink, dressing case and all, " because we're not *quite* in the stud-book."

It was rather wicked of him and certainly not the moment for a gleam of fun. " Anyway," he went on, " you've got me here and I'm not leaving until I've seen everything in the house. Really Dorothy, I must. Do you know," his voice sank, " there's a Renoir, a veritable Renoir nestling over there behind Queen Victoria? "

She knew then that it was hopeless to move him. It would be more difficult than extracting him from a good, unexplored junk shop. There is no such fevered blood as that which runs in a collector's veins. Its necessity fiercer than love or drink or drugs. But she could go on scolding: " Renoir! And what will happen to Yvonne and me while you're probing for Picassos among the Monarchs of the Glen in the back passages? "

He was off again, roaming and peering: " No doubt," he said, " the Bart. will look after you. He *may* be quite sane. He's only a nephew, she said."

" Oh *God*," the nephew suddenly grew monstrous in her mind, " Eustace, be human—I've heard of very queer happenings in these old Irish mansions."

Her back was turned to the door, her voice was strong and precise as only a well-trained English voice can be; it was not ugly, but it cracked a silence open like cracking the top of an egg.

Delightedly, Consuelo paused in the doorway. For all her size and height she seemed as light as air. She wore a dark cyclamen coloured jersey, big and soft, her tiny bird's head was tied in a man's purple silk handkerchief. She looked as rich and sweet as a very well-grown bed of violets—Princess of Wales—grown on lots of leaf-mould and old manure. She carried a basket and a walking stick and radiated aristocratic country activity. As she advanced into her drawing-room, wet hazel thickets, the district nurse, the music of hounds, your own grapes and peaches with the bloom warm on their skins, wood fires, subscriptions to the Church and *The Times* Library came with her, intangible and undeniable.

" *Have* you, Mrs. Thomas? " her melodious, commanding voice swelled out before her, " so have I. But nothing funnier than guests arriving on the wrong day. However, here you are. How do you do? " She pointed out and forgave the social enormity in the same breath.

The boats that only sailed on the wrong days, the aeroplanes that were the wrong form of travel for Eustace's delicate ears all came into Dorothy's mind and all seemed part of the general perverse horror of Ireland.

" I'm extremely sorry to be such a bore. But two days ago we sent you a very long telegram. No telephone directory disclosed your name or number."

" *Don't* apologise." She was again forgiven and then ignored. " How d'you do, Mr. Mills? "

" How d'you do? "

" It's so awkward and embarrassing for you, I know," her voice was all sympathy. " It's just the kind of thing I'm so glad I didn't do myself. But "—she looked about her vaguely—" weren't there supposed to be three of you coming tomorrow? "

" My daughter, Yvonne," Dorothy chipped it out, " after three years of hard war work, is now helping your housemaid to make our beds."

" Oh, dear," Consuelo sighed, the distracted hostess, " I do wonder if they'll be aired." She breathed out a great " HA " of blue mist and watched it dissolve on the drawing-room air. " You don't know yet what an Irish climate is like."

" As a matter of fact," Dorothy wrapped herself in her mink as in a bath towel, the same flinging gesture, and flinched backwards from the chilly breath as though it was an added cold contamination of the air, " I'm gettin' a pretty shrewd idea. Don't you find it a good plan to light fires sometimes? "

Hercules came trotting in to save his sister the embarrassment of a reply to this common thrust. He looked at Dorothy almost approvingly for a moment, then catching his sister's eyes, he shook hands politely and coolly: " How d'you do? How d'you do? " like a child who has been told to shake hands. " Bit unexpected, I'm afraid," he said with horrid geniality. " Hope they looked after you. By the way, has anyone told you about the sugar ration? Eight ounces a week, two taken off for the cooking and after that it's every man for himself in a lozenge box or pill bottle. Biscuits are so scarce, it's not worth dividing the ration. I usually eat the lot."

Eustace spoke for the first time. " I love biscuits," he said gently.

Happily Consuelo picked him up on it: " Oh dear, that *is* unlucky. You've come to the wrong country, haven't you? "

" I'm quite fascinated by the country, Mrs. Howard," he told her firmly, " and its inhabitants."

" My brother "—Dorothy gave an unmistakable look at the people, not the furniture—" is an ardent collector of antiques."

" Really? How nice, how nice." Consuelo accepted that in the gracious lady slumming manner. " Now," she went briskly on, " I hope we're all going to be great friends, so let's start with a clear understanding of the situation."

"My understanding of the situation, Mrs. Howard, would be so much clearer if it were possible to have our talk over a hot fire after a hot meal."

Consuelo was all concern: "Ring, Tots darling, please." And to the guests: "You must forgive any little lapses in organisation and comfort. My little daughter has only just succeeded me as housekeeper and between ourselves—well, the kindest word for it is inexperience. I fear the worst for lunch." She produced one egg from her basket, looked at it and put it back again. If lunch was to consist of one egg between four people, it was not hard to tell who would have the egg and who would have the curry sauce and raisins.

Dorothy, however, reacted brightly: "A fresh egg, how wonderful! Haven't seen such a thing for months—not for years as a matter of fact if the hen did it today."

"Your government," Consuelo gazed at Dorothy's hat as though the government were responsible for that little horror too, "seem to *like* making you all feel uncomfortable."

The strangers had the government they deserved. Hercules caught on to the idea, too: "I'd stand up to them a bit more, myself," he advised.

"You try standing two hours in a queue for a bag of biscuits," Dorothy almost spat it at him.

"Oh, I shouldn't dream of it. I'd use my brains and save my feet. I'd fox the beggars and send Bridgid. She'd love it, too."

"If you didn't live in such a neutral country you would realise that servants and fresh eggs are almost equally unprocurable in England. No drink, no petrol, no taxis——"

He stopped her halfway up the scale: "No taxis? Don't care. Doesn't frighten me. I can rough it. I can rough it. Nothing like a nice toddle up St. James on a nice mornin'. I suppose one can always get a drink at the club."

Eustace, who saw that Dorothy, swollen now with the righteous self-conceit of the war-worker, righteous and justifiable in contrast to these two useless old remnants of past extravaganza, was just about to be unsufferably rude, spoke for her quietly: "There are other, perhaps more far-reaching changes——"

"Yes, yes," Hercules agreed heartily. "Wire and plough and aerodromes everywhere—foxhunting finished, anything else?"

"Nothing on which I could hope to enlighten you, sir," Eustace admitted.

"Ah, I keep abreast of the times, don't miss much," Hercules agreed.

"Your grasp's phenomenal, if I may say so."

"You may, you may. And you young ladies," he turned prettily to Dorothy, "have had quite a time of it too?"

Dorothy suddenly thought there was perhaps quite a little something about the old boy. She flung up her chin and shook her pretty hair bravely, inevitably running a hand through its curls. "Well, all our nerves in bits and pieces. . . . Trying to keep a little glamour in our hair and a little varnish on our nails."

"My dear Dorothy," Eustace said indulgently, "bombs and barricades wouldn't keep you from your hairdresser."

"Certainly not. If red revolution ever comes to drop

my head in a basket, every curl will be in its proper place. That's how I happen to feel about it, Mr. Ryall."

"Oh, I should feel just the same, I'm afraid, shouldn't I, Tots?" Consuelo was sensitive to the faintest upward spark of interest where Hercules was concerned. She welcomed now Mrs. Guidera's arrival with a neat tray, a clean, pretty, little mid-morning fortification. A little food, a little drink. And with it Hercules was back within himself. No other interest could hold him for half a second.

Silently and ceremoniously Mrs. Guidera advanced and stood between her employers; her well-bred sense of her place allowed her to ignore even the presence of the two strangers in the room.

But Dorothy, cold, cross and hungry, was ready to snatch even a biscuit from the tray. She advanced, crying with acid gaiety: "Food! Food at last."

"William," Mrs. Guidera addressed Consuelo only, "is gone to town for the rations and Bridgid is above at her—unexpected—beds. So I just took your tray up myself. Your chicken broth, Master Hercules, and here's your egg-nog, madam, a dash of cream, a half a glass of rum, and I hope you'll like it. Drink it up now, while it's hot." She stood between Consuelo and the invader as though, a nannie, she protected her frail pampered charge from the assault of a street urchin.

Consuelo smiled up at her ravishingly: "Thank you, Mrs. Guidera. Now, Mrs. Guidera, this poor Mrs. Thomas——"

"Cleghorne-Thomas," Dorothy corrected.

"Leghorne-Thomas. Mrs. Leghorne-Thomas seems *very* hungry. Can you do anything? P'raps a cup of tea?"

"We're just out of tea, madam," Mrs. Guidera triumphed quietly. "But William ought to be back with the rations in a half an hour."

"Not another half-hour." Dorothy was quite near tears. The sight of these elegant morsels of food and drink was really too much. She lit a cigarette and isolated herself in a cold, furious silence.

Eustace was not defeated of his good manners. He possessed an extraordinary live interest in people which made him more anxious to find out the cause of rudeness than to be offended by it. Watching them sipping away at their nice hot potions, he said: "We spent the first half-hour of our stay with you having a very pleasant chat to your old friend in there," he smiled towards the sedan chair where the leather curtains were now drawn across the windows. "The one who's just off to Honolulu."

"By air, I hope," Hercules broke in anxiously. "Aunt Anna Rose would never stand one of those banana boat trips, though she's mad keen to try."

"She's your aunt, is she?" Dorothy knocked the ash sharply off her cigarette. "Very queer in her mind, surely?" The presumption was startlingly vulgar.

Consuelo stared back at her, puzzled. "How *odd* that you should get such an impression."

Hercules said quickly: "Rather wonderful for her age, don't you think. At least we don't really *know* her age. She cut the date out of every snob book farther back than we can remember and she won't tell anybody now—says *she* can't remember. Just her fun—her memory's bell-metal, sound as bell-metal."

"Her memory's too good, too good—that's just the trouble." Consuelo hated this consorting with the enemy, but it was for Aunt Anna Rose. "Please remember," she said, "don't call her anything but *Miss* Anna Rose."

"Really—what's her name?"

Consuelo leaned towards them and whispered: "The Baroness Schomanska."

"Oh, one of those little foreign titles. Why not admit it? No one's ashamed of them now."

"Well," Hercules spoke up smartly, "the last particular fool who called her that she dotted her one-two over the head and pushed her into the lake. Yes, before tea, too." He scooped a delicious teaspoonful of fragments out of the bottom of his cup and looked across it warningly before popping it into his mouth.

Eustace said quietly: "We shouldn't dream of calling her anything but Miss Anna Rose. How pretty it sounds. But the *other* name," he lowered his voice considerately, "Schomanska. It's Austrian, isn't it? I connect it with the Imperial family somehow, don't I?"

Consuelo warmed towards him. There is no solvent like snobbery.

"Not actually connections," she admitted, "but very close friends. "Hereditary positions at the Court and all that sort of nonsense."

"Then what . . ?" he stopped. Perhaps there was some sixty-year-old liaison, an indiscretion irremediable in those days. . . . Better not ask any more.

Dorothy had jumped to the same conclusion—"We won't forget the *Miss* Anna Rose," she said pertly.

Consuelo and Hercules both blushed together. They grew pink up to their hair. Consuelo said smoothly: "We don't often talk of it, but since you *ask*, he was the Emperor's closest friend. Their marriage was one of the great events and romances of that season. Vienna was quite at her feet. My grandfather was First Secretary at the embassy. 'The Rose of Dublin' they called her, I think, am I right, Tots?"

"Yes, Pets—and the Imperial white horses drew her carriage to church. Took 'em to the station afterwards, I believe. Quite a do."

"A coat of rose pink cloth, sables and a sable muff—I've got all the newspaper cuttings somewhere. Pretty she must have looked, mustn't she? It was almost historic, if you know what I mean. The little Irish beauty . . . *only* a duke's grand-daughter, we're a *very* simple country family, Mrs. Thomas. I 'member there was quite a thing about the Czar lending them his little summer palace in the Caspian for their honeymoon. The Czar before the Czar before the last Czar, it must have been. . . ."

"But what happened?"—now that the rude idea of illegitimacy was out, Eustace didn't mind asking. The story interested him.

"Died, poor chap. On his honeymoon—tough luck—such is life." Hercules shook his head sagely. "Bust appendix, I think it was."

"Yes, the *tragedy* of it, and in the train—the Orient Express."

"Imperial coach, I suppose," Dorothy put in. She couldn't help it.

"Yes, as a matter of fact it *was*," Consuelo admitted simply. "But that didn't help much. My father's told me about it often. They were very much in love and very young. She never really recovered from the shock. She's been obsessed by trains and journeys ever since. Round and round the world she goes, always thinking she'll find him. Sometimes it's trains, sometimes it's boats and now it's aeroplanes, and she never admits who she's looking for. She can't speak of him yet. So please, you won't say anything that would remind her."

"I should have thought a good psychologist——" Dorothy suggested brightly. The subject of Vienna still annoyed her faintly.

"I don't really think we'd insult our aunt with that kind of person." Consuelo might have been talking about an abortionist round a corner. "Anyhow, shall we change the subject? I don't want her to get you on her long distance."

"No, no, it's all right, Consuelo. Never uses her long distance gadget when she's flyin'—atmospherics bother her. She takes one of those Commando pills and just snoozes off," Hercules reassured them.

"But she herself mentioned Vienna to my sister—so gaily, too." Eustace was puzzled. Anything less romantically despondent than Aunt Anna Rose he had seldom seen.

"Yes, yes, but Vienna's much the same as Palm Beach to her now, you know. Her *mind* is so active, bless her." Hercules wrinkled his eyebrows into his hair, trying to explain Aunt Anna Rose without disloyalty or an unkind suggestion. After all, she was them.

"Let's talk of something else." Consuelo leaned confidentially towards the guests. "Now what's really puzzling me is, why you ever came here."

"Actually," Dorothy was delighted with the opening, "for food, rest, warmth and, we hoped, a little civilised society."

"Oh," Consuelo opened liquid, pitying eyes, "you're doomed to disappointment. You do know Ballyroden is the wrong end of a lake and the far side of a mountain from anywhere, don't you? "

" Yes, we realised that very clearly after our drive here today. Though not "—Dorothy paused—" from your advertisement in *Country Life*."

Hercules answered with innocent conviction: " We're twenty miles from anywhere and we love it."

" All right for us elders," Eustace hesitated, " but what about the young generation? Isn't it a bit isolated? "

" Yes, what does your nephew do with himself? " Dorothy leaned towards Hercules for her answer.

" Oh, poor fellow, he's—you know "—he tapped his own forehead meaningly—" completely ossified."

Dorothy indicated the sedan chair with a tiny gesture of dismay: " Not that kind of thing over again, I hope? "

" Oh, dear, no, he hasn't got one half of Aunt Anna Rose's brain."

" There's not nearly so much to go wrong, if you know what I mean."

" No, I don't entirely follow you. What *are* his interests? "

" Well," Consuelo didn't mind enlarging here, " he has a wild idea that he's completely broke, and he's full of crack-brained schemes for retrenchment and economy of all kinds—I mean, look at that fire. It's typical. And we haven't known what a hot bath is since my poor brother died. You know," her voice sank down far into the cadences of truth—" it's not a thing one likes to say, but sometimes we don't have enough to *eat* at Ballyroden. Of course," she looked hollowly into the basket on her knee, " every crumb I don't require to keep me alive I carry to the families of the old employees he has seen fit to dismiss since he came into the place. It hurts me to see everyone hungry."

Eustace and Dorothy gazed at her spellbound. The myth of a starving aristocracy with the walls of their mansions plastered in priceless old masters and their china cupboards bulging with sèvres and georgian silver was coming true before their eyes. Certainly the starvation part of it was no myth, and Eustace was prepared to vouch for two at least of the pictures he had already seen. There seemed no answer possible to this frank confession of necessity. Even Dorothy felt there was now some reason in drinking down egg-nogs and chicken broth in front of famished guests. There was only one thing to do about it—leave. Advance or no advance, waive the matter and go. She was clearing her throat to make the pronouncement when Bridgid came into the room, less sour and chilly, in fact, if anything, rather bustling and jolly.

" Your rooms are ready, madam, and I've popped nice hot bottles in your beds—two each."

The wish for rest and warmth was really overpowering. Dorothy shut her mouth on the words of farewell and stood up. Bed, blessed bed. There she would make her decision.

" Two hot-water bottles—how nice it sounds," Eustace smiled gratefully at Bridgid, " and if we might have a little something to eat."

Hercules interrupted like an imperious six-year-old: " Beebee! Beebee! Gummers. Gummers."

She took hold of the foot he held out to her and pulled at the heel of the boot. " Oh, Master Hercules, where have you been—look at the mud."

Consuelo waved her great white hands indulgently

towards the guests and the door: " Bundle off the pair of you, bundle off." She was quite gay.

The word ' bundle ' touched even Eustace with annoyance: " My dear lady—we can't bundle. We're weak from lack of food."

" I doubt "—Dorothy reeled slightly—" if I can actually make the stairs till I've had something to eat."

Bridgid stooped still over Hercules' gumboots, raised her head to say with dreadful brightness: " I've seen to that, madam. Hot tea, fresh biscuits and ham sandwiches."

" Biscuits," Hercules repeated dumbfounded; he collapsed forwards over his gumboots.

Dorothy clasped Eustace's arm with both ringed hands, she almost skipped like a child at a party. " Ham," she whispered, " oh, my dressing case, darling, quick, please."

" Don't think us rude," Eustace said as they hurried out, " we're only *dreadfully* hungry."

" Pull, Beebee—pull, ye divil, pull." Hercules was trapped halfway out of the boots. " Oh, me nice fresh biscuits. Blast these gummers, blast these foreigners." He sat in his socks, sadly. " I'm late to save them now."

" Why, may I ask, did you give them the ham and the biscuits? Are you *out* of your mind? " Consuelo asked in that chill, distinct voice she kept for fools and social aspirants.

" It's that William," Bridgid was trembling with thwarted righteousness. " Back on his bicycle with his rations and his nose into everything. The half your biscuits gone, Master Hercules, on to their plates—the half-moons with the pink sugar on them, too, if you don't mind, your little favourites. It's the young lady have him bewitched."

"God Almighty, I forgot the young lady. What next?" Hercules was very, very upset. "What's she like, Beebee? Awful, I suppose. Awful? Awful? Awful?"

"She's only like some low type on the pictures." Bridgid shook her good catholic head. "Oh, he looked at her as silly, and I didn't admire her at all, fancy, she wouldn't be my idea at all, nor yours, Master Hercules, only she was great to give a hand with the luggage, I will say, or I wouldn't have passed a remark to her."

"Where's William now? Send him along." Consuelo was marshalling her forces and readjusting her campaign.

"Willie—he's gone off on his motor-cycle again, scouring the snipe-bogs for Sir Phillip and Miss Veronica."

"Heaven send he doesn't find 'em," Consuelo lifted her eyes in pious request. "One hour more, only one, and these extraordinary people are out of our house and our lives. Mrs. Guidera is going to excel herself at luncheon. Bridgid, what about the beds?"

Bridgid paused for the exact words: "The mist that does be on the bogs is rising from them this minute. The hot bottles are nice and tepid and the stoppers in them very shaky."

Hercules looked worried: "Bit drastic," he suggested.

Consuelo was calm: "Did we or did we not decide on Total War?"

"Well," he cheered up, "we haven't begun badly. Great *coup* of mine capturing that telegram and a masterpiece of strategy getting the children off shooting."

"Still," Consuelo was far-seeing, "where are the P.G.s now? Tucked up in bed gorging themselves on your biscuits. It's not a decisive victory yet. Bridgid—

run down and keep an eye on the bath water. It's *not* to get hot."

"That's safely left to Mrs. Guidera, madam. Give them an hour now to chill off in their beds. Then Mrs. Guidera's beefsteak pie and steam pudding and I'd say they'll be catching that six o'clock express to Dublin."

"Well"—the matter seemed pretty well in hand—"I really think, Bridgid, as they are in bed, you might do a little something about this fire. We can let it out before they come down to luncheon."

"Indeed, Master Hercules'll catch his death." Bridgid was solicitous.

"I'm game, Beebee. I'll stick anything for one day."

"Did you put on the second hot socks and the little hot pants I left you out this morning?"

"I did, Beebee, I'm as warm as toast," he assured her like a rosy little boy.

She was pulling the fire together and inflaming it with some magic of her own. There was a sense of victory and ease in the room.

"Wot about a little nip, old girl. We need it after all we've been through. Takes it out of you, whichever way you look at it—and there's still half a bottle of our week's sherry supply. Do you good, I think."

Hercules was warming his bottom at Bridgid's fire, Consuelo had subsided, a great mass of peaceful achievement, on the sofa and Bridgid had gone out to her twelve o'clock cup of tea in the hand, when they heard the unmistakable sounds of an arrival in the hall. A familiar arrival. Things put down quickly in their usual places, the cloakroom door opening. Guns and game bags and cartridges lived there in the warmth.

"It's them." He paled. "Pets, they're back."

She sat up on the sofa as straight as a rush. They gave each other the desperate yet for ever together look of two children caught out in a real whipping business. They were over their heads in crime. They had eaten all the strawberries. They had flooded the house from bathroom to cellar. They had let the bullocks into the garden. They had put a match to the hay-loft. Nothing could save them. But she only thought of him: " Keep calm, Tots. Don't let them upset you. Remember your blood pressure."

And he of her: " I'm all right, old girl—you keep hold of yourself. They can't eat us, can they? "

" We don't know a thing, remember." She picked up the paper and put her feet up on the sofa.

" All right. I'll leave 'em to you, Pets. Don't let them bully you, darling, you give 'em stick. Don't admit a thing." He retreated to the farthest windowsill and got as much of himself as he decently could behind the curtain.

The tension of waiting for the policeman's knock was almost unbearable. At last it came. Fresh from the lovely air that blows over bogs: relaxed a little after their close relation to the real business of life (Phillip had shot six snipe with nine cartridges, and a whacking great cock pheasant had obliged Veronica by practically sitting on her gun)—they were, as it happened, feeling young and alive and close to each other and not at all seriously gestapo-minded young people.

" They've arrived? " was all they said.

" Yes." Consuelo put down her paper. " So unexpectedly." Was this really going to be easy?

" Tomorrow, you told us." Hercules poked his head round the curtain. Things didn't sound too bad.

" What have you done with them? " Veronica looked

round the room. The change from a wind on the heath brother to household responsibilities had not yet quite happened within her.

" We've put them to bed, dear," Consuelo spoke nicely and sensibly. " Wasn't that the best place after such an awful journey? "

" We've really done our absolute utmost." Hercules came right out from behind his curtain. " Went all out to make them feel comfy."

" That fire doesn't look very comfy," Phillip said. It was the first faint glimpse of suspicion.

" Only just gone down," Consuelo looked at it indulgently. " We had a cosy chat in here while Bridgid was arranging their trays and bedclothes and this and that."

"... And this and that," Hercules repeated, idiotically pleased.

" What did they have to eat? " Veronica queried.

" Oh, plates upon plates of ham," Consuelo lingered over the picture. They all saw the thin circles of pink and white; the dab of mustard; the plate with a red border and Leda and the Swan up to mischief as usual.

" And I sent up my biscuits." Hercules felt as warm a glow as if he really had.

" Did you, Uncle Hercules? That was sweet of you." Phillip was touched to the heart.

" If you stole upstairs now and popped your heads round their doors you'd find them as warm as toasts and as cosy as possible—just sleeping off the journey." Consuelo clasped her large, shadowy hands on her great solid bosom and looked benignly round the room.

Phillip was delighted with the picture: " Shall we go and take a peek, Veronica? "

"Oh, I wouldn't." Hercules could not restrain himself.

"Why not?" Veronica felt the tension. "Aren't they nice, Mummy?"

"Quite nice, we thought. . . . Quite nice. . . . Quite decent sort of people. . . . Pleasant surprise, really. . . . Shouldn't be surprised if she plays Bezique. . . ."

* * * * *

Upstairs, Dorothy Cleghorne-Thomas was screaming. She stood on her bare, manicured feet on a thin red carpet, colder than glass, colder than the air of her room through nightdress and cloud of bedjacket. She held her eiderdown by the corners and flung it to the farthest side of the room. When it landed a cloud of feathers went up and two more mice popped out and scuttled away. From the bared hollow of her bed there rose a gentle cloud of steam. She snatched her mink coat from the single coat hanger in a vast mahogany wardrobe, bundled her feet into her fur boots and whipped the hot-water bottle out of her bed. Held upside down against her stomach it let go a sullen gush of tepid water. It was that, even more than the mice, which called forth her scream of rage. Her scream died in the air of the great room, unheard. Unheard, it melted powerlessly into the hearts of the great joyous cabbage roses that lapped and overlapped each other's red and darker red petals all over the walls and up to the gilt picture rail; beyond were the blue-white depths of the ceiling. The two high windows seemed full of the shining lake waters; stiff white curtains patterned with red faded roses and thickly, soundly braided in pale, unworn cotton braid, hung from brass rings on brass poles. The blinds were old and strong and white and had deep expensive fringes. In the middle of the thinly carpeted floor a huge ottoman as round as the world with a hump in the middle, as smooth and regular as if a bucket of sand had been turned out there, was covered in the same material as the curtains. The dressing table was plain Victorian mahogany of a vast and useful size and the great bed had a canopy of ribbed red silk. The eiderdown, lying now in a bunch in a corner, was red too. Thin red silk on one side and a paisley pattern on the other. It was about eight yards square, yet it hardly weighed more than the mice inside it, so superior was the eider of its down and date. On either side of the bed two entrancing pieces, combining the offices of *Prie-Dieu* and *Commode*, reared up their modest, comfortable proportions. Among the pictures on the roses was an excellent engraving of Queen Victoria, Albert the Good and all the royal family. Also, a surprising German prince with his medals and a delicate, grey blue ribbon like a flash of water on his tunic. He had a map under his hand and there were snowy mountain peaks behind his head. Besides these there were many cosier family portraits—gentlemen as pretty as Hercules in brown serge coats and creamy stocks. A smooth headed child with bare, sloping shoulders and a bird on her finger. Shelves full of fat novels, none of them published later than 1914. 'Lady Betty across the Water,' 'The Real Charlotte,' 'The Arrow' by A. E. W. Mason, 'The Rosary' by Florence Barclay, 'She,' 'The Light That Failed,' 'The Road to Rome' by Zack, 'Dromola' by George Whitely-North, and mountains of Blackwood's Magazine with the list of contributors from the Empire on their bran coloured covers.

None of the significant timelessness of these things did worse than irritate Dorothy. She was exhausted. She was cold and disappointed. She was far away from a suite at Claridges, or a game of bridge, or lunch and a matinée with a girl friend or an amorous colonel. It was all a bad, bad egg and the sooner it was flung away from her the better. She was just about to shudder her way down the icy corridor to Eustace's room when her door opened and he came in, looking rather too frail and chilly inside his camel hair dressing gown.

" My dear," he said, " I agree, you needn't say another word. It just won't do. My bed is soaking, too. Not just the leaking hot-water bottle but natural plain moisture, and there's a pane broken in my window and the blankets are made of lead, lead, lead. I really think before the young man gets back from his shoot we'd better tell them (quite gently, *please*) that an hotel would be the thing. It's my ear, you know. If that starts I'm lost and I think it's beginning to grumble a bit."

" Eustace, thank God." She forgot even her soaking nightdress in her relief. With the splendid energy of England's women she clasped her coat round her and set out to cut her losses. She didn't even pause to put down the hot-water bottle.

It was like this that Veronica and Phillip first saw them. A handsome lady with the make-up cleaned off her face, wearing a desperate air of exhaustion and middle age. A beautiful nightdress dragged over the tops of fur-lined boots and her mink coat was wrapped so that its lines were gossamer round her excellent figure. Beside her an old man rather tired and ruffled and obviously about to make a protest of some sort. But it was the lady who swept forwards, empty hot water-bottle in hand—a symbol of horrifying discomfort.

" This is the end," she said. " The *End.* I can't stay —not for any reason. Could someone please order a car. How do you do? How do you do? " Without looking, she shook the hands Phillip and Veronica held out to her. " Forgive me, it's *too* boring—a damp bed, a leaking hot-water bottle and a mouse, *two* mice, curled up in my eiderdown. It's far from what we hoped for and I can't bear any more."

" Please forgive all this fuss," Eustace tightened the cord of his dressing gown and looked a little paler, " but my unfortunate ear is hideously susceptible to damp. I'm stone deaf on one side, you know, so I really have to treasure the other, and I'm not sure I haven't caught cold already. So perhaps if you gave us the name of the nearest hotel—much as I'd like to stay—it might be the best solution," his eye included Consuelo and Hercules, " for us all."

Phillip and Veronica came out of the ghastly trance in which they had listened to protest and explanation. One light only burnt clearly in their minds.

" We can't possibly let you go to a hotel." Phillip rang the bell. " How awful this is. What has happened? Veronica, can you understand it? We thought you were arriving tomorrow, you know."

" All the same "—Veronica looked faintly like the insulted landlady—" I aired all the beds my very own self—— Oh, I did think everything was quite nice. I'm desperately sorry, too——"

" Nice "—Dorothy collapsed shuddering in the chair nearest to the fire—" nice, I must say."

It was then that Willy with a true sense of situation answered the bell and brought with him the comforting rattle of a tray of glasses. " I thought this was what you rang for, sir," he said a little shyly, not as though he was the genius of the lamp.

" William, how right you are. Mrs. Cleghorne-Thomas —gin, pink gin, do you think? That mouse must have shaken you to the core."

Still she did not yield. Not though his type of good looks were the kind to make Harry's exotic photograph look like an advertisement for razor blades or furniture by instalments. She was really disgusted and her night-dress felt more like a cold compress at every moment.

" It wasn't only the mice, Sir Phillip. I'm afraid the whole thing's impossible. I must wake up my daughter —God knows how she's got to sleep—and pack."

" Veronica, darling, bring Miss Cleghorne-Thomas up a drink and find out what's happened." Phillip pressed vast gins into his guest's cold hands and kept on talking like a desperate young A.D.C.

Veronica was really stupefied by the truth of all the housekeeping horrors she had foreseen: " Willy," she said dully, " what's gone wrong? Do you know? "

" I don't know if you intended it, miss," he said with a gentle look at Hercules and Consuelo, who sat rather upright on the sofa, rather silent, rather po-faced and dignified, " but the guests were put in ' Frigidaire,' the ' Old Nursery ' and ' Blue Beard.' "

" Don't be silly, it isn't true." Veronica reeled, thankful at the enormity of the business; it set all her little heartfelt preparations back in focus again. Then her eyes and Phillip's met and communicated and turned together to accuse.

" Oh, Mother, how wicked of you. . . . No one's slept in those rooms for years. The old Nursery's full of wild cats and kittens."

" Oh what a hideous mistake." Consuelo made a great, regretful movement of extreme grace. " It's all the muddle of having so many mistresses in this household, I'm afraid. I thought Bridgid *knew*. After all, you give the orders now, dear children, don't you? "

" Do we? " Phillip was cold (he was like someone looking at a picture of which he disapproved, in fact, a little bit Albert the Good). " Do we? I'm glad you think so, Aunt Consuelo—because I'm now driven to desperate measures. You've absolutely done the dirty on us, darlings. Very well—no pocket money, no sherry, and no biscuits for one whole week."

Immediately the whole world retreated into the black diminishing glass of absolute microscopic depression. They had been so good, so good not complaining about the drink ration, making the utmost fun and importance out of their two glasses of sherry in the day, actually feeling rather better without the rich supply of other days, and much better for the fresh invention of virtue and economy.

" No sherry? No sherry at all? " Her eyes filled up like a child's. " My darling "—the rebuke was inspired —" how am I to swallow my pills? "

Phillip was outwardly unmoved: " You'll swallow your pills in water."

" Your aunt can't *drink* water." Hercules came flying to her rescue, he was horrified—" you know water chokes her."

" I can't help that." Phillip's mind was on nearer things. " Now—listen to me, Aunt Consuelo," a nasty possibility shot up to certainty, " you go down to the kitchen now and see to it that your slave, Mrs. Guidera, sends up a decent luncheon or it will be two weeks without sherry."

Veronica took up the cue quickly: " And Uncle Hercules, you go and chase Bridgid about her business or your cigarettes will be cut too."

Out in the hall they stood together, Hercules and Consuelo, in the hall of their own house, where all their lives they had had fun; seen the money fly; their only responsibility to enjoy themselves as much as possible, with easy charity, kindness and good nature thrown in. They had always been the children of this house—the younger sister and brother, the babies with their talent to amuse and their tremendous love for that elder charmer who was dead now, safely out of the cold confusion in which they were turned round about like sticks in a flood. In the hall they questioned each other: " What now? What next? " The familiar places seemed changed as the whole world changes when schoolroom and governess succeed nursery and nannie in life. A time-table instead of the misty nursery day; walks instead of playing houses in the rhododendrons; sums for stories and a great uncertainty in the new discipline taking the place of a nannie's bosomed and unhurried world. They looked at one another again, and parted wordlessly as they heard the drawing-room door open and the voices of the terrible young once more like the wolves behind them.

Within the drawing-room, comforted by gin and fire, Dorothy and Eustace sat and discussed the affair from a different angle.

" What do you think? " Eustace held his hands to

the pretty fire, pleased again by such things as the basket grate with all its brass knobs complete and the shining cut brass fender. " Obviously the poor children are as keen as possible to make us comfortable. The whole thing looks different—don't you think? "

" Yes, I do rather agree. The boy's a charming person. The girl's all right, plain as well. But the old people are torture and Auntie ought to be in a bin, shouldn't she? "

" My dear, *please* "—he indicated that far country in the sedan chair.

" That's what I mean," she lowered her voice, " one's practically got it oneself in a moment. I really feel as if she *were* in Honolulu. And where does that feeling end? A bit more persecution from Hercules and Consuelo and I might be over the edge myself—too ghastly. Now, what do you bet they didn't suppress our telegram? "

" Oh, I wonder." He was all sensible indulgence.

" Well," she was her strong active self, fortified and ticking over as usual, " I think I'll just ring the post office and find out. D'you suppose this telephone works? It looks the original masterpiece, doesn't it? How ghastly, I hate the thing you squeeze, it makes me go deaf. Hullo—hullo. Oh, my God, not a whisper! Oh, hullo. Post office? Yes, yes—I'm speaking from Ballyroden. I haven't got the number, it's not on this machine, you must know it—Ballyroden, Sir Phillip Ryall—I want to enquire about a telegram sent from Liverpool, eleven-thirty, yesterday, thirteenth November; what time you received it and whether it was ever delivered? "

A tiny thread of a voice, faint as a bad line over mountain lakes could make it, answered her:

" Ballyroden? Telegrams *never* get there—too much

interference. I've known a telegram arrive five years late at that house—he-he-he. Nobody cares. There's only one sane person in that house and you won't see much of her. You take my tip—get out of it quick—before they *get* you—skip!"

"Eustace"—Dorothy was really white to the lips now; she held the telephone, which still quacked and whispered gently, at arm's length, one hand over the mouthpiece—"I *knew* my instinct was right. Even the post office say they're all blazing—and the post office *must* know the form."

Eustace was on his feet, too. After all, the local country post office is at least a solid point of reference in an unknown world.

"My dear," he said, "Yvonne—have you seen her?"

"No—not for an hour." Terror mounted in the moment.

They did not hear Phillip come in again with Veronica. They did not see their spellbound trance within the doorway, eyes on the telephone and the frightened faces; did not see them clutching each other's hands at this new *impasse*, whatever it might be.

"The post office must know," Dorothy repeated.

"But that's not the post office," Phillip shouted.

Really, this was bedlam. Dorothy screamed "Help! Help! Help!" into the instrument, hoping somehow to convey the dangers of her situation to an outer world, before she dropped it with a clanking thud and got behind an armchair. Obviously the poor boy was the same way as his elders. Not the post office, indeed—then who did answer telephones in Ireland?

Eustace stood his ground grimly. "Now, now," he soothed as Phillip and Veronica came rushing forward,

" take it easy. Don't upset yourselves. Nothing really matters, you know. . . . There's always tomorrow. . . ."

Veronica picked up the telephone quietly. The quiet ones were always the most dangerous, he remembered.

" It's all right, darling," she said. " It's Phil and me. Yes, we've got everything under control. . . . Yes, we won't stand any nonsense. . . . Yes, we'll give them stick. . . . Yes, *and* who began it. Oh, yes, we'll make them wish they'd never been born. Certainly, darling——good-bye." She hung up and put the telephone back on its little tray-topped, inlaid table and turned sweetly to Eustace who was by now longing to get behind the armchair with Dorothy.

" That was only Aunt Anna Rose," she explained. " You were on Aunt Anna Rose's private line. I don't know if you've met yet——" She indicated the sedan chair. " She's the greatest darling, you'll really love her. She was so keen for you to come, too."

" Good God Almighty, child." He pulled Dorothy out from behind the chair and collapsed with her on the sofa. " How could we know that? "

" Please—another drink? " Dorothy held an empty glass out in a shaking hand.

" Of course—and a strong one, and for you, sir." Phillip eagerly refilled their glasses. " Now, before Aunt Anna Rose gets off her boat——"

" It's not a boat "—Eustace corrected him precisely—" it's a PLANE—B.O.A.C."

" You have caught on quickly." Phillip gave him a direct and grateful look. " Before she lands, let's apologise humbly for our other relations. We don't know all they've done to you today, and said to you today, but if you could somehow manage to look on it as a bad joke and let's all start fair, we would be so grateful. Veronica and I so want to make you comfortable."

Dorothy sat up straight, the better to let him have it: "Quite frankly, your elders' attitude is that we are most unwelcome intruders and I don't imagine they're prepared to do anything to make our stay pleasant. Paying guests we may be, but at least let us pay where we're wanted. They were"—her voice almost broke—"so *ghastly* to us."

"*Not* Aunt Anna Rose too?" It was a real cry of defence.

"No, no," Eustace smiled enjoyably, "Miss Anna Rose genuinely mistook us for passengers. *Third*-class passengers."

"It's only her muddle, you know, she *never* means to be rude," Veronica defended solemnly.

"It's all right, child. She was charming to us." Eustace liked the humourless little creature. "And as far as I'm concerned, I'm very intrigued with the other two—but it's rather a different thing for my sister and niece—they're much more sensitive plants than I am, as you'll see."

"We'll keep our relations in order," Phillip promised. "You must be a bit patient. Their trouble is they're not grown-ups, they're two spoilt, naughty children still."

"Do they really have pocket money?" Eustace probed on delightedly, "and can it be true you're going to dock them?"

"I'm afraid I must," he was shy and pained at the admission.

"Oh, fascinating—utterly fascinating. Dorothy, we *can't* leave." Eustace implored her not to spoil his fun.

" Promise me one little week," he pleaded, " and then if it's all too difficult for you, we'll go."

Dorothy was not to be won over too easily. She had not, like Eustace, the kind of mind to recognise the qualities of genuine truth and sweetness when she saw them. In Phillip and Veronica's gentleness and good manners she was only aware of the starving Irish gentry clinging obstinately to three times ten guineas a week.

" Well," she said, " I'm willing to risk it only if we may really have your guarantee that the old people don't molest us—but I'm not really prepared to answer for my daughter—and it's the end so far as I'm concerned if anyone's rude to her."

" Oh, Mom, but everyone's been lovely to me." She stood in the doorway, almost as tall as Consuelo and of the same extravagant build. The tiny perched head had a face as pretty as a butterfly pinned on it, eyes as disproportionately large as those on a butterfly's wing and dark hair to her shoulders. Her great big body flowed into meagre wrists and tottering ankles. A tiny little voice came tripping and whispering out from far away, absurdly attractive and nonchalant and unexpected out of so big a girl.

" You haven't met my daughter, Yvonne, have you, Sir Phillip? " Dorothy genuinely forgot Veronica in her anxiety to see the impression exchanged at this meeting.

Phillip shook hands with the significant, polite lack of interest his kind show so proficiently towards women.

" This is my cousin," he said, undoing Dorothy's rudeness, " Veronica Howard."

Veronica shook hands silently, overcome by all the glamour: the dark man's dressing gown with its pale monogram: the hair, unwaved, cut and set so near to the natural growth: the long painted nails: and then the flat, soft slippers, a child's comfortable bedroom boots: through all, the terrifying ease conveyed in the little running voice. . . .

"That sweet boy, William, woke me up and said there was a drink going so I came down to see what was happening. Oo, don't you look silly bundling about in your overcoat, Mom. Really dear, bedsyby's the place."

"Darling, what horror did you find in your bed?" Dorothy asked mildly, delighted with her child.

"Only a cat and her kittens—very warm and cuddly—I *liked* it." Yvonne somehow managed to convey this information as though it was confidential and for Phillip only. Also, somehow it sounded like a child's unintentional indecency.

"I'm so sorry you were all put in the wrong rooms by mistake." Veronica sounded as stiff and apologetic as any young manageress—no wonder Yvonne ignored her.

Phillip cut across to say warmly: "Do have a drink."

"Oh, no," she was hugely serious about it, "I'm terrible when I have a drink."

"Better have a little one," he said.

To Veronica the words sounded suddenly portentous, embarrassed, persuasive, gently insistent; yet what were they but the most polite, common words? It was some quality in the girl's hesitating acceptance that gave them importance—as though only he could persuade her. She had that power of isolating herself and her beauty to one person, of excluding, without undue emphasis, others from the circle. In childhood, that power had been militant in her. Never a friendship of three for her, always one of the little trio must be cast forth and by passwords and secret signs, made to feel the outsider.

You said little rhymes about them under your breath when they were near, loudly when they were out of sight but not out of hearing. The secret house in the bushes was kept from them. The new slang word was used ostentatiously between the initiated only. The adored grown-up was besieged and prevented from communication with the outcast. And then in the course of a holiday or school term the outcast was wooed and seduced and the Great Best Friend cast out. Shameless, strong, always warm, always successful, always on the winning side, always gay even in her cruelties, she had proceeded in years and beauty, but had hardly developed beyond being the success of the dormitory, the picnic, the game of sardines. Her conquests in life had come to her with such ease that she had substituted a pervasive, easy good nature for the strident unkindness of childhood and school-days.

Now, when Phillip had mixed for her exactly, but exactly, the tiny little drink she wanted, she turned to Veronica to say: " Do you do the housekeeping, because let me tell you, I'm mad about cooking and I'd love to get loose among a few dozen eggs. I've just done a course with Mrs. Spry "—her eyes went round the room—" I could give you a few ideas about your flowers, too, and " —her eyes had circled the room and come back to Phillip again—" there's nothing I don't know about pruning fruit trees."

Veronica felt violently defensive about her mother's flowers and her own housekeeping. Even the wild extravagance of the past seemed human and forgivable beside the uninhibited offers of assistance from this strange beauty—offers implying an assurance and a criticism nearly intolerable from a stranger.

Consuelo and Hercules came back looking smug and tidy as though they had just had their hairs curled round a nannie's fat finger and their faces washed with a flannel. Ready for lunch they were or a drink if anybody cared to suggest it. Things were so upside down today that the sherry ban might reasonably expect to take a little holiday at the expense of the gin and vermouth. But before they could really ripen the situation, indeed, while they were still exchanging rather dazed how-do-you-do's with the enormous young gipsy, the door of the sedan chair opened and all Ryall eyes turned to it with the affectionate expectancy of something to interest them, to cheer them, to change the difficult moment into a moment that flowed—a moment before which one could not arrange an acceptance or a bored acknowledgment—because one never knew in what extension of her life Aunt Anna Rose would expect and get their astonished and loving interest.

"Ah——" they breathed, as the sedan door opened and Aunt Anna Rose came smartly out. She had discarded her overcoat to reveal a tropical suit of fine shantung. The chiffon veil which had been tied over her hat and bunched under her chin was now wound gaily round the crown of her tuscan straw, its brim bent down in a slight suggestion of the Solar Topee. The swathes of chiffon were bound about it to withstand an equatorial sun, as well as to provide a pretty background to Tito, who spread his wings on the brim, abandoning himself to the languors of the tropics. She carried a long-handled white and green lined parasol and pointed it laughingly at the guests in their dressing gowns as she advanced: "Ah ha, what did I tell you?—always go by air. You poor people do look as if you'd had a night of it—dirty, unwashed, dishevelled—look at me—bandbox fresh after 10,000 miles."

Reality and the other world of her own united themselves in the visible situation. She went up to Veronica and bent to kiss her, aware of something outside the little girl's life. " And who's that curious young person? " she whispered, indicating Yvonne who gaped entranced. " Not quite—quite. Not quite—quite—*quite* the job, I don't fink." No one but Veronica could hear. With some confidence she said, squeezing the gloved hand: " This is Miss Cleghorne-Thomas, Aunt Anna Rose."

" Well, well," Aunt Anna Rose shook hands, " you look as if you'd had quite a doin'."

" Made a good trip, darling? " Phillip interrupted. " No adventures? "

" A little bit bumpy, we had to corkscrew all over the Caribbean, but it was worth it to see the sun. I love the sun."

A kind of glory of gaiety and enjoyment shone from her. The sun came out as she said: " I love the sun." And with the sudden lift in the light her sense of well-being imparted itself to everyone. From top to bottom of the hand-blown panes of glass, heat came beaming widely into the room. It caught the group between their shoulder blades and sent a shudder of rapture through them. William brought the moment to an appropriate climax: " Luncheon," he said in the doorway, " is ready."

" Thank you, boy." Aunt Anna Rose beckoned him forward. " Now, tell you wot," everybody was included in her brilliant smile, her very great pleasure was manifest —" you shall all lunch with me at Ciro's. Boy, hot langoustes, fried chicken and curried yams." She clapped a gay little dismissal to the black boy and turned to Eustace, singling him with absolute self-possession from the crowd. " Do you like yams? "

" I'm fearfully keen about yams. May I sit beside you, Miss Anna Rose? And will you excuse my déshabillé? You see, unlike you, I didn't travel by air."

" It's the only way," she told him seriously. " Pop out of your plane in your best hat, ready for anything."

" And in that hat, Miss Anna Rose, any adventure might arise. Such a beautiful bird."

" You like my Tito? " She was charmed at her new friend's good sense. " It's mother's Love Bird." Her great eyes swept upwards and she whistled the sweetest note. " Aren't you mother's Love Bird, Tito? They called a General after him, I believe, yes, in the *last* war. Now come on, everybody, luncheon's waiting and everything's on me, remember. Come, my darling," she put out a hand as she passed Veronica, " you shall sit on my other side and we'll have such fun. I've ordered a table on the veranda overlooking the aquarium. I love looking at fish. I tell you what we'll do after lunch, we'll walk up to the Salmon Hatchery. Very amusin' up there in November, very amusin' indeed. . . ."

The dining-room shared a certain quality with all dining-rooms in old well-cared-for houses. It was cleaned and cared for and used only for its own purpose. It had the calm of a pair of manicured, massaged hands scented with violet soap and lying idle in a satin lap. There was not a flower of any kind as a background for the sweet-smelling air. The first thing to strike a stranger's notice —this strong, sweet smell. It is a smell like very good, dry, winter apples put away in a cupboard and watched carefully—not one bad one left among them; yet it is sweeter far, and hangs on the air that is dark, not damp, quite fragrantly. It is only in dark rooms that this smell is complete. It goes with turkey carpets and very ugly mahogany furniture and plenty of clean silver on the sideboard. It should go with a white tablecloth, but at Ballyroden these had been abandoned and there were rather unpretty mats instead. They were made of baby samba skins with the stripe down the middle, and these were laid on top of other mats of crocheted straw.

There were some pretty portraits on the walls—one of an admiral in palest blue with an order as big as his head on his ribbon. There was a dark secret-looking girl, suspiciously like a misery of the past and a ghost of the present, but not at all, she had married happily and well, had eight children, all satisfactory, and died at eighty-four.

The windows were the same height as those of the drawing-room, but the square panes had been, most unfortunately, removed and great dark spaces of plate glass put in their places. These had been so buttressed outside by well trimmed evergreens that, looking through them (and their lace and velvet curtains) was like looking through a giant diminishing glass. The world retreated to a third distance. The sky and the hills could not flow inwards, breasting the room like a swan on a flood, as they did in the drawing-room and in the hall.

" No——" Phillip was saying in reply to Yvonne's murmured questions about Aunt Anna Rose, " she had a dazzling sort of love affair, I think. I don't think anyone could have been happier."

" She seems terribly happy this minute." Yvonne looked up the table. " She brought us all in here on a sort of wave of joy—you'd think it was one of those big surf waves out there where she is. I bet she's got a surf board—don't you? May I ask her? "

" Oh, no," Phillip said quickly. " She'd never do anything that seemed ridiculous, I don't think. It's best not to ask her funny questions, if you don't mind."

Yvonne took his rebuke quite well. " She probably won't speak to me, anyhow," she said. " But I'd love to ask her about old Vienna. Did Strauss write a tune for her, I wonder. Gosh, she must have looked a dream, waltzing away under the chandeliers. What was the chap like? "

" We never, *never* talk to her about that time," Phillip said. " I've never even seen a picture of her husband, they were all destroyed so that she could try to forget. I've always heard he was very good-looking and rather a one for the girls. The only thing connected with him she does sometimes mention are her rubies. She always says she's left them to Veronica."

" Oo, my favourite stone. Are they lovely? "

" They don't exist," Phillip said shyly. " That's why I wanted to warn you to take it easy if she says anything about them."

" Oh, I see, they're just a little phobia? " Dorothy looked up from her really excellent curry for the first time.

" Or a kind of dream," he corrected. " She'd love to have them to give Veronica, bless her."

" You must find it all a bit of a bore at times, I should think."

" Do let me get you some more curry." Phillip got up and went over to the sideboard.

" Mom, you old cow. Darling, don't you see they all worship her? "

"I think it's all damn silly, but what a good curry. If all the food's like this things won't be too bad." She shouted down the table: "Jolly good curried yams, I'm having some more."

Aunt Anna Rose gave a polite, unsmiling little wave of her hand, the hand held towards herself like royalty in a carriage. She accepted, she passed over the advance, she did not allow it to increase her intimacy with the Person. She continued to talk to Eustace. They were discussing the migration of birds—a matter on which she was less prosy and better informed than any correspondent to the *Field*, The Country Gentleman's newspaper.

3

A NOVEMBER morning of still, sparkling, intoxicating sun and frost followed the first really cold night of the winter. It was Dorothy's twenty-eighth night in the premier guest room of Ballyroden, and for twenty-eight nights she had suffered quite considerably. True, her bed was not damp and a great weight and quantity of blankets had been put on it. The fire had burnt until eleven o'clock when she had been too warm and lazy to get up and stoke it. Much later she had woken out of a dream, stiff and chill and slightly drugged with cold. The many blankets seemed as though woven of tin. With nervous resolution she got hold of a thin, blue cashmere rug of her own and wrapped it round her shoulders. Better. But after a short time a kind of thrust of cold seemed to be hitting her below the rug in the middle of her back. Her head was cold, too. The hot-water bottle was an icy weight. The electric pad that worked intermittently on the archaic electric light system seemed to have died. So had her bedroom light. The idea of a hot-water bottle was like water to a thirsty man. She put the idea away. She took deep breaths—a very warming exercise. It only woke a kind of unpleasant activity in her stomach. She rearranged her rug so that it wrapped her around. Its soft wool fingers and the spaces between them reminded her of icicles. She put her dressing gown over her head. It seemed the only really woollen thing on the bed. By now she knew that all the blankets were washed-out, servants' under-blankets, reinforced with concrete. She could have got out of bed and shut the window, but she would as soon have jumped into the lake in the moonlight. She could have tried to read herself to sleep, but even had her bed-side light been working, it was an idea impossible to face. She breathed deeply again with the awful resolution of one who has for years kept her figure under control by conscientious exercise. She drowsed off as people do in the snow, and woke with a cruel pain in her hip bone. She turned cautiously on to the other hip bone so as not to disturb the faint warmth that sleep had gathered round her, and then her stomach felt awful again. She was so strong-minded that she breathed deeply, strongly, urgently at least nine times. An extraordinary warmth was born after she had struggled with the breathing. She slept again. She slept until she was called. She woke with a red nose and crooked, electrified hair. She was still obsessed with the idea of her night's suffering and single-minded enough to complain to Bridgid on the subject.

Bridgid, of course, was enchanted: " There's eleven blankets, only, on this bed, madam," she said, acid but polite, " maybe I could knock up a few more."

Dorothy sat up to receive her breakfast tray. She shuddered among her glassy pillows. Her mind dived away towards her flat with its civilised heating. She thought of the three perfect and sufficient satin-bound blankets on her own bed, the eiderdown light as a cloud —pale pink and a tea-coloured lining, weak china tea— a mushroom and its underside. She thought of the morning air, warm as milk to a bare arm. She handed out a rubber hot-water bottle: " Would you be kind enough," she asked, " to give me my fur cape—in the wardrobe."

On her way to the wardrobe Bridgid caught her foot in a trip wire which connected the electric pad in Dorothy's bed with a sèvres vase (pink, with grey and white cupids and lyres on it) that had been fitted for light—for greater convenience, also, because the wiring of her pad was inadequate in length for this mausoleum, Dorothy had taken the lamp off its dressing table and laid it on its side on the floor, where it looked curiously pathetic in its prettiness, like burning rosewood pianos in starving Russia. It looked still more pathetic after Bridgid had dashed it into the foot of the wardrobe.

" Well," she commented, picking up the bits, " Mrs. Howard was right, as usual. She told Miss Veronica it was the height of common-minded ignorance to use a valuable vase for a lamp. " Of course," she conceded, " even Miss Veronica couldn't have known any person would have put it on its side on the floor to trip another person. That's William's work, I suppose, and about all he did do, too. On my evening out if you don't mind." She brought the fur cape over, elaborately stepping across the wire, and gave a start of affected surprise as she saw the end of the flex leading into the bed. " In God's holy name, what has he been up to? " she inquired.

Dorothy snatched her cape and flung it savagely round her shoulders. She knew that Bridgid knew all about the electric pad, that carefully kept guilty secret that she had untangled each morning before she was called. She had always known that it would be supposed to fuse the lights, and now it had.

" All right, Bridgid," she spoke with a carelessness she was far from feeling. " I'll explain the whole thing to Miss Veronica. And it has nothing to do with William."

" I wonder, had it anything to do with fusing the lights, madam? " Bridgid ventured in her most respectful voice. " Twelve o'clock last night when Sir Phillip woke me for a candle to sit up with his prize Jersey cow, and she calving."

" Calving was she? How ghastly. When the post comes I should like mine up here as soon as possible." Dorothy poured out her coffee in the most decisive way. It was hot and quite excellent. She prised a Worcester saucer off the top of her bacon and eggs, which were depressed and on the cool side. However, she ate them up ravenously and was into her second cup of coffee and her first cigarette when Yvonne came into the room.

Yvonne was wearing a beautiful pair of whipcord trousers and a loose brown and white check tweed coat with a flap back. She looked quite all right, at least as good as any tall, fat man dressed by an expensive tailor.

Dorothy brightened a bit. The ravishing child. And so well and so burning bright.

" Hullo, Mom." Here she, too, tripped over the flex and saw the pink disaster on the carpet. " You seem to have had quite a night—breaking the place up."

" Terribly awkward, isn't it." Dorothy pointed at the broken sèvres pot without looking that way.

" My dear, it's so ugly, don't give it a thought."

" Yes, it's ghastly, so it *must* be good. Eustace will be hocked and cross and the old people won't let up on it ever."

" Let's just bundle it away in a drawer. There are hundreds more, far uglier, in the house."

"That dreary Bridgid knows. What's more, she's got the form about my electric pad. I was so exhausted after last night I forgot to disconnect myself from it all. Too boring."

"What happened last night?" Yvonne was sitting on the edge of the bed eating a piece of her mother's toast with wonderful greed and indolence.

"Didn't you notice? It was arctic."

"Was it?"

"What were you young people getting up to?"

"My dear, we couldn't go to bed on account of this cow."

"Oh, don't be silly."

"I didn't actually look on at the business like Veronica. She's unbelievable. But I made tea for them in the kitchen. We didn't go to bed till four."

"Who's 'we'?"

"All three."

"How too boring. I wonder you didn't get the cow in as well."

"She couldn't leave her calf."

"I see. Pity. Oh, here's the post. That's something. You can take the tray, Bridgid. By the way, do you mind telling them in the kitchen *not* to put icy saucers over my breakfast, it doesn't keep the breakfast hot and it only flattens the egg. I thought they might like to know. And *please*—if I may, as soon as possible, and *hot*. You know what I mean—HOT." She delved in the bed and held out her natural rubber hot-water bottle in it pink bag.

Bridgid took it from her with the tray and left the room in silence.

Yvonne looked up from the post with brilliant eyes: " My dear, it's come," she said.

Dorothy combed the post with that avidity new every morning: " Do you mean this letter from Harry? " she asked resignedly.

" No, is there? God bless him. Actually I meant this." She tore a dismal paper covered booklet out of its wrappings. " ' First Principles of Farming: a simple introduction to the keen Novice '—that's me. Couldn't be more keen."

Dorothy settled back among her pillows in a dreamy, brooding Mother-Trance. After the child had gone, still reading the book on farming and with Harry's letter unopened in her pocket, she lay still, warm with hot coffee and optimism for the future. This change in Yvonne's enthusiastic love life had been beyond her dreams.

If only, she told herself with an inward tremor, the young man holds out on her she'll marry him. She accepted Veronica's chaperonage gratefully. She welcomed Phillip's absorption in the farm. She could almost tolerate Consuelo's veiled barbs of malice. Everything that could add a little something rugged to the path of love drove Yvonne's enthusiasm for Phillip towards the edge of ecstasy. Never before had so many simple codes of living lain between her and what she wanted. She would defeat them all and she was starting at rock-bottom—this farming. She would gain a sort of mastery of the subject, too. Dorothy dwelt rapturously on the thought of her child intent on that terrifying sage green booklet. . . .

The connection with the future inspiring her, she let her eyes roam round the room while she played that luxurious irresponsible game of altering other people's houses. This bedroom to which they had moved her was the most important in the house and as such had suffered enough from redecoration in the years immediately preceding the first world war. Since then money had not been lavished on such triviality. Here she lay and considered her surroundings. She had absorbed quite enough of Eustace's information and knowledge to know just how well proportioned and right the room was. She could appreciate the great windows, streaming with rain or sun, the marble chimney piece so light it was like a thin bow of ribbon tied against the wall. The decoration on the ceiling, after some Italian master by the estate mason—blunt in execution but airy as a garland of river flowers in feeling. She yielded to perfection when she saw it. In her mind she retained the aubusson carpet, but felts and double felts should line it to the walls. She had yet to experience a sensation more damnable than the feel to the bare foot of aubusson carpet on bare boards, a quality only comparable to steel in a black frost. Having dealt with the floor, she debated the question of the windows and their curtains. Never had she known a room potentially capable of holding light, contain so much darkness. The windows themselves were curtained rather charmingly in a shiny chintz with a pale pattern of carnations and roses over it, well lined and braided in the delightful cotton braid of 1900. The curtains hung on brass rings on good brass poles and ran smoothly; not one had come off its ring. But the line of light above their tops was grim and chilly to an eye accustomed to deep pelmets. Dorothy scrapped the curtains remorselessly and allowed her mind to revel freely in the horror of the wallpaper. This was the monster which ate, drank and soaked into itself all the light and colour of the room. It was green, not a smart, modern spinach green or in any way related to such a green, it was a deep bad blue green with a watered satin surface covered in yellowish green garlands. Where damp or sun had changed its colour it deepened towards prussian blue, the prussian blue of the student's water-colour box. Over and between pictures were hung five tiny elaborate gilt brackets. Each bracket had a large bottom shelf, two smaller shelves above and a wee mirror at the back. Each shelf held a little bit of dresden china —frilly, gilded bows supported these *bijouteries* against the towering heights and deeps of the wall space. Dorothy thought about the glamorous new bride giving generously to church jumble sales—the thought included the book-shelves. There were several of these and all of them had the look of the carpentry class and the little boy at his private school. Little lockers beneath the shelves emphasised this. They were small and very light for their load of big Edwardian novels. The chairs—she itched to attack with a razor blade, for beneath their unlikely looking upholstery (chintz covers of a different pattern to the curtains and giving the chairs very much the appearance of a semi but permanently invalided lady in an enormously loose bedjacket) reeded mahogany legs peeped barely forth. She sighed and decided to ask Eustace about them. He would know what to think. She was in no doubt as to what she would do with 'The Horse Fair' by Rosa Bonheur, hanging high beyond eye level above the gilt Victorian looking-glass, its base almost wider than the shallow strip of marble beneath. There were one or two attractive silhouettes, the Ryall profile unmistakable, and a great many water colours, of the peeps and views order, by travelled aunts. On the whole it was all much less interesting than in Blue Beard, her first bedroom. But, at least, the dull mahogany battlefield of a bed upheld some sort of pretence at a spring mattress. While she complained that the fire was so far away that she could not see it when she lay down, it did not smoke or belch rocks of ancient soot out of its pretty mouth. She decided she would keep the fire. With that and strong central heating as a starting point her mind hovered pleasantly over the room's redecoration.

She was interrupted by Eustace's morning visit, a daily episode that had marked value in her life. Like Yvonne, he was looking so well, she warmed towards him happily. She was never more peevish than when they looked pinched or nervous or had earache or influenza. But here in this frightful cold house he looked so well, with an open-air rosiness like a gardener or the healthy gnarled look of a very beautifully pruned and trained and sprayed fruit tree. He was ready to go out. She saw that he wore soft natural coloured wool mittens and a scarf that matched them.

" But what about your feet? " she said, looking at his slippers.

" Oh, Bridgid says she's got a surprise for my feet."

" My dear, it's a disgrace how well you get on with Bridgid. She doesn't do a thing about me."

" Well, she's a witch doctor and you haven't got anything for her to cure. You're sickeningly healthy and good looking. I play my ear up shamelessly—sometimes I'm a bit nervous of her herbal cures. She might be Hamlet's aunt, one never knows. But anything for peace."

" What are you up to this morning? "

"I ought to go on cataloguing the library, really. It's great fun."

"Now why do you want a surprise for your feet for cataloguing the library? Don't try to deceive me—you know Miss Anna Rose is waiting for you somewhere."

"Are you getting worried about it?"

"You haven't been so interested in anyone for years, have you?"

"She's enthralling. Don't you feel there's some eternity of love alive in her? It's never begun, it's never ended, it's never died—there it is—there she is—1888 breathes the air of 1948—no older, no younger. Don't you really feel it?"

"No, I don't. I find her pretty tiresome pretty often, if you want to know. She makes me as nervous as a kitten. What are you doing with her this morning—own up."

"We're off to the river, hounding down the poachers."

"There are no poachers on the river at this time of year. Even I know that."

"Maybe no. Maybe yes. Whether or not, they give me a remarkable appetite for lunch."

She gazed at him from her pillows, not unperturbed: "Don't get into it too deep, old boy, will you."

"I'm head over ears—oh, here's my other danger."

"*That's* where you are, sir." Bridgid disposed of the hot-water bottle as a hospital nurse deals with a boring patient, the same cold uncomplaining competence, before she turned to Eustace, a look not unlike the one she kept for Hercules in her eyes—"And how did you sleep last night?"

"Very well, thank you. But my head was a bit cold. In the first frost I always feel like a dahlia."

" Now, isn't that too bad. I hope you didn't get a chill in the ear on top of the little remedy we put to it."

He shook his head like a spaniel, testing out the ear. " I hope I didn't."

" I'll leave a little something on your hot bottle tonight and you can just roll your head in it nice and cosy."

" Oh, thank you, Bridgid. Didn't you say you had something for my feet today? That's where the chill starts, if you ask me."

" I'll meet you in the boot room," she trysted him mysteriously, " I have a wad of sheep's wool heating for them—it's the wool of a *black* sheep."

" Splendid! Not a *black* sheep? "

" Leave it to me now, only, if you'll excuse the liberty, come down the back stairs, I'll settle you up in the boot room and Willy has Miss Anna Rose dressed and ready on the gravel sweep at the side door."

" To me, the whole thing smells of witch doctoring and plain, old-fashioned intrigue." Dorothy lit another cigarette.

" Doesn't it? " he agreed. " I never thought I'd have so much fun again."

" Why must you at your time of life have your fun in the boot room? "

" Oh, don't be common—I'm jolly lucky to have any fun anywhere. My dear, I don't suppose Master Hercules is too keen on new favourites, and Bridgid is tact itself, God bless her. Now, is there anything I can do for you before I go? "

" Yes, I did want a good talk to you about Yvonne."

" Let's thresh her out this evening—I really can't keep Miss Anna Rose waiting any longer. You stay nice and warm in bed till lunchtime."

"There's nothing else to do and nowhere else I can do it, as far as I can see. Unless I get up for an icy hour before lunch and listen to Consuelo reading her letters of sympathy aloud to Hercules—I think she invents the people who write to her about Sir Roderick. Yesterday we had the Bishop of London and the day before it was the Aga Khan. I expect it'll be the P.M. and Elsa Maxwell today." She put on a vast forbidding pair of tortoiseshell spectacles and moved herself round far enough to kiss him with unwilling affection. "I'm glad you and Yvonne are enjoying yourselves," she said almost christianly.

"I don't know why you don't try seducing Master Hercules—you might find it very heartening."

She shuddered and lost herself in the American House and Garden. She could no more follow Eustace in his spiritual excursion, spirit salted with unwearied human interest, than she could know by what lore he told himself that a picture or a piece of furniture was right or wrong.

The boot room was a dusky no-man's-land sandwiched between the kitchen and the servants' hall. It was nearly as big as a billiard room, and ever since the house had been built pieces of rubbish, small and large, had found their last halting place before the church jumble sale, in here. It was heaven to Eustace and he only shuddered to think of the brittle treasures that must have gone from this clearing house to perish, their value or prettiness ignored or despised. Literally everything had got in here. Trunks, stacks of pictures, empty picture frames. It was a much commoner, more warm-hearted dump than the cloakroom off the hall, and as a collection, rather a better piece of social history. Anything perishable, Eustace felt as he waited for Bridgid, surrounded by the hunting boots of three generations and three generations' supply of Day & Martin's empty blacking bottles, could have reached its final dissolution here. The contrary was equally true. Who knew what priceless article might not still survive amongst and beneath the mountains and wilderness of junk. He longed truly for one strong ardent man with whom he could go mining and prospecting in this treasure field. He was not very good at lifting things himself, his heart was not a very sound one. He sighed as he gazed at a great, bulbous basket trunk, at a safe older than any make he knew, at pretty basket grates, their brasses green as spinach, leaning broken one against another—they had been ripped out here and there throughout the house for the existing Victorian substitutions. He saw, perched afar on crags of broken china, a birdcage, an affair as elaborate as the Crystal Palace, and inside it, he thought, a dead bird, until he looked closer and saw it was a black cock's feather boa—caged for no earthly imaginable reason. A separate pile of leather-covered brass-nailed baggage with a beautiful, sprawling coronet and monogram held his attention, for they were practically unused or worn by travel, as new as though they were due to start to-morrow on some wedding journey. He gave a little surprised jump of romantic understanding as he placed them in his mind—Miss Anna Rose, of course, her luggage that had started out on that romantic honey-moon. His mind blinked in a charmed delight at the sudden picture of a pair of lovers travelling for ever towards the Summer Palace of a Czar—the picture for him had more than clarity—it was water clear and actual as breakfast this morning; as full of the absolute joy and absolute despair of life as a Chekhov piece. Why drag in Chekhov? This *was* the stuff of life itself, the terrible eternity of objects outliving grief or joy. These beautiful trunks and bonnet boxes sat here stationary for fifty years in the boot room of an Irish house, somehow dark and derisive and still while their owner gadded madly round and round a world of fancy. He leaned his hands on a table and really wondered that life allows so much lease to pain.

Bridgid interrupted him briskly: " If I was you, sir, I'd take my hands off of that table. That's where Willy mixes poisons for the rats."

He looked down and saw that he was leaning on a half-hoop mahogany table, solid, plain, early Irish Chippendale with a deeply reeded front—one leg was gone so that it sat on a packing case, and it was covered in empty tins and jam-pots with pieces of stick in them. " Yes," he said, " of course—how silly I am. Thank you for the warning, Bridgid. One never quite knows, does one? " He dusted his hands vaguely together and smiled at her, his dream of the past splitting suddenly open into this dream sequel of the present. The happy, mad bride was waiting for him. God bless the bride, and he must not keep her waiting. He saw that Bridgid had brought him a pair of gumboots and a pair of dark, thick, brown socks, warm from a fire. The boots, too, were hot and dry—not the soggy, expected cold of a rubber boot. His heart blazed at this warm goodness. It made him feel tremendously happy and spoilt. It was out of this world of today altogether.

Aunt Anna Rose had not waited for him but she had left a very distinct message. She would be in the garden feeding her robins by the potting-shed. He felt quite a familiar of the place so he saw without effort exactly where she was to be found and set out along the path to the walled kitchen gardens, some distance from the house. Such a pretty and intended distance, a nice little walk, and the path had been made and drained as well as a high road for the ladies of the house to go up and down. Beside the path and planted back from it were azaleas and rhododendrons, the white and green azalea and the honey-coloured, and three giant Tibetan rhododendrons with great rusty limbs enclosing dusky air. They flowered one after the other in strict, yearly rotation—March, April and May. There were groups of other shrubs, too: spireas and kalmias, great mats of heaths and camellias growing in the most sheltered spots, their dark glossy foreign leaves a hidden surprise. Besides all this and spotted by awful white rocks and holed limestone rocks like great fungus, there was the pink bluebell glade. Miss Anna Rose often remarked to him upon the prolific beauty of the pink bluebells which some aunt of hers had planted here. And he always refrained from expressing his absolute preference for blue bluebells. Only the very young prefer pink bluebells to blue. Equally, they prefer pink primroses to yellow. Behind the shrubs and bluebell glades and seas of winter heliotrope, beech trees grew close on naked ground. The aspect was bare and open through their distances and bosky and hidden as they closed into shrubberies and further woods.

* * * * *

Greenish face and greenish eyes, hair the colour of a linnet's back, greenish too. Always tweed coats and skirts, badly made, which shortened her body into a duck's body. The long-waisted coats linked with a single button; the aertex shirt collar always out over the neck of a fawn coloured jersey. She lived in gumboots. She had a maidenly way of wearing gloves, always gloves out-of-doors—it was like something a once-spoilt woman saves and clings to out of the past, an aunt's hands, white and padded pink with healthy great almond nails unvarnished and strong. In the cloakroom there were baskets of different kinds of gloves that belonged to Veronica, leather gloves and rubber gloves and cotton gloves and string gloves, all well mended and washed, and very seldom an odd man out, for if she lost one glove she searched diligently until she found it.

Here she was, gloved and gumbooted as usual, walking up from the garden with her baskets of brussels sprouts and a handful of herbs tucked into the top. By herself, out of doors, her unpainted look lost the green shade it had beside Yvonne's brilliance. It was no longer sickly, but a child's healthy pallor. Even the lips appeared reasonably coloured against the evergreens which grew beside the little path for busy aunts.

She was thinking away like mad: wondering if liver would be enough for luncheon so that the chickens could be kept for dinner. Mrs. Guidera had said there wasn't enough liver. Veronica had said it could be sliced thinly and cooked in cream and herbs with a lot of fried *croûtons*. Mrs. Guidera had looked grimmer than death. Mrs. Guidera had given all the sour milk to the chickens so that there was no brown bread, and that meant all the baker's bread had been used for breakfast and what about your *croûtons* then, unless Willy would go into town for a loaf—fifteen miles for one loaf. That was what it was like to housekeep with Mrs. Guidera. Veronica, who was not an hysterical subject, was twisting and turning the matter to its best conclusion in her mind when she met Eustace.

He was part of the household worry that she fled when she had put on her gloves and gone to the garden with her basket. Here he was again. Seeing him, she could only wonder desperately how much liver and how many *croûtons* he would require and consume for luncheon. They all became consumers and devourers, assuming the irritating avidity of chickens reared intensively.

She remembered the girl who had spoken out so smug and pat on the day of Uncle Roderick's funeral. . . . We can supply eggs and butter and cream and game. . . . We sleep in the best bedrooms. . . . They must have them . . . whisky too. . . ." What had she seen when she rushed on her fate like this? Eager, hungry English, longing for nourishment, quietly grateful for her ministrations, her gentle ruling of the household in sober new economies, no more champagne, no more apricots in brandy, otherwise good food and hot water (every other night) and Phillip, her darling, increasingly conscious of her, his indispensable, his little money-spinner for Ballyroden. But how could she have foreseeen these smart, greedy, beautiful women, who knew more about good food and comfort than she had ever dreamed of? Or her awful jealousy of that great glorious girl which crept in and ate her heart, no matter how she exorcised suspicion. That she had fallen in love with Phillip was so obvious as to be laughable, it was something like a child's body and soul worship for an adult. It was not the way to win a monk with an object—Phillip. An overworked religious with a goal in view, a beloved friend, whose recreations were shooting snipe and nursing the dogs and dreaming over the evening fire of bull-dozers and tractors and day-old chicks in thousands: whose mind hummed with pedigree shorthorn herds, pedigree wheat, dried grass and methods of castrating Aunt Anna Rose's robins, if he could have used the idea somehow to further the salvation of Ballyroden. Veronica's pinch of anxiety over Phillip and reaction to Yvonne's advances was not yet acute. Strangely, it was Yvonne's success with Mrs. Guidera that confused and angered Veronica out of all relation to its importance. Yet it was a daily infringement of authority, this romantic invasion of the kitchen by the guest. To come down briskly to the slate and the store cupboard (lately locked after its years of freedom) and interrupt a conversation on the blue ribbon heights of gastronomy with plans for roast beef or young rabbits in parsley sauce, was somehow difficult and belittling. Beating the air with words to make the gastric juices flow, or beating sauces, cakes and mayonnaises in bowls, Yvonne loved the kitchen and seemed to fatten on its air. Mrs. Guidera welcomed the stranger, taught her, talked to her, listened to her, and accorded Veronica only the coldest respect and distant attention. It had all boiled and developed in the passage of the days into something wounding and nerve racking. Any power or charm in Veronica seemed to evaporate, leaving a harsh little automaton in its place, a robot, a loveless familiar of the house, unlike the great, flowering, rich, young female who stirred the pots and licked her fingers and praised and laughed and suggested expensive little amendments to Veronica's menus. . . . " My dear, take out every bone and soak them in brandy and you won't ever dream they were rabbits. . . ." She rather guessed, although she had not made the accusation, that the scarcity of baker's bread for *croûtons* was due to a delicious course strangely named '*Coques m'siu*' that they had eaten the night before.

And here he stood in her path, one of the embodiments of her anxiety, a consumer, a devourer, paying through the nose. Unlike his niece and sister, never suggesting or protesting or demanding, only by his patient presence expressing all the new unsolved difficulties of life.

"Hallo," he said, "brussels sprouts? I love them."

She felt as defensive as though he was about to suggest soaking them in champagne or serving them with caviare. That was how far she had gone along the nervous road.

"Do you?" she said and ducked her head sideways to pass on.

He could see that she was upset. "Don't think me boringly greedy," he said suddenly, "but I do feel a completely different person after five weeks of your delicious food and this lovely place. . . . I'm sure it's awfully tiresome for you, this food obsession we all seem to have, but you do take such trouble and it is so good. It's such a relief to get away from dear little tiny Yvonne's ideas of stewing mice in wine and lacing milk with some awful ambrosia. Promise not to let her loose in your kitchen."

Veronica was so taken aback by this that she turned slowly red up her forehead into her hair like a child surprised in a secret. Then, with a click, she was shut in her box again and answered with dry sub-human propriety: "Oh, she's very helpful . . . very kind . . . thank you."

So no one was allowed to set a foot within her strict confidence. He thought of that great, cannibalising beauty he had brought here with him and a small wave of pity went over his heart. He did not say any more. He looked down at her in silence from his gawky height; his forget-me-not blue eyes were as kind as a gardener's or a doctor's.

Veronica met the look, it was a look never before encountered, and it filled her with a sort of dismay that her trouble should show so naked. Yet, beyond the dismay, there was a dawning relief that there could be understanding or care for her beyond her own bound life. It seemed dangerous. It was a new idea, and she fled it, frightened.

" Aunt Anna Rose is waiting for you," she said in a voice that suddenly shot without her leave into a treble, " waiting for you before she feeds her robins." There was nothing roguish or funny in the statement. He nodded acceptance and went on, satisfied that she was so well aware of his assault. It was a beginning. He walked on to the high wall and the dark green latched door, as solid as a door into a convent. He opened the door into the kitchen gardens where for numberless years four or sometimes six men had worked and idled. Now there was to be one man and some hideously complicated little plough, he understood. It seemed rather futureless in this great deadly expanse of cold winter garden—flatter, wider and more endless because, with summer borders cut down, there was no height to qualify the distance except the high, dreary plantations of brussels sprouts and broccoli. At intersecting paths, bushes of box were trimmed into great cold, pale eggs, and the box-edgings were so wide that two children could have run abreast along their tops.

At the very end of the garden the diamond-paned windows of the potting sheds were pasted close as pictures in a scrap-book to the unbroken spaces of brick wall. All the depth and width of the sheds and their slate roofs were behind the wall. The gardener's house was built in the same way. The wall seemed to run through the house and become part of it. The house front, door, and curtained windows were like a false clock face painted on china, all partaking of the life of the garden, all subservient to the necessity of the garden wall.

"Hullo, there you are—good!" She stood in the dark doorway of the shed, an archway big enough for the entrance of a cart. Her cheeks reflected the pinkish bloom of the walls. She was wearing her bird watching Inverness cape, reed pale and heather red, he noticed. For poachers, it was the mannish covert coating with wide shoulders and a sort of matching deer stalker. "The idea is, you see," she had told him, "in this hat, they don't know which way you're walkin'. That's the way I fox them."

Today it was a less warlike affair in violet felt with Tito peacefully spread upon a whole bed of rough double violets with silky leaves.

"These ruffians are tearing me to bits." She threw some horrible meal grubs to a dreadfully calendar specimen redbreast sitting on the handle of a mowing machine inside the shed: "That's all for you." She peeped into an Allen & Hanbury black currant lozenge box: "We've got four more of these ghastly chaps waiting for us in their terrains. Don't let's waste any more time. I've got to knock up some sort of a hide-out in the Kilahala bog before this afternoon. Willy saw something he can't describe down there yesterday and it's a nice day to watch birds, so let's. Hurry—we'll go through this way—shorter."

He followed her down the passage-like length of the sheds, smelling their deep earthy orderliness. Along the tidy shelves for apples the smell was sweet as in the dining-room. Strawberry nets were twisted and looped and hung on nails—everything that can possibly be hung on a nail, a gardener hangs on a nail: bunches of gladioli, unknown seed heads, strawberry nets, boxes, little tools, great flowing trusses of bass matting, withered pasteboards with '1st Prize, Vegetable Marrows, 1924.' The long rabbit-warren darkness became an easy pallor. He could see all the stored up yesterdays and tomorrows of this garden, and stopped with a startled exclamation before something that had less than nothing to do with today, tomorrow or gardening. Hanging on a nail (like everything else), beside the shelves of Cox's Orange Pippins was a small, pretty and practically undamaged eighteenth century looking glass. Its glass was a bit tarnished, so was its little golden bird; the piece of soft wood which backed it was riddled with woodworm.

"Stop a minute. Stop a minute," he said to Miss Anna Rose, who was sailing before him down the length of the sheds like a ship driven through narrow straits. "You must let me look at this I've found."

She looked too, for a moment. "Stiff with worm, I expect," she suggested practically.

"Only this bit of seed-box nailed across the back." His thumbs were feeling over it gently. "Oh, it's a little beauty. We can't leave it rotting here."

"My dear man, this place is full of junk," she said impatiently. "If it wasn't so cluttered and crowded up with rubbish there might be a chance of my rubies turning up some day."

It was the first time she had mentioned the rubies

directly to him. Collector that he was, he had asked everyone in the family about the probability or improbability of their existence. After the extensive inquiries his conclusion was that the rubies had in fact existed. Their value was legendary, but beyond question there had been rubies. Hercules and Consuelo spoke of them with complete conviction. He formed the idea that they were convinced their darling brother had got hold of the lot and disposed of them for less than a quarter their value. They did not propose to go into that matter. It was all part of their jolly past belonging to cricketing weeks and months at Monte Carlo and gambling losses which really had to be met. They had had quite enough scolding and unpleasantness about those days lately and they certainly did not propose to enlarge on any subject to their brother's discredit. Again and again they reiterated that nothing must be said to recall Aunt Anna Rose's tragedy.

Phillip and Veronica were uncertain on the subject. For them it had retreated into the obscurity and fantasy of the past. Their outlook, he sometimes thought with a certain sadness, was not unlike that of two plumber's mates looking backwards without much interest or rancour to an illegitimate ducal grandfather. The present struggle to live and continue to live blinded them to the colour and glamour of their family's yesterdays and days before yesterday. They were depressingly factual and sensible in their acceptance of the present; sane and indulgent to a degree towards those glamorous, spendthrift elders. But no shaft of lightness ever broke through the poor children's respectable endeavour. They could never deal grandly and lightly with minor or major crises. Never entrance him as Consuelo had entranced him when she said—of some major world-crisis: " Well, *I* don't know—we seem to be used to wars in our family —our uncles were always muddlin' their battles so shockingly."

Without emphasis, she claimed a share in disastrous importances. Or, the other extreme of importance, as she studied the pages of Debrett anxious to pinpoint an intimate friend: " *Dear* Susan Wainbridge—but I can't think who she *is*." Eustace had seen his sister flinch before that well-defined importance.

The children seemed to him like the Victorian age succeeding the age of Elegance. They were so nothing. So without naughtiness. So kind. When he had asked them about the rubies they had only shaken their heads doubtfully, passing over their loss as Consuelo had glossed over her uncles muddling their battles. Thousands of dead soldiers. Thousands of lost rubies. Rubies that had never been, so let Aunt Anna Rose enjoy them till the end of time. " We can't have anything like an enquiry," Phillip had said anxiously. " If they're real they'll turn up, and if not, things are no worse than we know they are. We really can't worry Aunt Anna Rose. That would be the last thing." It was strangely immaterial from such a limited, overworked young creature.

So now, he went on dusting and thumbing the glass, wondering whether she would say more, wondering whether to ask, whether she courted a question, whether a question would upset or excite her; afraid to go near this subject of which he had been warned gently by each person in the family. It was odd how coolly she mentioned them, standing here as if only yesterday she had worn them and put them aside and some person had popped them into an unknown safe-keeping. He looked up and met her eyes—the beautiful calm eyes of a child untroubled by its fantasies.

"They'll turn up," he said easily, accepting them in their round, actual existence, put away, most likely, in chamois leather—not in any morocco and velvet case. He longed to take a nearer step; he had some idea that if she got closer to the truth of the rubies, then too, she would become more a person. It would be like catching a fairy or transforming a child into the entire being it was to be. It would be an intensely exciting experiment. Then, looking at her turning from him and his precious little find, keyed only to the importance of feeding those prinking birds before they gave up hope of her arrival and bundled off sullenly to their little wilds, he wondered if anything could justify such an experiment. Those who knew her longest were probably right. Let the past sleep; let her perpetual youth be sufficient; why waken any sense of loss or pain for her? With talk of these rubies, real or phantom, the tragedy and love of her life would break into reality once again. Now the brown, bright nightingale amorous is half-assuaged for Itylus. . . . He put back the glass on its nail and followed her without further question. . . . The Thracian ships and the foreign faces, the tongueless vigil and all the pain. . . . Out again in the real life of the cold garden, he itched to probe; after all, he was a treasure hunter, an expert on jewels and pictures and furniture, and the idea of these jewels mislaid and this past forgotten was almost too strong for his fortitude. It was something in the contented way she counted over the grubs in the lozenge box and snapped shut the lid on the remainder after she had fed the second robin, that stopped him. Let her dwell in her present. There is no rival to content.

They short-cutted again through enormous glass-houses, warm round their dark dripping of water, warm from the sun, for there was no other heat. Here there was perfect order without any sense of prosperity. Peach trees were trimmed and tied in as beautifully as a piece of needlework. Vines and nectarines had their houses, too, and the same care. Throughout the length of the glass were great plants for the house: camellias and the winter *rhododendron fragrans*. It was a tree, that huge luxury bell of peppery sweet. He thought of it carried into a warm hall and could smell its lemon-rind scent in his mind. Obviously it had stood every April for years past in the hall at Ballyroden intoxicating diners as they passed through bathed and dressed for evening, ready for drinks and food and love. There was a climbing double pink geranium and beside it a great wuzzy asparagus fern, all set to frame the little bouquets for ladies; the usual greenhouse rose, china pink and soft petalled, grew up its trellises, darkening the light. There were fifty pots of cypripediums, definitely prepared to produce fifteen blooms between the lot of them, and a house full of primulas, all without exception going to be pale mauve. There were fuchsias of all kinds and a fine collection of azaleas, salmon pink and salmon pink, and salmon pink again.

In the domed central house where the rose and the white wisteria climbed and pots of healthy, sandy malmaison carnations were ranged on the green stages, Phillip stood with one foot up on a pierced ironwork garden seat, his head bowed over a notebook and pencil, talking at weary length to the gardener—erect and stubborn and pale as death beside him.

Phillip looked very tired and very grim as though he

had been talking for hours. His pipe had gone out and he was tapping it like a nervous woodpecker on the back of the seat. There was something other-worldly about the greenhouse gloom, the inner moony light, the warmth and the sad drip drip of fern darkened water, as though these two were exhausting themselves purposely in a jungle. Eustace was not sure that both were not near tears.

"... That vine made twelve-pounds-ten last September, Sir Phillip, and I've pruned it and thinned the grapes for twenty years, besides my peaches brought in fourteen pounds and more with all that went in to the house. Master Hercules would eat three in the day, every day. You know he's very fond of a good peach."

" But, Tracey, we must grow tomatoes and tomatoes won't do with peaches and vines and rose trees. We've got to harden our hearts and sweep the lot out."

" But I'm telling you, Master Phillip, I made fourteen pounds—fourteen pounds on the peaches alone. And that asparagus fern is a yearly fortune for funeral wreaths."

" All that doesn't pay your wages for two months out of the year, Tracey."

" Well," there was dignified rebuke in the tone of voice, " we all have to live, Sir Phillip."

" Exactly, Tracey, that's why I'm growing tomatoes in quantities. Here's the glass and we must make use of it."

". . . But not the muscatel vine, sir—we'll chance the muscatels on——"

" We can't. All the vines must go."

" Muscatels, too——" They stood together in pure anguish.

As Aunt Anna Rose went by light as a chain of bubbles,

Phillip looked up, absently good-mannered, but the gardener stood with dropped head, a little stocky man like an over-pruned apple tree. Eustace did not pause. He passed from the 1890 atmosphere of the domed and shady central house and out through the last little cold one, full of boxes of cuttings, into the garden. Aunt Anna Rose, that romantic irresponsible beauty, was flying on before him, gay as a white duck head down in a pond, and he felt again an impulse to catch her, to speak to her sensibly. To hold her mind and force it back through despair and heartbreak and death and beyond death back to the great happiness she fled. From such an analysis the truth about these jewels might be proved, to the relief of the situations he envisaged throughout Ballyroden. This little scene which he had witnessed was typical of many such. Why, if it were possible to forestall it, should the axe be laid to the roots of green muscatel vines and white wisterias? Why should a sturdy gardener cry about it in his twenty-fifth November? And why must this bitter struggling with possessions be all Phillip's inheritance? She was old, this fairy being from the past century. Even though her great rainbowed bubble of happy existence should be shattered, there could not be many years to come of depression or suffering, while there looked to be a life-time of both before those stern young people, Phillip and Veronica.

* * * * *

At three o'clock the sun was off the drawing-room windows and Hercules and Consuelo sat as near to the fire as they could squeeze with a small card table and a game of Bezique between them. The splendid air that surrounds those who make an unashamed business of amusement overhung their game as grandly as it does those games where fortunes come and go. Fortunes had, in fact, been won and lost in that room, but not this afternoon—although the snapping up and down of markers and the final calculations were as precise as if hundreds hung in the balance.

Consuelo put the cards away: " You owe me ninepence, Tots, really you do."

" You're sure, Pets? " He wrinkled his eyebrows up and down and slipped his money up and down in his trouser pockets, delaying payment.

" Yes," Consuelo spoke firmly, " and it's a lot of money these days, so please pay up."

" You wouldn't wait till Saturday when our allowances are due again? "

" No," she said sadly, " I can't. I need it. Come on, dear—ninepence."

" Oh, my dear—very well, very well. But I wish I could find a beziquer who was more unlucky than myself."

She put the money in her bag: " It's not that you're so unlucky, dear boy, but I'm a better player."

" Yes, bless you, you always have been," he looked at her with loving admiration, " *and* lucky. Do you remember the night we were cleaners—absolutely out, at Monte, and you left everything on red and it came up fourteen times."

" Oh, my dear." They savoured that past moment together. It was not a memory—it lived for them, it was present. He sighed, letting it go at last.

" I wonder," he pondered, " if that chap, Mills, plays,

or Mrs. Thomas. I might be able to rob them. You're too good for me."

"Now, Tots, no collaboration with the enemy. As it is, Mr. Mills gets quite enough encouragement from Aunt Anna Rose."

He stood squeezed between the card table and the fire, too idle to move the little table six inches one way or another. He warmed his behind. "What does she see in him?" he asked in a cosy gossiping way.

"Heaven knows, but she's taken him out again this afternoon to watch birds in the Kilahala bog."

"Kilahala bog—he'll be up to his knees in water after last night's rain." He spoke with evident pleasure.

"That may damp his ardour. Really, Tots, the situation is getting out of hand. They've been here more than three weeks. They look like being here three years. They like it—all but that woman."

"She's a shocker. She's a shocker."

"The other two are more dangerous. And look how they're undermining the servants. Willy has been Yvonne's slave from the first day. Even Mrs. Guidera encourages her into the kitchen, and I suppose, though I hate to say it, you can't help noticing that Bridgid is very obliging and unnecessary with Mr. Mills."

"Oh, what a nasty idea," he was really surprised and distressed. "I feel sure you're wrong there, Pets, really. You don't often make a floater but that can't be the right form. No, no, my own Beebee. But have you noticed how keen that Yvonne is on Phillip? Talks about nothing but farming. Poor little Veronica."

"She brought the whole thing on herself," Consuelo pointed out with triumphant coldness and truth—"and for what? For money."

" Money—sordid business. We never bothered much about it, did we, Pets? Not at her age and Phil's age. We had a different way of lookin' at things. Perhaps it wasn't nicer, but it was different. Now, I can't see you or I putting our Uncle Hercules, the old major, on an allowance of ten shillin's a week, can you imagine such a thing? Or stopping the port going round after dinner. How I wish this Mills chap liked port. It's most unlucky he don't. He says he's gouty—how can he be gouty? You know what I mean. Poor chap. I'm not a snob, but he can't have had a grandfather. Can he? "

Consuelo shook her head, vaguely denying the grandfather. " I wish someone would do something about this fire."

They both looked at the fire which was burning low. Hercules looked at the basket of logs on the right of the grate and at the basket of turf on the left.

" Pity someone doesn't do something about it. There's no method or organisation about this place now. None whatever. It's pathetic really, the way these kids muddle things. They don't know the value of anything."

" Not an idea—or they couldn't imagine we could get along on ten shillings a week."

" My dear girl, we must raise some ready cash somehow. We've had our ups and downs together, but we've never been in such an appalling jam in our lives, and what's really bothering me today is how I'm to get myself to Powerstown Park races on Friday. It's my favourite meeting and I've got a certainty for the Clonmel Chase."

Suddenly she changed from the spoilt, dignified, grumbling woman into an eager child: " Oh, but we must go, Tots. We haven't missed a Powerstown for years. Don't you think the children will have a car to take us if we're good?"

"P'raps they will, and we can always bet on the nod with Phil Feeney."

Their pretty eyes met and promised each other the outing. It was unthinkable that anything should stand in its way.

She stood up: "I must answer some of my letters about darling Roddy—before post time. Five more to-day from five more old friends, and each says she knows she was the *one* woman in his life. That makes seventy-five."

"Oh, the *dear* old boy. How many letters have we had now?"

"More than two hundred."

"Oh, much more. Jolly sweet of the P.M. to write, I thought. And the Archbishop. Funny I should get one the same day from the Aga and Cardinal Taormina and that little bowsie who runs The Box of Tricks."

"How many have you answered, Tots?"

"How many have you answered, Pets?"

They shook their heads at each other and sat down again under the acknowledged weight and press of work that lay before them.

Yvonne came in, saw two old things sitting dreamily on either side of the fire. She knew nothing of the brilliant gaiety that lived between them or of that intimacy which held them inviolable. Nor did she realise the iciness of their critical spirit towards such people as herself.

"Hullo," she said, "could someone hear me my tables, please? I've just got them off by heart and I want to be word perfect when Phil comes back from buying the new farm tractor." She thrust a book into Hercules' hands. It was all rather like an awful child in bows and ringlets coming in to insist on reciting its beastly piece. Hercules lost the place and dropped the book and sat back in a dazed way. She picked it up, found the place and gave it back to him. He still did not look at the book and even seemed faintly disgusted at its touch.

" Multiplication? " he asked faintly. " I'm not very clear about them myself after Five Times."

" Not that kind." She took a breath. " ' Periods of Gestation on the Farm ' tables."

Consuelo opened her eyes:

" Good gracious! I've lived in the country all my life, but I wouldn't dream of knowing anything like that for certain. So unattractive."

" I'm keen. I don't think one can go in for old-fashioned repressions these days. I want to look at it all from a real, clean, scientific point of view, and I want to start at the beginning. It's all glorious Nature—so will you hear me."

" Oh, dear, all right," Hercules twiddled the pages unhappily. " Well, if we must, let's start with the birds."

" Why the birds? "

" Oh, I don't know. They seem less real."

She laughed indulgently: " You'll be back at the bees and flowers next. Ask me a real one, you silly old man."

" Very well—I will. Ducks? "

" Ducks, ducks? " She was puzzled. " They don't give ducks, do they? "

Hercules' attention was riveted on the page in front of him. He did not answer. Consuelo sat withdrawn in apathetic disgust.

"They don't give ducks," Yvonne repeated impatiently.

"Don't they?" Hercules turned a page without looking up. "Read *that*."

"Where?" She leaned over his chair. "Gracious, you're on the wrong page. That's the start of the business —we needn't go into *that*."

Consuelo opened her eyes—suddenly she wore the look of the one who is out of the fun.

Hercules went on reading avidly. "Why not?" he said. "It's all glorious nature. Oh dear, now you've lost my place. This bit's very boring. Ah"—he was now warmly interested—"here's a teaser—this'll puzzle you—Rabbits?"

"You're cheating. It doesn't say rabbits, does it?"

"Yes, it does."

"Where?"

"There."

She leaned nearer the book, reading. A thread of joint interest was between her and Hercules. In their silent attention they were equal and Consuelo was the outsider. When Yvonne raised from the page eyes like stars and said dazedly: "Oh, aren't they awful?" she could keep apart no longer but picked her huge self as quick as a cat out of her chair and joined the group round the book, her absolute charm making it easy for her to yield: "I'm missing everything. It's not fair. Where? Show me . . . *Fancy*!"

"Not a dull instant." Yvonne gave a great sigh. "Ask me cows now."

"Cows?"

"I know! I know!" Consuelo's hand almost flew up.

" Don't tell me! Don't tell me! Nine months." Yvonne leaned nearer him than Consuelo.

" Wrong! "

" Eleven," Consuelo sniffed, " it's elementary."

" Wrong again "—Hercules himself became pregnant with triumph—" nine months and seven days."

" Are you sure? " Yvonne said. " I truly want to get this business straight."

" And why? " Consuelo asked her directly. The question came like an arrow through all the slack, fat, easy manner: an arrow that pinged into its mark and quivered there.

Yvonne answered with that frankness so foreign to Consuelo's generation: " Because they're Phil's favourite subject after tractors."

" How nice of you to take so much interest in our poor nephew."

" Oh, I think he's pure heaven. I'm tremendously keen."

" Well, I think you'd be more sensible if you let him talk cows and tractors to Veronica as he always has done," Consuelo suggested. She sounded almost helpful. The very last thing she intended.

" Oh no. You must meet a man on his own ground."

" But that's Veronica's ground," Hercules insisted, " fair do's. Mustn't poach. No crosslining. No stroke-hauling."

" Tell me, tell me," Yvonne murmured rapturously, " tell me all about *stroke-hauling*. It sounds wonderful, much easier than this dreary gestation."

" It's Aunt Anna Rose's subject, really, but I can give you a rough idea."

" Oh, I don't mind, I like it rough." She looked quite

lovely with her great arching white teeth and rogue's eyes. Consuelo was reminded of herself and her youth. When she was young they had dared to look even more than this child had said. " Ah," she sighed, and wished for a daughter like this. Differently bred, of course, different worlds. But the same gorgeous dewy looks and little clipping voice and the same greediness. One could have lived with such a daughter, there were common grounds, an identical approach to life. Her little, dark, governess of a daughter could never dream of the pleasures her mother had known . . . the terrible temptations . . . the joys of yielding to them. . . .

She was plunged so entirely into the past that when Phillip came into the room she very nearly shared Yvonne's spasm of pleasure at his approach. She felt a sort of admiring horror at the lack of technique, at the frank avowal of the girl's greeting:

" Hullo—Wonderful! Did you buy your big red engine? "

He answered in her own silly way: " No, Gorgeous, I couldn't. All the money in my money box wasn't enough to pay for the red engine. The man put it back on its shelf."

" Oh, poor lamb. What a disappointment."

They sat down together on the sofa, obviously pleased to be near each other. He gave her a cigarette. She took it as though it was a *gage d'amour* in square-cut emeralds. She leaned for the flame of a match as if for a kiss.

Hercules was very bored. He was longing to get on to the subject of Powerstown Park races. Unlike Consuelo, he had never been in love and found the whole thing pretty good nonsense. He glanced over at Consuelo, confident that she would find some auspicious opening for their little project. He knew his Pets. Tact and diplomacy were her strongest characteristics. He heard her say:

" It's terrible to be so short of money," and sat ready when his turn should come to take advantage of this brilliant tactical opening.

" Isn't it? " Phillip answered gloomily.

" Dear boy," Hercules said gently, " could you spare me a cigarette."

" Certainly, dear Uncle Hercules, but I did give you twenty before lunch."

" Oh, I'm sparing those," he answered with righteous frugality, " I shall need 'em. P'raps someone could give me a match? "

Yvonne struck one and held it away, teasing him like a great sly bird: " You wouldn't give me a teensy bit of chocolate, would you, Mr. Ryall? Baby likes chocolate."

" Oh, my dear, I haven't a morsel. I'm longing for a piece myself. Wish you hadn't mentioned it. Makes my mouth water."

" You must have a nice lot salted away somewhere," she said rather sulkily and commonly as she lit his cigarette.

" Only wish I had. No money to pay for it. Can't buy a biscuit. Can't buy a thing."

This was where Aunt Consuelo said with dreadful casualness: " That reminds me, Phil, dear child—what arrangements have you made about getting us all to the race-course tomorrow? "

He looked up: " What race-course, Aunt Consuelo? "

" Why, Powerstown Park, naturally. I've put English meetings right out of my life."

"Never thought of it," he answered with a sort of false brightness, "and we're not going, anyway. You and Uncle Herky always lose a packet there."

"Oh, my dear boy, my dear child," Hercules was desperately fussed, "just a trifle, only a trifle. I've got three certain winners tomorrow. Oh, we must get there somehow. Can't bear to throw good money away."

"My darlings," Phillip spoke strongly, "we are not going racing tomorrow. Please understand. I'm afraid I do mean it."

"Oh. . . ." Consuelo's face wore the white, hopeless expression of a child. Blood drained from its cheeks. The skin was left white and papery. In her defeat she was withdrawn and entirely resentful. Hercules was more articulate. He had to explain the wrong-headed nature of the restriction. His little notebook was whipped out. "But old boy, old boy. Let me show you—it's like this. I put two pounds on Golden Disk in the first race at three to one. . . ." He calculated, sucking his pencil, and wrote happily for several minutes: "There you are in black and white. I show a profit of forty-seven pounds on the day—can't help myself."

"Dearest Uncle Herky, we aren't going racing."

"But——"

Consuelo put her hand over his: "He means it, Tots. We can't have our little toot."

"Oh," his eyes fell open as deep as a bloodhound's. "Oh, *dear*!"

"Look—don't cry. Please——" Phillip felt every sort of male Goneril. There were no old people like his. He wanted to put his arms round them and hire cars for them and buy champagne for them and see them happy and easy. But always his foolish generosity was bounded by sense and also by that ascetic endeavour that might become a luxury with him. It is the danger when the young take to hard living. " Please be good about it. I want things desperately, too, you know. I do want things to save the place from the jungle—tractors, flame throwers, circular saws, New Zealand winches——"

" But that's thousands and thousands. Take it steady, dear boy. Remember what darling Roddy always said: a stitch in time saves nine. Look after the chutes. See the down pipes aren't blocked by leaves and the roof sound, and you'll have your home for ever in good order. That's what he always said and did his best to carry it out, dear old man."

" But the chutes are perforated, Uncle Herky, spouting water on your head, and the roof wants a thousand pounds spent on it this minute."

" We only want a car and our entrance. We don't want a thousand pounds. Don't blame us, we've all done our utmost best. We don't want one thousand pounds, really, old boy."

Phillip said rather hopelessly: " Please could we forget it."

" Look, the sun's coming out. Why don't you two go for a little toddle-woddle to get up those appetites for tea? "

They looked at Yvonne as if she was the kind of revolting specimen that one can scarcely endure to grind under foot: " What a funny idea," they said, " it's pourin'."

It was then that Bridgid came into the room, hurrying and fussing prettily and careful for them: " Now—lovely sunshine. Master Hercules, your thumb stick—Mrs. Howard, your goloshes."

Hercules got up and looked out of the window: " Oh,

all right," he agreed, "if you say so." The day really seemed changed.

Consuelo joined him. They stared out against the wet panes. They would not make any fuss. "We'll look for eggs in the cowshed, Tots. It's nice and warm in there."

"The farmyard's pretty mucky," he said. "What about my gummers, Beebee? Then I can go in the puddles."

"Your gummers are on the damp side." Bridgid looked a little confused and spoke rather tartly to hide it. "Just keep your feet out of the puddles for one day, sir."

"I've got a lot of dreadful things to think of, Beebee, and I don't want to have to keep my mind on puddles."

"Just keep your feet out of the puddles and you'll do," she repeated. "Look at your shoelace, gone again." She knelt and tied it with that little, dry, firm sound nannies make with shoelace bows. "Knot it *twice*, that's what I've always told you."

"Gimme me stick," he took it from her and smiled a little thank-you over his crossness.

"And my big umbrella, my green umbrella." Consuelo rejected the one Bridgid offered.

"Oo *me*—I left it somewhere funny," Yvonne plunged towards the door. "I'll get it."

"And the dogs," Phillip said, "I'll get them for you."

Everyone had to organise Hercules and Consuelo when they took an airing. Bridgid was bustling Hercules out with a whispered admonition about running along the passage, when Dorothy came in, her chin on top of a balanced pile of writing material, Vogues, library books and *Petit Point*. She was insultingly warmly dressed, her mink coat on top of tweed: fur boots still swallowed her pretty ankles.

Consuelo paused to say solicitously: " Oh, you've got your feet down very soon after that huge luncheon, Mrs. Thomas! Shouldn't you have stayed in bed a bit longer—think of that chin line."

" To be candid, Mrs. Howard, eight hours out of twenty-four on your mattresses is quite long enough for me. Last night I was so sore and stiff that I couldn't turn over in bed—I had to get up and walk round and get in the other side."

" And that "—Consuelo had her hand on the door knob ready for a triumphal exit—" is about as interesting an adventure as you are likely to have. Good-bye, I'm just off to get some fresh air."

" Well," Dorothy was undefeated, " if fresh air is all you want, you've only got to sit at this writing table for ten minutes—you'll be practically blown out of the house."

Before Consuelo could find the right answer, William came gaily in. He carried a hot-water bottle in a soft bag and a green cashmere rug.

" Master Hercules is waiting on you, madam," he ventured, " and Bridgid says if you please, let yous hurry, for he's standing on the gravel with his two feet in a puddle to provoke her for the loss of his gumboots."

" Oh dear——" She sailed off, delighted to be saved the effort of further repartee.

" Where's that hot-water bottle going, William ? " Dorothy asked jealously.

William answered from the sedan chair: " In the nest, madam." He was inside it himself, stirring round and fixing things like a thrush moulding its nest with its body. " Oh, it's very nice and snug in here," he put his head out through the window, " her fur rug, and her green rug and her hot-water bottle and her hat-box for Tito."

"Tito"—Dorothy experienced a pang of that absolute jealousy which the elder child can know for the pampered baby—"Tito—really, this house is paradise for second childhood, but Hell on earth for the normal adult. I was kept out of the bathroom for two solid hours last night—and why?"

"Why?" Willy asked with his usual humanity and interest.

"Miss Anna Rose in there—swimming the lake after a poacher."

Willy's eyes shone: "Ah, but she got him in the wind up. One of the Wild O'Donnels from Lyre, too—oh—a tough crowd."

This complete acceptance of the unreal against the actual sent Dorothy reeling: "My dear boy, are you, are they or am I—entirely crazy?"

Shutting the door of the sedan chair Willy reassured her gently: "You'll be all right, madam, when you get into our little ways. You'll be as steady as any of us."

She looked at him, slightly frightened: "Your little ways are rather catching too. I get quite worried about my brother."

"Ah now, and himself and Miss Anna Rose the greatest pals out," Willy soothed her reasonably.

"Exactly." Dorothy came nearer. "Off to feed the robins every morning, and now he's out in an arctic wind watching impossible birds in a bog with an unpronouncable name. One thing, his bad ear will never stand it."

"Don't you fret yourself about his ear at all, madam," Willy spoke with sober assurance, "Bridgid knocked up a right little potion for that ear—fernseed she got at the turn of the moon and stewed seven hours in the milk of a black goat."

Suddenly Dorothy put both hands up to her breast: "He didn't *drink* it?"

"He did—why not?" Willy's light, sweet voice held the very essence of unexaggerated truth.

"This is going *too* far," she was genuinely concerned, "we must really get back to normal life." She groped for some reality. "I'll write to my agents about the flat immediately." The solid resolution comforted her and she moved across to the writing table, a vast Buhl affair, where one sat with one's back to the airy window.

"Oh, madam." With clasped hands Willy took a step towards her. "You're not going to take Miss Yvonne away from us. I'd say she'd be terribly lonesome after the farming." The suggestion was made with extreme restraint.

Dorothy accepted it. She was learning quite a lot about good manners from the servants at Ballyroden.

"Yes," she said thoughtfully, "well, I know *you'll* take care of Miss Yvonne for me, William, if she decides to go on with her farming. Now," her dismissal was reluctant and gentle, "I really must write a letter, if I can hold down the paper." She shuddered in the draught that caught the back of her neck as she sat down.

"I'll come for your letters at four-thirty." As William shut the door a swirl of air sent the writing paper skating on to the floor. It annoyed Dorothy as acutely as though she chased a spring hat down a gusty pavement. . . . Oh, the agony of it all. . . . On her feet to retrieve the paper, she took a sudden resolution: after all, why not? It was a very sensible idea. Nothing against it whatsoever. She gathered her belongings together, handbag, writing block, cigarettes, lighter, stepped into Aunt Anna Rose's sedan chair, closed the door and sat surprised in the strange, strange little inner world of warmth, like the country-under-the-bed world of childhood. As she put the fur rug—nutria and blue—over her knees and felt the warmth of the hot-water bottle penetrate her clothes and pulled across the leather curtains on the side next the public, she saw for the first time something of the divine sense behind Aunt Anna Rose's fantastic escape from living.

Back to the empty room came Phillip and Yvonne. Yvonne—shamelessly resolute. There was a warmth in her determination like the child that knows what it is going to grab, and grabs. No hesitant amorousness, half afraid of a denial, but a great odorous sensuality filled the air round her—a heavily flowering Portugal laurel on a wet, warm afternoon—within its shelter proven peace and darkness.

She was talking about Hercules and Consuelo. A frigid subject, but behind all her words to him her eyes were heavy with other meaning:

" Poor old pets—you're so *strict.*" The words were cross but her voice rounded and flowed with admiration —" You'll be making Aunt Anna Rose travel third class by slow train, soon."

Within the sedan, Dorothy debated whether to declare her presence. She knew that tone in her child's voice. She knew that sunken attitude on sofas, as intimate as weed in water. Looking at Phillip, arms on chimney piece and puzzled eyes, she decided to rely on his resistance. Yvonne's light, tiny voice went on in its minor key clatter: " I simply think it's such a shame not to let them have their little toot. Couldn't you see tears? I could see tears. Think of them now, getting the eggs in that gloomy old cowshed, or don't you give it a thought? You're so tough, and p'raps those hens haven't laid any eggs to amuse them. Really, you go too far. I must say I do think you go too far." The compelling look she gave him as her voice clicked out and stopped was as strong as the current in a river.

He stuck to the spoken subject with sullen determination: " They'd absolutely lose a packet. I know them."

" You aren't nice to anybody, are you? I'd like to go. Why don't you and I go? Why don't you take me? "

" Yes, that's quite an idea." He smiled over at her on the sofa. " Drinks and dinner afterwards, I suppose."

" *Please*. Why not? "

" But how can I cut everyone's allowance down to ten shillings a week, refuse to hire a car to drive them thirty miles and then take myself off for a jolly with you."

" Need they all know? "

" Don't be so silly."

" William could take me on his motor bike and we could meet at the races and come back *very* late and walk up the drive. Oh, it would be fun. Oh, I'm keen to go."

He looked at her heavily. " I must start tilling the fifty acres tomorrow."

" Fifty acres, what a lot. What is it? "

" It's Virgin Leas."

" What hard work. Poor you. I *know*. I'll stay and help. After all, I'm truly, truly trying about this farming and you can't get nearer the bone than Virgin what's it."

" You'd hate it. It's a very long, cold, tiring business."

" Couldn't we have a teensy rest every four hours? " She moved inevitably farther up the sofa till he came over and sat in the void beside her.

" Why are you so forward and naughty, Yvonne? " Her name sounded as though he had never spoken it before but taken it straight out of his mind.

" I like being forward and naughty best, I suppose." Her voice was rough and low. The tinkle spent itself like the ring on glass.

" You're upsetting me."

" You don't think it's rather nice? "

" No. It takes my mind off the circular saws and tractors and bull-dozers and combines." The pages of bright circulars flew open.

She gave one of her cat's yawns. " Even combines? I do feel like a combine. Are you ever feeling like a bull-dozer? "

" Sometimes." He confessed it.

" What does a bull-dozer feel like? "

" Simply terrifying."

" Would it frighten a combine? "

" They never meet," Phillip said resolutely. " One works in spring and the other in harvest time."

" Maybe," Yvonne leaned nearer to breathe the question, " they get into the same shed in November."

" Well," he admitted, " I have heard of it."

She leaned back again. " But what do you think happens when a keen combine and a good bull-dozer meet in November? "

" I don't know." He met her eyes. " I don't know yet. . . ."

Dorothy was spared the necessity of dropping something or coming out of her cuckoo's nest by Veronica's great schoolgirl entrance. For a tiny person she made more noise than a classroom full of fourteen-year-olds. She came in, head down, arms swinging, and went straight to that certain point of irritation—the fire.

" Oh, hullo." She thought they were rather quiet on the sofa. " Oh dear—couldn't one of you have put a log on the fire? "

" I am sorry." Phillip looked bored and guilty. " I never noticed it was so low."

" I did," Yvonne was experiencing that horrid moment of disappointed love, and illogically blamed her discomfiture on Veronica, " but you see, I thought it was William's job."

It was quite a little challenge to the housekeeper. Veronica looked up from her efforts with the fire.

" Oh, did you? Well, he has rather a lot on his hands now since he's taken you on as well as Aunt Anna Rose. I think he wasted about an hour this morning teaching you to ride his motor-cycle, and he's awfully tired after it, too. You're pretty heavy to pick up and keep straight."

" Oh, he's divine." Yvonne accepted the rebuke as a tribute to her attraction. " I'm mad about him. We're going to the Pictures tomorrow, too. It's a date."

" Thursday tomorrow. Aunt Anna Rose will be very upset if she can't go to the ' Queen of the Jungle ' serial on Thursday afternoon. You can't go tomorrow."

" Tomorrow, he said," Yvonne reiterated with all a spoilt darling's ugly weight and intention.

" That's a bit awkward," Phillip tried to bridge the difficulty.

" Everything's awkward today." Veronica spoke in that high-pitched dreadful little voice. " Mrs. Guidera's used up all the eggs and all the cream, Phil. I can't think where they've got to."

"Can't you?" Yvonne snuggled down like a full fed cat.

"Oh, I *am* so tired! And Mother has broken out and bought fifteen rabbits and the man wants half a crown each for them. He's waiting." She turned to Phillip. For the moment she exemplified all the domestic ties and drab responsibility and straightforward righteousness which had seized, with inheritance, upon his life. His little, faithful friend made him feel faintly sick.

"Good God," he said with a new impatience, "tell him to take them away."

Veronica looked at him nervously. A grieved Phil she knew, and a tired Phil and a strong sacrificial priest, but irritable and impatient she had never seen him: "I can't," she whispered, "they've been here since last Thursday, and they're stinking."

"My dear Pet, I thought you kept quite a check on the larder."

"Well, I do, I do, but you see, she hid them in a big bag where she keeps her black hat behind the dairy door."

"How sweet and sanitary," Yvonne threw in unpardonably.

"She's always kept it there, hasn't she, Phil?" It was a defence of Ballyroden.

"How should I know?" he answered wearily, cutting straight through the sense of close companionship in which she held him to their past.

There was a silence during which Yvonne did her hair and looked at her nails before she said: "I can't really see why it's all so difficult. If I had four servants I'd have time on my hands to do my nails and set my hair and play the gramophone."

"I don't expect you to understand anything," Veronica had tears in her eyes, "but you do, Phil, don't you?" It was one of those unanswerable cries from the helpless, the unwanted.

He passed by her complaint: "I'm in a sea of troubles too," he said. "Do you know, I've just had to turn down a new combine."

"Oh, my poor, *poor*——" pity streamed from Veronica for the disappointed one. But it was to Yvonne that he turned.

"D'you ever get your wishes?" her light voice dropped a tone.

"Yes," Veronica watched their eyes find each other, "twice, I have."

"Ah, which two?"

"A tip-up lorry and a football." Like all his kind, he was past master at evasion of the serious. At a nonsense answer that got nobody anywhere. He did not want a serious issue. He was glutted with responsibility. He was incapable of taking anything in the shape and size of love lightly. He had a rather charming innocence and immaturity—attractive up to a point and wildly annoying beyond a point. Yvonne had not yet reached that degree of intimacy. This was the most childlike flirtation she had known since the age of fifteen. The tip-up lorry and the football put her back in the sulks.

"All right, all right. I may be silly, but that combine would pay for itself over and over again. It's wasted on its shelf, poor little thing, breaking its heart up there."

"What on earth are you talking about?" Veronica was puzzled and appalled.

" Don't you know? I'm studying farming? I'm mad about it. Phil's going to teach me everything."

" He'll hardly have time." A governess spoke unfortunately: " We don't play at farming here, it's pretty deadly serious—isn't it, Phil? "

" Mmm—don't discourage our new pupil. She's a fine, strong girl, we might knock some work out of her if we take her the right way. Do you like being taken the right way, Yvonne? "

" Oh, yes."

" Come on then—we're putting out lime on the top of Kilknockan hill this afternoon, and it's raining. I'll see how much you can stand."

They were at the door. Veronica was alone, alone in an afternoon drawing-room. Other people were going out together spreading lime in the rain.

" Phil," she called faintly. She did not know what she was going to say.

" What, dear? " He turned.

She saw her own hand out, asking for something. She had to explain the hand away: " Just—the money for the rabbits."

In the hall Yvonne's voice was flying, light as a little bird. Phillip hesitated between the two streams of living. He hardly knew the hesitation was pleasurable: " Oh, darling," he said gaily, " tell him to call again." And he was gone.

Through the window of the sedan chair, Dorothy watched the change coming over Veronica's face. She was not a very sensitive person but she knew women's emotions backwards, and for the first time Veronica took shape to her other than as a disagreeable managing child with the mind of a small sea-side landlady in July. Now, she was reminded of one of those awful unchosen children in that party game, 'I wrote a letter to my Love' with its clear touch of horror. . . . It isn't *you* and it isn't *you* and it isn't *you* and it isn't *you*. . . . She saw the stiff upper lip and the trembling lower lip and the darting, anxious eyes of the unchosen child. She saw the knowledge and realisation spread itself and the young-old face take a definite shape of ugliness in its pain. It was mortified rather than pitiful. There is no attractive quality in failure. Only a sense of exasperated detachment is born in the witness or confidante.

When the girl, suddenly as if in some sort of rage, set to tidying the room, lifting heavy chairs about like a poltergeist, beating cushions, pulling covers savagely to rights, she realised smugly that things were out of hand, but saw no possibility of helpfulness in this hysteria, nor any need whatsoever to make her presence known—until —a clownish tragedy—some savage piece of Veronica's tidying set Aunt Anna Rose's telephone bell ringing, ringing, ringing, with the robot insistence of a telephone at night. Veronica picked it up and it rang into her face, magnificently imperturbable. "Shut up," she said, "shut up. Oh, my God, do *stop*." She pushed it back on to its hooks and raced across the room to the sedan.

Realising the offensive as her best bet under such circumstances, Dorothy popped her neat head, fingers in ears, out of the window: "For heaven's sake, child, control this ghastly machine or I shall have to get out."

The effect of shock reacted on the telephone and on the immediacy of Veronica's grief. Both ceased together. In the whole course of her life Veronica had never seen anyone enter Aunt Anna Rose's chair except for its cleaning or arrangement, and that was done with deference and usually in the early morning hours when the house is no one's. This trim lady with her curly head, her pretty make-up and her great sleeved mink coat was as truly shocking as to find a cow in your bed, or to see a fish swimming in a haystack.

" Mrs. Cleghorne-Thomas "—it was a gasp of horror—" get out, please, get out at once."

Dorothy was really rather anxious to get out. The genuine horror of Veronica's reaction had got through to her as well as the telephone. She began to feel as though the fairies would start to tweak her and beset her with ugly tricks if she persisted in this violation. But the stronger this conviction grew, the more determinedly her good English middle-class courage forbade the retreat.

" *And* why? " she asked. " I'm actually farther off from pneumonia at this moment than I've been since I left England."

" *Get out.* This is Aunt Anna Rose's own place. It's where she lives. None of us goes in. It's her train. It's her aeroplane. It's her own own fancy. It's her own fun. It'd be better to take anything from her than do this. Get out, please."

" My dear girl, are you all right? It's really the most shaming, neurotic exhibition I've ever seen. Quite too embarrassing. Quite frightening. Not what one's accustomed to." As the words came smartly out in a jeering, grumbling way, Dorothy was actually gathering her belongings together and preparing to get herself out, reluctantly, but as certainly as one gets out of bed to catch a train.

It was bitterly unfortunate that the birdwatchers should have viewed their evening's special quarry after a wait of only twenty minutes instead of the expected two hours. Having accomplished this purpose, it had been Aunt Anna Rose's idea to go home before pneumonia set in; this brought them into the drawing-room without warning and while Dorothy was still scolding and fiddling about inside the nest.

Veronica shut the door of the chair on her quickly and stood defensively and unimaginatively in front of it. Not that Aunt Anna Rose noticed anything. She was bubbling over with delight at the success of the afternoon's observations. She and Eustace were both gay and flushed from the mountain breeze blown over the lake. A smoke of chill air came into the room with them like the fine vapour on a fresh glass of champagne, an out of the way air of celebration and gaiety.

"Very funny, very funny, wasn't it?" she was saying in her wild young voice. "Such a wonderful day. Never had such sport. My dear Veronica, two yellow crested grebes in a most compromising situation—weren't they, Mr. Mills?"

"They were indeed," he corroborated.

"Yes—in November, too. Tito was surprised," her hands went up to the deer-stalker where Tito floated head down, veiled in russet and wearing rather a sullen out of it all expression. "Oh, it *was* cold. The day has changed. I'd have stayed out till tea-time myself but I was bothered about Mr. Mills's ear." She came farther into the room.

"Get warm by the fire, darling." Veronica tried rather obviously to shepherd her away from her sedan.

"It's out." Aunt Anna Rose spoke nonchalantly. "I'll pop into my carriage. These trans-continental expresses are really overheated. I'll be all right."

"I hope we didn't stay out too long in the cold." Eustace thought Veronica looked cruelly bothered and anxious. "We've really had quite an exciting day with what I found this morning and what we saw this afternoon."

"What did you find this morning?" Veronica asked in a desperate voice. Anything for delay. Anything to get Aunt Anna Rose out of the room even for a moment. Finally and desperately no reason occurred to Veronica. She was like a tone-deaf person asked to sing an air in tune. It was not possible.

"Aunt Anna Rose, what did he find?" She caught her arm, whisking her round towards the fire.

"Ask him." Aunt Anna Rose was thinking of her close, warm carriage rushing through the evening, rocking a little on its wheels; and of a sympathetic fellow traveller, dark-skinned, astrakhan-collared, taking sleeping pills out of a silver snuff box; settling down for the night and the journey. . . . 'Si madame permet je ferai une petite lumière. Je ferai une lumière bleue. . . .' She longed for the warmth and the little floating light and the soothing, speeding train. "Tell her quickly," she said.

"Hanging on a rusty nail in the apple house—guess what?"

"She's a bad guesser. Tell her. Tell her."

"Believe it or not, behind the Cox's Orange Pippins, an eighteenth century mirror, in perfect condition, too."

"Oh, yes," Veronica seized on the subject, "Tom, the gardener's dreadfully vain, he must have pinched it from the boot room—don't you think so, Aunt Anna Rose?" She caught the inverness cape and spun her round again.

"But, my child, it's Chippendale." Eustace could not help demanding some interest in his find.

"Really," the little, dead voice went on, "who *was* Chippendale? Was he nice? Aunt Anna Rose, do come upstairs and take your cape off, love, to please me."

"I may need it for the night."

"Chippendale, Chippendale," Eustace was off on his favourite horse, "just a word for some of the loveliest things in some of the dustiest corners of this house; a word for mirrors with little golden birds fluttering for ever in dark toolsheds and for tables with reedings and mouldings where clothes are brushed and boots are cleaned and Willy mixes poison for the rats."

"How exciting! Aunt Anna Rose, your hat."

"No. Just take my boy's veil off. Now I'll just get in and have a nice, warm nap."

"But your boots." Veronica had hit on it at last. "We must go upstairs and change your boots. They must be wet. Mr. Mills's gummers are absolutely soaking —look at the pools and footmarks on the carpet."

"I am a savage," he apologised. "I'll change at once."

She was content. "All right, I will if you will." It wasn't so bad if they did it together.

Veronica sighed with relief and flew to open the door.

Left alone, Aunt Anna Rose went straight to her chair. "Me slippers," she said over her shoulder, "I know the valet's left them in the luggage rack. Always does."

The door was open and there sat today the brutal and absolute contradiction of that foolish, happy world which Aunt Anna Rose had maintained so long and so beautifully. Veronica and Eustace both saw something as complete and perfect as a bubble floating on light, about to break: about to end in nothing. They had forgotten Aunt Anna Rose's readiness and steadiness of mind. Her defence of her violation was light and whole as the bubble she kept in the air. She stepped closer to the chair and spoke with chilly politeness: "Really, madam, you astound me. Surely you must be aware that this carriage is engaged. . . . Reserved. . . . Loué. . . . Besezt. . . . Reservato. . . ." She hardly seemed to know to whom she spoke and tried each language separately, seeking to explain the mistake the ignorant traveller had made.

Dorothy could have allowed the dream to continue. She only had to apologise, pick up her suitcases, get out and call a porter. But, no. She was a coarse, matter-of-fact woman and she had suffered enough from the indulgence of a whole household for this old woman's crazy world. "I'm aware it's the one warm place in this house." She refused to play the Train fantasia.

"Out you get, Dorothy, and quick too," Eustace came across to her, white with anger, "and remember, for God's sake," he whispered, "you're in a TRAIN."

They were all surrounding her, all shocked, all against her. Inspired by an unfortunate access of bulldog spirit she sat back firmly in her seat, oddly like an angry traveller in the train she denied.

"You're a bit touched yourself, Eustace. I got this seat first and I'm not going to move."

Aunt Anna Rose on the other side of the chair was still composed and in command of herself. "There seems to be only one thing to do with this person." She turned to Veronica: "Call the guard, me dear," she said gently.

At last accepting the Train myth, Dorothy laughed over her shoulder, mammoth in her mink and air of opulence: " Call away. The guard won't come. It's not a corridor carriage."

" Take care, take care," Veronica's distress suddenly mounted to terror; " don't say that—don't remind her. Get her out, Mr. Mills, get her out."

" I've stood enough nonsense." Dorothy was too angry to retreat now. " Even if this is the Orient Express, goodness knows, I've paid over and over again for my seat."

Quick as a cat Aunt Anna Rose was in the sedan too: " Out you get," she said dangerously, " or I'll dot you one, two, three."

" Don't you dare——" Dorothy, genuinely frightened, caught her by both arms.

" Don't touch me. Don't insult me. Out! Out into the snow with you." Possessed for a moment by entire strength, Aunt Anna Rose, with one vicious thrusting push, had Dorothy out of her train and flat on the station platform. This accomplished, she got herself rather elaborately into her seat while Dorothy screeched her way out of the room.

" Oh dear," Veronica was round-eyed at the disastrous goings on, " now she'll leave and Phil will be so worried. Thirty pounds a week gone bang. Oh, Aunt Anna Rose darling, you've done it this time. Do you hear me, Aunt Anna Rose, you'll have to apologise, sweetie. Do you hear me? "

But Aunt Anna Rose had escaped into her dream.

" Aunt Anna Rose. . . ." Veronica was afraid for their darling.

" Run away, little one," Eustace said. " Trust her

to me, will you? She has flown our lives, she has flown our speech and ways." He fumbled after the lines.

"All right," Veronica felt the great calm of one who trusts a doctor with the Beloved, "I'll go."

He was grateful that she left him no advice; no hints or tips for dealing with this mad lady; this lady to whose tragedy he had felt appallingly near in those words: 'Out, out into the snow.'

He lit a cigarette and sat down on a little chair, a little Victorian sewing chair, lower than Aunt Anna Rose's seat but close to her. He did not look up to see the storm pass over her. He felt he was too near to her truth and her sorrow.

It came rather as a surprise to hear a tidy little voice from the chair above him: "That was *nice*. Did I kill her?" He looked up to see her wipe her mouth on the back of her hand. A cat-that-swallowed-the-canary smugness and calm possessed her.

"Nearly," he assured her, adjusting himself to this new aspect, "very nearly."

"I haven't enjoyed anything so much, not since my honeymoon." She spoke as one who has been last week to Deauville, and not one on her first or last honeymoon either.

Eustace was filled with curiosity. Was she speaking of the sacred, tragic wedding journey of the past? That trio of beauty and love and death on which all questions were forbidden?

"How interesting," he said mildly. "Do tell me, why does killing my sister remind you of your honeymoon?"

"Because she's fat." The words came spitting out.

Then she hesitated and spoke more slyly, " I'll be sent off to bed at six if I talk about it."

" Why mustn't you talk about it? " Eustace was looking at the smoke of his cigarette. He was burning with interest. It would have killed him not to pursue the matter. Here was an irresistible slant on the past which he must follow. " Why mustn't you talk about it? " he repeated when she did not answer.

" I can't remember." Her voice was growing young again. The impenetrable bubble was reforming round her, within its pretty sphere there was a shadow of a different shape from the accepted shadow.

" Tell me," he persisted.

" No." She sounded more peevish, more of an old lady than he had ever thought. She huddled herself in the chair without any of the spreading ease with which she usually sat.

" I mustn't bother you," Eustace sighed, " I'm getting as tiresome as my sister. But you've finished her off. She won't come back any more. I expect your train is leaving soon, so I'll say good-bye."

Aunt Anna Rose looked at the enamel watch pinned in her coat lapel. " Don't leave us yet," she said anxiously, " what about the dinner basket? It's a long way to the Bosphorus."

He took a great chance: " Ah, yes. Champagne do I see? . . . caviare . . . *and* peaches. Is this a wedding journey? "

She looked at him so helplessly that he grew afraid of what he was doing. The voice, changing, changed him, too, into another person. She spoke quickly with an anxious sort of gaiety. " Don't go, Papa," she said.

"My flowers too. Be careful. Shake out the confetti—we don't want people guessing——"

"No, do we?" He had gone too far now to stop. "And your jewel case." He handed it up. "Take care of your rubies."

"But they're not in the jewel case," she said, crafty again, "they're in a far safer place."

"Where?" He asked it insistently. Out of all this, if he destroyed her, he would have something for those two who lived so austerely in the present.

But she had him beat: "*You* know," she gave him a long-edged, doe-like glance, "you hid them. We're going to the Czar's little summer palace, you said, and one *can't* be too careful with royal servants."

Now Eustace knew where he was and where she was. He would play his part, walk on a thread in air and cross that abyss in her mind.

"True," he said, "quite true. And how lovely they looked to-day on your white dress, on your skin." He spoke with real shyness. He was ashamed to play on her so—who was he to dare impersonate that dead lover? "My Rose, my Rose of Dublin, I see you coming up the church to me—lilies and rubies and the dark music of the organ."

She leaned towards him. What now? he wondered, and trembled for his next move. But she sold him the moment again: "And did you hear me hiccupping?" she asked.

"Hiccupping?" He was taken aback. "Hiccupping, my heart?"

Aunt Anna Rose threw up her pretty hands. She laughed and went on, half apologetic, and as the past took shape, identifying it dangerously with the present.

" Blind drunk on champagne and doped on sal volatile. That's me. Look!—here I sit in yawking hysterics with me Brussels train spread out on the bed behind me—nailed to the bed with steel pins." By some curious backwards twist of her neck she assumed the position of that bride. She looked gayer than any bride should look. " The rubies," she touched her breast—" the bracelets are sliding down my fat arms. . . ." She held up her hands, looked at them despairingly: " Will the wine help me, Papa? Oh dearest Papa, don't let him have me. It's not too late, Papa. Don't let me be married."

Eustace was instantly that wanderer in a graveyard who comes to an open grave and in the grave a coffin which now he must see opened. He was that ruthless, kind father. He took her hand with fatal benignance.

" Now, Pet, steady yourself, my angel. All girls feel like this on their wedding morning."

" But Papa, I can't. Oh, I can't, I can't. Oh, must I do it, he's old, he's so old."

" He'll be husband and father both to my little girl. Drink this, my dear."

" Oh, look, I've spilt it on my dress. Good, good, I can't be married now."

" Quick, pin a spray of flowers on the stain. Dear, it has to be—all Vienna is waiting in the church to see the Rose of Dublin married. Another glass of wine? Yes. This little tablet too."

" *And* another glass for luck. I'm better. I'm better now. And after the honeymoon you'll take me home to Ballyroden. You'll keep your promise, Papa? "

" Of course, my Rose."

" And Mama——" He was immediately aware of the

third person. “There was something you were to tell me on my wedding morning. You haven't told me yet, Mamma.”

After a moment's wait for the answer, Eustace spoke with decision: “She can't, my child. Not with a gentleman present.”

Listening to nobody, Anna Rose raised her voice: “What, Mamma? Speak plainer.”

“She says,” Eustace raised his voice desperately, “just ignore it. It's quite, quite customary.”

“Oh—I see. I'm better now, Papa. Unpin my train, Mamma. Put it over my arm. Give me the lilies. No, I'm not sick any more, Mamma. Let's go, Papa. One more glass perhaps—ah ha-ha, you do look funny, Papa. And the rubies—bullock's blood they are—oh dear, where's the floor? Your arm——”

“Quiet! Quiet!” He put her back in her seat. “And now?”

“Where are we now? Is the weddin' over? Oh, the train's rushin' on—I'm getting afraid again. Papa has gone—you're not Papa.”

“We're alone now, dear. Husband and wife on their wedding journey.” He leaned barely closer.

“Don't come near me.” Her revulsion was frightening. “Don't. What will people think? I'll call the guard.”

“Our carriage is reserved. No one can come near us for two wonderful hours.” He leaned near again, desperately determined on the last truth.

She struck at him and as he staggered back her angry eyes changed to frightened eyes and her voice minced and pleaded. . . . “Guard. Yes, Guard, yes, he was leanin' out of the window. The door opened I suppose, wasn't it awful? I can only imagine the door opened.

Is he dead? He is dead, you say? He is dead? Oh, get Papa—Oh Papa, Papa, Papa."

" All right, my child, my little girl. Forget. Forget." She gave her hands to Eustace, abandoned to his guidance. . . . " It was an accident." Such a cruel accident to happen on her honeymoon. The poor little bride, the Rose of Dublin."

Now that she was so terribly entranced he would ask her, he would get all the truth. Perhaps, since the romance of that marriage was so monstrous a disaster, the rubies, too, were thrown in as decoration to the lying of two lifetimes. " Now, tell Papa, tell him before they come back, my dear, for your own sake—*where did you put the rubies*? "

" Oh, Papa, he put them somewhere so safe, so safe."

" Yes. Where? Where did he put them? "

He was too eager. He saw it as she shrank from him, avoiding the hopelessness of effort. The truth was falling away on a tide, floating every second farther from her mind.

" I can't remember," she said. She looked exhausted. Tired out, like a cross child hours beyond its bedtime, as little open to reason. " But they're safe. Safe all right, yes—safe in my—in my—in my . . . Oh dear, oh dear, please let me come home. Please let me come home."

He gave it all up. Never had he felt more thwarted, exasperated and ashamed; as though he had broken open a child's money-box to buy himself a drink and found not even the price of a drink inside.

" All right, Miss Anna Rose. All right. You've been safe home at Ballyroden for fifty years."

She brightened, her voice resumed its vitality:

" Forgive me, but I rather forget your name—though I never forget a face."

" Your new friend, Eustace Mills."

" Of course, of course. You're not a scrap like the man I——"

" Married? "

" Did you say ' married '? "

" Yes."

" Did I say ' married '? "

" Yes."

" Married? That's safe enough. Oh, I'm a cagey birdie, I keep cool. I say nothing. There's no harm in saying ' married,' is there? And I'm *not* on my honeymoon? "

" No, you're not on your honeymoon."

" Thank goodness." Her voice was back to its usual serene fluting level now: " Pretty ghastly business when all's said and done, aren't they? "

She looked with bright gratitude round the familiar drawing-room. Never might she have left its chaos and beauty for any further adventure than a ball at the Vice-regal Lodge or a country garden party; wet beech trees and beds of begonias; games of croquet and strawberries for tea; all leading to a marriage into some right and suitable local family. Her beauty certainly was guarantee of that probability—only her life had been terrifyingly and absolutely different. He wondered whether he knew a little bit more than anyone else about that train journey to the Bosphorus, to the summer palace—or did they all know? Whatever he guessed, whatever risk he had taken with her, whatever unlooked for discovery he had made, he was no nearer to the truth about those rubies. Yet he was nearer reality. He knew now that she had worn them once at least. There was no dream in that actual memory of heavy, slipping bracelets. The line of the necklace had been exactly remembered in her touching fingers. He looked at her helplessly, blankly now; asked her nothing; gave it all up; sat beside her, a tired, silent man—even without interest. And as such she went on talking to him, slightly bound by the good manners of her date—the manners that abhor the vacuum of silence.

"Of course," she volunteered, "mine was exceptional, I realise."

Still he bowed his head without an answer.

"My husband, you know—Baron Schomanska—had a nasty fall out of the Orient Express on our honeymoon." The words dropped out, lightly and precisely.

"Really, was he killed?" Eustace attempted the same delicate pitch but felt in his voice the drive towards dull reality.

She retrieved the situation, nodding her pretty head decisively—sane and hard as a nut:

"Oh, yes—*quite*."

The whole tone of the episode was so in another world from that which they had just shared that he persisted as one might pursue polite enquiry into some aggravating little contretemps of the past. "How did it happen?"

"Well, we'd just had dinner—such a good dinner too. The poor Baron was a weeny teeny bit tiddley"—she used the little modern word with indulgent hesitation—"if you ask me. Anyway, he went to open the window to get some air . . . he must have opened the door by mistake." Her voice lifted like a bird in air. "I never saw him again."

" What a terrifying experience," Eustace said thoughtfully.

" Yes, wasn't it? " Again she gave that little nod of the head as though she was biting off an end of thread. " *And* he was so fat," a tiny scream of laughter, " I don't know how he fitted through the door. Anyhow "—she gave him a narrower look—" I was dreadfully upset about it all. Father brought me straight back to Ballyroden, and here I've been ever since. At least," she looked up and round her, " it's me headquarters, you know—must have a clearing station and a dumping ground—somewhere to repack your suitcases when you travel as much as I do."

He nodded agreement: " Do you find you mislay things at all? Those rubies . . ."

" Oh, those rubies." She laughed indulgently. " I said to myself at the time: ' I know I'll forget where I've hidden them '—and I never spoke a truer word, for I've never seen them again."

So, with masterly indifference the story was rounded off. He felt quite moved by the skill which had manufactured this airy version of the truth and terror. This was the story built up in her mind. This pure trite *histoire* for *jeunes filles*; cool as a stream; full of sympathy for the little bride and widow. This respectable narrow caging of the truth which only hopped, a tamed bird, from perch to perch in her mind, had equally forced on her forgetfulness of such a blinding reminder as the rubies. They were too much a part of that old terror she fled up and down the railroads of the world. By train and car and by ship and plane she fled. He was appalled at the magnitude of this great evasion. His mind recalled by degrees the charming fantasies of Consuelo and

Hercules. . . . The Rose of Dublin. . . . The handsome couple. . . . The Emperor's friend. . . . The Romance of old Vienna. . . . The final, unspeakable tragedy of the wedding journey. . . . All her family must know the truth, even the children, or they would not shield her as they did. He looked at her as she sat there dreaming of some fresh adventure, and he found himself quite outside their love for her. As a spoilt child becomes a little monstrous to the kind stranger, so he found this old enchantress for the moment affected him. His great experiment with her had failed. He felt like a disheartened surgeon stitching up a hopeless piece of work. He could go no farther. Her condition was unchanged.

" Well, well," he spoke reprovingly, " it seems a pity—those jewels would mean a lot to Ballyroden and the children."

" But they are here—Roddy never got them out of me. They're for little Who's-it, my niece. Nice little dowry they'll make her too—poor little thing. High time Consuelo did something about her. When I was eighteen I was going to balls at Vice-Regal Lodge. They had a silly little name for me."

" The Rose of Dublin? "

" That's it. . . . Oh, I can hear the bands playing as if it were yesterday. And such gay partners—Beau Longfield I remember, and Julius Connery. He was clever . . . and he can *stay* clever, I said, most unattractive chap. Then there was that desperate tough, Lord Stratford of Slaney, very sweet, though, and Billy—Billy Wildbore Blood—but I've forgotten Billy." She laughed nervously.

" He was a special friend? " Eustace insisted.

" Oh yes—yes, indeed." She looked round.

"You were engaged to him, perhaps? Or just a boy and girl affair?"

"I can't remember," she said quite angrily. "But one thing I do know—that child, little thingammy, should lose no more time. Why doesn't Consuelo have some of these young men for shoots? Or cricket teams? They always came in my day—and for Hunt Balls—great fun, great fun."

He said: "I think that would be another classical extravagance for Mrs. Howard. The young man Veronica wants lives here. Don't you know she's in love with Phillip?"

"But he don't look at her," Aunt Anna Rose spoke with final good sense, "since you brought in that other little beauty."

"Yes, that's true," he agreed, "but he don't look at Yvonne much, either. I think Veronica's an even money chance, if you ask me."

"Oh, I'd back the other myself. Common but pretty, lots of money, very keen too, I know the look."

"Very like her mother, don't you think? A go-getter. A good dresser. Good looking. Always has what she wants out of life—whether it's someone else's man or someone else's seat in a train."

"Oh," Aunt Anna Rose sat up, "a seat snatcher, is she? One of that kind? I've met them, up and down the world."

"We've all suffered from them, dreadful types. Coarse grained, thick skinned—always have the legs of you. Shove in first, fling down an armful of expensive picture papers, unpin the reservation number, and they're home and dry."

" You're right, you're right. They're the mischief to get out once they do get in. Nothing but unpleasantness." She tapped her teeth with her fingernail, young arched teeth, clean as stainless steel, the teeth of a healthy woman. " What d'you suggest? " she asked.

" I'd venture to give the other little affair a push in the right direction if I saw the opportunity."

Aunt Anna Rose sighed: " There are no opportunities nowadays. No balls at Vice-Regal Lodge—no soldiers, I believe, at the Curragh, now. Nor a tent at a race-meeting. Not a hat fit to be seen on any girl I see. Or a nice lace dress. Or eight-button gloves. Poor young things—I don't know how they ever get married. They look so awful, too. They really do seem to try to make the worst of themselves, don't they? "

He wondered. His mind, without any trouble, skipped from her presence, poised as though a parasol was open behind her head, her chin tilted up above a boned, magical little structure of net and lace—from that to those trunks he had seen in the dark today; those black leather, basket-lined, coronetted coffins, holding, like tombs in Egypt, every necessity for beauty and pleasure. The dress that was never unfolded, the paper had not yet fallen out of its sleeves, its braiding curled like snails in shells on cuffs; stiff net tacked under hems that had never swept the dust and been untacked and put in fresh by patient maids at night time. The idea of that virgin trousseau was as appalling as his understanding of the mythical romance which had ended in death and madness. He looked at her sitting there, pretty as a pigeon in a wicker cage, and remembered the tiger's heart he had seen when, briefly, truth had faced her after half a century of pretty figments and forbidden subjects and graceful forgetting.

*   *   *   *   *

William came in: "Post time." He looked for someone not there and his eye lighted gently on Miss Anna Rose. "Ah," he said, "I'm off to Clonmel. Would you care for a little spin, miss?"

"Yes, yes." She was radiant. "We'll book our seats for the Jungle Queen tomorrow, shall we, Willy? We left her in a terrible pickle last week, didn't we? Hung out by her two heels over a sixty-foot drop, in her leopard skin. Where's me hat? She shouldn't trust that big, black sambo, Willy. That's what I've said from the very first instalment. Wouldn't trust him meself." She was up and off. Hat, veil and gloves adjusted in a minute. She was ready for her next adventure.

She was escaping him now as she had always escaped any link with that past; fleeing up and down the world; meeting strange people, real people, and those shadows still more vital—the porters she tipped; the monarchs to whom she bobbed; pilots of transatlantic flights and old sea captains of banana boats. All her contacts were fresh and suitable to her age. She had grown old in her dream world but she had kept abreast of the times. She was in no sense a shadow of that desperate child-bride she fled. She was alluring, preposterous, amusing, teasing, adorable, what lady you would have her be. And she was carried, upborne, isolated on the air and breath of beauty. It glorified unfairly every little action, amplifying and enhancing all she did. Exaggerating all she was.

Now, before she whirled away with Willy, she recollected this friend she left behind. Aware and pitiful of his tired looks, she came back across the room to bend over him where he sat discouraged and disappointed, to say: " You look tired. Tell you wot—sit in my nest till I get back and rest yourself."

Eustace felt as if a queen had handed him some little piece of pretty nonsense to remember her by. He bowed: " I'm very honoured."

The reality of the favour only became poignant when she looked back again across the room to say in her most direct, most matter-of-fact manner: " But don't forget, me dear man, it's a non-smoker."

She had him beat. He would never catch up with her. Hearing the pulse and putter of the motor-bicycle engine at, he supposed, the hall door, he went over to the window, where rain now streamed against the panes, and looked out to see her run down the steps, her coat caught charmingly round her, the veil securely tied under her chin. She gave a triumphing, fleeting look behind her at the loving absent nobody who could not stop her spree. She nipped into the sidecar combination and as Willy let in his clutch and the fine gravel spattered, she leaned forward, her posture demanding all the speed he could make—her wish for it like a shadow flung on in front of them.

4

THE STONE-BUILT cow-byres at Ballyroden provided excellent accommodation, but none of those nervous modern tricks where the cow touches something and water spouts smartly into her mouth while an inexorable machine pumps her dry of milk—no languid sensuality left about the business. Phillip had not got so far as yet, but he had ordained a great new nonsense of hand and udder washing before the milking business started.

At four o'clock the cows had not yet slobbered and clanked their ways into their stalls; the great length of the house was like a cathedral, but warm with the morning and evening body warmth of animals and food and the steam and stream of milk and splatter of cow pats. The light came gently across the straw through low, gothic arches of doorways and high, arrow-slitted windows. The rafters had little things hidden in them by men; cans with nails and broken screws; forgotten swallows' nests patted into the sides of them. White doves with little feathers turned on their smooth backs, piped white sugar on a white birthday cake, sat about in the warmth, making a terrible mess of everything and eating all before them.

Hercules and Consuelo came in out of the rain and a gust of pigeons met them face to face: "Dirty little things, don't know why Phil doesn't liquidate them."

They both knew it was because of Aunt Anna Rose and they were in complete agreement with Phil, but it was nice to look at each other and condemn something cosily.

Consuelo had her purple scarf on, matching the vaporous dark of the interior and a man's over-coat. She looked gloomy, but her gloom lightened as they stood together in the absolute centre of the shed. A shaft of splendour was piercing through the gloom, a gamester's quickening to the game.

" Now, me little Bucko," she had Herky by the elbow, " we'll start fair. My turn for the dark end, if I remember, and sixpence to the winner—one, two, three, GO."

They went their opposite ways, prowling and poking along the racks of hay and straw-filled corners and hollowed earthy places as they had done since they were five years old. They knew they were better at finding eggs than any two people in the world and of all things they loved the game. A hot egg in the palm of the hand sent shivers of pleasure through them. As they went their separate courses they kept silent. Neither would tell, till the end, what luck they had met. This system they had evolved lent a sustained suspense to the game.

Now they met and turned out their pockets gently, sitting beside one another on a smooth pole dividing the cow-stalls. Apart, they had been thinking. Though only apart for ten minutes, each had a new turn of mind to show the other.

" I think," Consuelo put two bantam's and one hen's egg back in her pocket and Hercules let go a tortoiseshell kitten, " we'll have to take the matter into our own hands for once and simply hire a car."

" Old girl, you know they've got very cagey about us

lately at the garage. Ignored my last message entirely. There's something behind it."

"Well," she said gravely, "if I had time to go into the matter with Phillip again, I should. As it is, I'm going to send them a telegram in his name. For his sake as much as ours we've got to get to the meeting. We'll pay for the taxi out of our winnings."

"Well, of course, of course. That's only fair. But how are we going to get the wire off? I'm afraid William . . ." He shook his head. "*Colaborateur*, rather, don't you agree?"

"We'll have to nip over the fields to Annie Hearn's and get her to send it—she's a decent old thing."

They looked out at the rain.

"The Hereford bull's in the field between us and Annie and it's three miles round by the lake road. We'll never make it."

Consuelo looked absolutely implacable: "We're going through the field with the bull," she said, "and if we're killed, Tots, that'll teach 'em."

"So it will. But I wish I had me gummers."

"Gummers, my dear chap, you wouldn't stand a chance in your gummers. Remember, we may have to run for it."

"No good hanging around," he said, "let's get on with it."

They were both terrified of bulls, but gamblers first, last and all the time, they took a chance on that too.

The rain was coming down in great slopes of water when Phillip and Yvonne came together to the shelter of the cow-sheds. The cows were in to be milked, twelve of them standing in huge, mild expectancy, great steaming bodies and clattering reptilian tails.

"I see what you mean about this washing business," Yvonne eyed an udder, crusted with dirt, "most necessary."

They had left the lime-spreading mercifully early because Phillip said the chaps won't expect me to get round to the milking on a day like this. He had not suggested that she should go back to the house and have the hot bath which seemed almost heaven to her. She looked quite magnificent with the rain streaming through her dark hair, hanging on her eyelashes and staining great peachy triangles under her cheekbones. Her tweeds were soaking. Her jersey was soaking. Her feet in their expensive country shoes were completely and absolutely wet. Never had she known that out of a bath or a swimsuit one could be so wet. Some glory upheld her. The desire to excel, to show off, to prove to him what a girl she was. An inner glory for herself, too—that love could bring her to this—held its own magnificent satisfaction, almost its quelling of appetite.

Phillip's mind had gone from her into his work, into that ascetic endeavour for Ballyroden which might become for him a dangerous luxury. It had really come to him quite as a surprise to see this drowned beauty, at the end of two hours, still shovelling lime beside him. Once he had said: "Shouldn't you have brought a mackintosh?" Twice he had said: "I must buy a lime spreader next year."

She shook her wet hair out of her eyes and did not answer him. She had learnt the value of a great exuberant silence indoors—so why not in the rain? But quite sincerely, she found it hard to believe it when on their way home he had turned aside to catch out somebody not washing his hands. It was the most exulting ignoring she had ever experienced.

Now, relatively, the cow-byre was warm as a bed. After the wind and the rain she felt housed, surrounded by warmth. She would have welcomed love. Possibly that was what he intended. She waited. Then followed him up to the darkest end where he had gone. " Do you mind my asking you to keep quiet," he said; he had a little notebook in his hand and was looking at this cow's udder in a disastrously clinical way. He added: " I'm really rather keen to straighten up this business."

Then they came, the two men in oilskins, and to his great shining pleasure, to his warm delight, they carried great buckets of hot water with them.

" Good boys," he said gently and plunged his hands in water and fell to washing the cows with them.

" I can't milk," he said regretfully when the washing business was over.

She watched the men's hands in a trance and the cows relaxing and the pails filling. It was all so different from the children's picture books and milkmaids and may-day stuff, I love you pretty cow who gives . . .

" Won't they hate it," she spoke to him with an effort, " when you get that milking machine? "

" Oh, I don't believe one has any trouble. They say they get used to it in no time."

" Poor loves." She looked at him out of her big, liquid eyes. It worried him in front of the men milking and so did the change in her voice. Veronica slapped the cows and took it all like the district nurse. It would hardly have bothered him had they witnessed a bull and cow mating together. There it was. But this great, pulsing beauty had got the thing from another angle altogether, the wrong angle. " Come and see the calves," he said suddenly. He wanted to get her eyes off the men's hands.

They staggered round in the straw of their shed—innocent and awkward, roaring for food. The bolted door was very high but he did not shut it. He left it open and stood with his back to it, keeping the calves from escaping. It would have been much simpler to shut the door and ignore the calves.

She gave the calves a finger to suck and they took her cold hands into their mouths and she cried out in her rich, giggling voice: " Stop it. I like it," quoting from some wanton little saying.

* * * * *

Veronica was running back to the house in the rain, heavily as a little bear. She, too, had thought an evening of such rain the probable moment to catch somebody not washing his hands or his cows' udders. She had thought Phillip was far off at his lime and had set about this uncomfortable inspection with a cosy little feeling of virtue and indispensability. Her usefulness put her nearer her own niche.

She had seen Aunt Anna Rose's departure with Willy and felt sure that somehow the train incident had been cleared up for her by Mr. Mills. She herself had smoothed over the affair with Mrs. Thomas. She hardly guessed how easily that lady had been overpersuaded from catching the night mail or ordering a car to the airport. At least, her yielding had left Veronica with a little feeling of diplomatic importance and an ache to tell Phillip all that had taken place.

And now she had seen him: seen only his beloved, familiar back and stooped head in the calves' warm house: heard from the darkness that rich, giggling voice: felt with horror and grief her own place outside it all. She had thought there was something averted and somehow slyly amused in the milkers' eyes when she had left the cow-byre. Why had they not said: Sir Phillip is in the calves' house. Ordinarily they would not have hesitated. They knew, of course. They all knew. They were all inside life and part of the game while she, poor virgin solitary, poor useful one, poor dry-eyed aunt, must consume her heart away. As she went wordless back to the great rain-washed house, through the streaming rain, past all the well-known, ignored places, the old ice-house, the back of the kitchen garden wall with its warren of toolsheds, and through the black iron gate and the clipped tunnel of Portugal laurel and so into the pleasure grounds, the walk for single ladies of the house, her grief was so whole within her it drained all meaning and colour from the world.

She did not feel the rain in her face. The soaked green grass was as white as salt to her. She felt only that what she had never had was no more hers. She was the ghost of all her aunts, and knew their pain.

* * * * *

Eustace, looking out into the rain, already impatient for Aunt Anna Rose's return, saw Veronica's drenched figure in oilskins coming up the steps, walking heavily like children do in trouble.

She raised her face once with the black oval of the sou'wester round it and it looked to him like a drowning face under water; or the face of one lost, rejected by life, and not yet taken into death. There was quite a terrible look in the eyes as though they knew the truth, that the struggle could be very long.

Eustace went straight out into the hall to meet her as she came in. He would have her at once. He would not allow his help to be put aside with that frigid fearfulness he knew in these young. So he said, without preamble: "Tell me, child, did she do the thing? Miss Anna Rose? Did she murder him?"

The blood rushed into Veronica's face. "What has she said to you? It's only her nonsense—you know that."

"No, I *don't*." He was not going to be turned out of any valuable intimacy. "As a matter of fact, I believe every word she said to me."

"Oh." Veronica tore off her wet oilskins; her greenish fair hair was unexpectedly dry and smooth as a bird's back. "Don't let's talk about it here," she said, her eyes flying anxiously up the staircase.

"All right," he opened the drawing-room door, "I've got the fire going, rather fun it was." He shut the cage door on his linnet. "There's nobody here, so please come in and explain this dangerous myth to me."

Again he was ashamed of frightening her. There was no need at all to make so much of Aunt Anna Rose's story, but through it he hoped to establish some right to her confidence.

"Was it the truth?" he asked.

To his surprise she answered him in a just, considerate kind of voice:

"We don't know—we simply don't know. Even

Uncle Roddy didn't know and he might have been told. If anyone knew, he'd have known."

"But the bridegroom's family—the Schomanskas? They seem to have nurtured some very ugly suspicions?"

"Ah, yes," Veronica agreed quickly, "but they were trying to frighten her into giving up the rubies. That's why they started the story."

"From what she said to me, my dear, they seem to have had remarkably strong foundations for their suspicions."

"What did she say to you?"

Veronica listened anxiously to his exact account of that translation he had shared. To his surprise she accepted monstrous bridegroom, doped bride, assault and possible murder with absolute calm.

"Her marriage wasn't really her tragedy," she said with some hesitation.

"It seems enough——"

"Nothing's enough if you're unlucky. No—you see, when she got home to Ballyroden and back to the man she really loved, *with* a widow's dowry *and* the rubies tucked away somewhere, perhaps—he, he was afraid of her. He was afraid of the story: of the whole thing: he avoided her, he didn't what you call come up to scratch."

"But can't you see how what she told me affects you today. This wet afternoon your whole future changes if you believe in the rubies as I do."

"I haven't got any future," Veronica said stubbornly, "on this wet afternoon or any other afternoon. After all, the rubies haven't done much for Aunt Anna Rose, have they? They didn't help her when she got back to Ballyroden, did they? That was her real tragedy, you know—not whatever happened on the honeymoon—you see that——" The linnet's head dropped forwards to the clasped hands between trousered knees. "She'd let him down first, of course. But I always think she's lucky he's not a grandfather living near. He was killed in the South African war. I think that's why she won't face the real, old, empty life again. She pretends she never came back. She's still on her way home to him or she's going to meet him somewhere preposterous."

He said directly: "*You* won't allow yourself any gay refuges like Miss Anna Rose, will you? Don't set off to the Bahamas when you lose Phillip, please. You'll lead a sane, useful, unhappy life, won't you? I want to offer you two chances—will you consider them?"

Completely startled out of all her protective colouring, she looked him in the eyes and answered straight: "What are they?"

"Help me to couple up the link I nearly made between Aunt Anna Rose's two minds to-day. Help me to find the rubies. For you—they're yours—they may or may not make the difference I hope for you."

"What difference? You don't think Phil will marry me because of those fairy rubies, do you?"

"No. I'm not quite so optimistically old-fashioned. But such things help. Face it. There's nothing like a few thousand pounds to put a girl on her feet. A bit of drama helps, too. A change is good—something to set you in a frame for him to see you better——"

"And if we don't find any rubies, if we make a silly failure of it all and hurt Aunt Anna Rose—what do we do then?"

"We," she had said, "we." Eustace warmed absurdly: "I have an alternative to offer you," he said, "it's all to my advantage if you fail."

" No ? Tell me."

" I'm going to buy a house here and a parcel of land. That's what I want. And I shall need a comptroller of house and garden and Kerry cows. You'd be worth a big wage to me . . . let's put it on a purely business footing. . . ."

Veronica took a quick breath. " If I had to leave Ballyroden," she said, " there's nothing I'd rather do."

" Would you promise to bury me by the lake," he said, " or scatter my ashes on the Kilahala bog on a night when the curlews are crying? "

" Why do you want to help me? "

" I'm a collector."

" Yes, I know—jewels and furniture."

" All rare and delicate pieces interest me."

She looked at him like a baby owl: " But we haven't found them yet. They've been lost for fifty years—why should we ever find them? "

" Ah, of course—the rubies—you're going to find them, my dear, you'll apply the next turn of the screw."

"——To Aunt Anna Rose? I'd rather lose everything."

" I'll let you into a secret. *I believe she rather likes it.* She led me such a dance today, and she won. Hands down, she won. She isn't really mortal."

" She doesn't know where they are. She has forgotten." Veronica cried out from fear and pity.

" She does know and she must remember. I believe if she did she would settle in peace—come to rest in peace at last. As things are, she'll haunt the place. We must help her to find her soul, don't you think, while we still have time? "

" What does she want with a soul? " Veronica protested. " The darling is perfect as it is. God bless it."

"The darling, 'it,' 'the pet,' the everlasting doll of the family. Three generations of you have joined hands in her madness."

"How dare you say she's mad?"

"Mad as a hatter to most of us. But enchanted, of course, to the rest, it sounds prettier. More Mary Rose, doesn't it?"

She laughed at this and he liked her for it. "You're only just teasing. I know you love her," she said. And, as she said it, became a variable human child. The little tormented landlady ceased in her. It was as if he had cleaned deep scales of dirt off half a picture, and what he could now see held exciting promise.

"You'll come in with me on this?"

"I will."

"You'll do what I tell you?"

"Cross my heart, Mr. Mills."

"If it frightens you?"

She looked at him again out of those queer child's eyes. "I'm with you," she said.

He knew quite certainly that she was holding something up, keeping something back. A plan had been conceived which he had not fathered. She was incalculable as any silly, loving woman is. For this plan, this secret, whatever it was, she would go through fire, burning those with her, destroying herself, even, if she saw a reason for it. Aunt Anna Rose—for the first time he saw her as Aunt Anna Rose's flesh and blood.

* 5 *

Phillip opened his morning's post standing up in the hall: staggering statements from the Co-operative Stores (could wire for a European war cost so much?): that monthly sheet he insisted on the bank delivering: a small cheque for straw: an enormous bill for coal: the grocer's bill (in which the words Biscuits, Biscuits, Biscuits, seemed to have shot the total up to forty pounds for the month). He remembered the paying guests and his heart opened a little towards Veronica. He remembered the bullocks ready for the next fair. They weren't looking quite the thing either. Why don't they want to go in and eat their hay? he asked himself and his mind was in the field with them, hungrily, drearily breaking down a fence to get out on to the avenue. Yesterday Yvonne had said: "Those bullocks don't seem to have anything to eat except their own footmarks." The ruthless truth one got from the ignorant. He thought of the separated milk, and what happened to it all? He could not make a statement on that to save his soul. In this hour of morning depression the whole estate seemed like a terrible wall of cotton wool on which he could never impose his will. Cotton wool and briars. The cursed briars. He had cleared acres of them, stubbed them up and ploughed them out. They made way for light, hungry patches of gorse. A thistle cutter might destroy these if he could afford to buy one. All the bright machines he wanted buzzed and shone in his brain. He knew the place must have them. If he could lay his hands on five thousand pounds today, tomorrow—Ballyroden had a chance. He heard Willy and Bridgid clattering gently with trays upstairs and he thought of all the people in his house dependent on his effort, and he sickened. He sickened in the aloof height and grandeur of the house his forebears had built him. His eye reached no rest in its pretty distances. The sweeping staircase, the mahogany doors with their pediments, the great, elegant window faces, the huge, pale rugs that swam on the floor spaces and had resisted the feet of generations, so fine and strong was their quality. All these possessions were for him gathered and concentrated at this moment in one tiny point of sound, a sound that held in its little completeness, all the sense of struggle and responsibility and desperate effort and failure, and worry near to madness.

It was the sound of a drip of water, dripping from the roof, falling all the way down the beautiful hollow height of the house, falling like a body through the air and landing punctually as the tick of a clock in a tin basin at the stair foot. He thought of the two workmen who had been on the roof for two months; their wage bill and the material they had used. He was glad Bridgid had put the basin back in its old place; but again, her experienced lack of confidence in anything done to the leaks in the roof depressed and disturbed him. No one had any optimism, no one could trust him.

He stood alone in his house with the dreadful bills for all his ventures in his hands and he felt exhausted and appalled at his undertakings. Who was he to drag fortune from the air? All had been breathed before him: all spent: all enjoyed: all lost: nothing was retrievable. He was savagely aware of his impotence, the tired lover of some great demanding beauty. He longed for something undemanding, small, gentle, easily satisfied and careful. Such a thing as he could compass. He looked about the hall and entrance of his house and life, undefiled so far to-day by the feet of guests and others. That awful morning lack of feeling towards things and people left him sick and empty like an outgone tide. No doubt, in the evening, when work was done, the old, known warmth for house and relations who were like children would fill into his heart again; but now their coldness and pressure was almost more than he could stand. He fled their dependence, their love, their treachery, all their mistrust of his efforts. In this *tremblante* morning hour he felt vulnerable to all their mistrust and headshakings. There was but one, the little one who would never fail him, whose understanding filled the day's work, whose lack of demand left peace to his sleep at night, whose mothy looks only pleased and did not disturb him. He thought it might be good if she came in now. Out of all this terrifying muddle of bills she would help him to calculate a justification, a reassurance from the future sale of the bullocks: the wheat: the eggs. He found himself listening for her return from the morning encounter with Mrs. Guidera, putting off the moment when he should set out for the day's work until she came.

At last she was there, a mammy turban on her head and a coat and skirt. No corduroys, no gummers, no air of out-of-doors. An abstraction was upon her and he resented it. " I'm just off to the fifty acres," he said.

" Oh, yes, of course, today we're starting. Well, good luck." She turned to the staircase.

" When are you coming up? "

" I've just washed my hair."

What had that got to do with it? " I'll be there all day," he said, " I was wondering if you'd come along round one o'clock and bring me some food. I don't want to come back to the house for lunch if I can help it."

" I'll arrange for William to do it," she said with deliberate, planny brightness. " As a matter of fact, Phil, Mr. Mills has asked me to go racing with him."

He gazed at her appalled. Could she not see what a nonsense, what a light thing she was making of his ascetic rule for the community? She, his classic good example, could take what he denied them; if she could take what she did not even want, and fall into a silly, jolly outing, how could he maintain any sort of discipline with his giddy elders, how keep the balance of proportion in such things, if his own serious young contemporary was thus light-weight? All the tumult and aggravation that had been on his mind a moment ago were concentrated in this awful climax.

" You know it's true," he cried out like an angry little boy, " I'm not being a swine just for the hell of it. They will lose seventy pounds there. They always have."

" Eustace isn't dreaming of taking them," she said, " he's only taking me and Bridgid and Mrs. Guidera."

God, God, the great coloured circus-like quality of the outing overwhelmed him. There was a silence into which water plopped down to the thunder of the tin basin. For the first time since together they had taken on the burden and the fast, knotted the cord and worn the hair-shirt for Ballyroden, he felt the terror, the weight, the shapelessness of the future that any religious faces for the unknown good. He did not know his need. He could not tell his fear. The admirable restraint engendered by a good public school turned him now into a splendid, tearless pillar of salt.

"Just as you like," he said politely. "By the way, I think I owe you at least fifteen pounds, don't I?" He put his hand in his pocket and took out his note case. "You may find you need cash. . . ." When he raised his head from counting the notes she was gone, nor did she answer his call. He put the money down on the top of the barometer, dropping down to nothing within its glass case, on the centre of the octagonal rent table, and put a 4-oz. brass letterweight on top.

"Oo, what a lot of money," Yvonne said. All her hair was hidden under a tight waterproof cap. Without the rest of her hair, her eyelashes looked six inches long: "For who?"

"Veronica," he didn't see what else to say, "she's going racing with your Uncle. Aren't you?"

She shook her head. "I thought the Lord Abbot ordered all the young novices into the fields today."

Righteous, injured, hurt, jokes appalled him. The walls of his house were swaying and he was, as it were, offered a box of chocolates. His woman had shown him that she, and if she then all women, were his antagonists in the scheme of life he envisaged. . . .

Yvonne's eyelashes shot back into her head like a doll's when it is lifted off its back, and her great eyes looked into his. Their blue-grey glass was quite immeasurably pretty:

"Oh, all right," the walls of his house were swaying and he was offered this box of chocolates, "come if you like, but it's a busy day." The thought of it increased his dreadful feeling of pressure and sickness. Did no woman realise what work meant? He had thought one went with him all the way in his striving and denials, and how wrong he had been. He did not feel in any sort of holiday mood to enjoy this great, willing beauty. Responsibility and worry and nervous strain had more or less made a monk of him and he bitterly resented her determined approach.

* * * * *

As their car neared the race-course Hercules bounced a little delightedly on the seat. It was a great big car and smelt of other people's wet boots and dead cigarettes and faintly of drink. The windows were permanently stuck up and had sticking plaster across a crack. A St. Christopher medal swung by a safety pin above the driver's head, other medals were affixed more permanently here and there in the car's structure.

Consuelo shut her eyes and sighed. They were very near their hearts' delight now. She opened her eyes as they slowed down in the stream of race traffic and began re-sorting the newspaper cuttings in her handbag. Hercules shoved off a programme seller who was jumping on to the step of the car. He had no intention of wasting his substance on expensive things like one shilling race cards. One must not be extravagant and he intended to have a good bet on the first race.

He sighed and said to Consuelo: " Lucky thing Phil settled those little accounts. We can bet as we like."

" Ah, my old bucko "—she gave him a look that was nearly a squeeze of the hand—" it's quite like old times, isn't it? "

" Ah," said their driver, " we didn't have any little

outing since the war at all. Or since your trouble with poor Sir Roderick. Oh my, dat was a tundering tump, a very sad ting—dat's definite."

" Terrible times," Hercules agreed absently. He and Consuelo were collecting from their persons five shillings for the car park. He found half a crown, so did she.

" In my opinion, we'll have another war; for in my opinion they should have left Germany longer to walk through Russia—another couple of years couldn't harm anyone and would quench the Russians."

" That's true. Very true. When shall we lunch, Tots? "

He considered this: " After the first race. Then we'll be twenty pounds to the good at least. A bottle of the Golden, I think, old girl, don't you? "

" In my opinion, you should go easy. 'Tis an acid ting, champagne. A glass of malt now, is nicer to the stomach. Not that I'd touch it. Out. It's Out. There's no pleasure in life with stomach trouble. No pleasure at all. Nothing fried—nor a rasher, no—nothing in the pan—nor a drink. No. Nor a cigarette. Just watch yourself, you may say. That's what you may say."

" Terrible ting, tummy trouble," Hercules had caught the alliterative infection, " no pleasure in life. Do you ever have a bet these days? "

" Well, the excitement upsets me too much. I'm very upset if I back a loser and I'm only too trilled if I back a winner—isn't dat a funny ting? "

" I'll give you the first winner to-day—Vanessa."

" King Clarion," the driver riposted sharply.

Consuelo sat up: " Doesn't get the distance."

" He wasn't able to give Irish Knight seven pounds and beat him over the same distance, was he? In Mallow, was he? Don't excite me now, contradicting me, I'm afraid of my stomach."

They subsided again among their snowstorm of newspaper cuttings. It was raining heavily when at last they found themselves in the car park. But they were adequately and tidily equipped for the weather. Years of race going had left them that undecorative modicum of utility, so right as to be a poem, a poem that the ignorant can never learn.

"If only I'd found my gummers," Hercules said. "That's the only little thing, Pets, that makes me nervous."

"Ah, dat's de ting—nerves—mind you, I'm very nervous myself. I have to sleep with my aunt." Their driver's heart was in this trouble too.

They left him murmuring it out to himself and hurried on, seriously, absolutely intent on the pleasure and business which combined happily before them.

Hercules started the day beautifully by walking in at the trainers' gate with a friend. When he met Consuelo inside they shared the money thus saved. It was an auspicious beginning. They trotted about between the bookmakers and the saddling enclosure. Old friends spoke to them warmly, trysting them to drinks after different races. How happy they were, leaning on the rails. How beautiful it was to see the horses led round: to see the jockeys mount and ride down to the start: they were at home among all the busy preoccupied faces: they knew exactly what they wanted to do and the time and place to do it. They never spoke an unnecessary word: they ignored all fools and questioned no friend awkwardly about his horse's chance: they were in their own world, divorced from any other importance or responsibility.

"Where shall we watch our race?" Hercules asked her as they turned from the enclosure with the crowd.

"From the rails." He knew she must feel as close as could be to the awful magic of horses galloping. It was like love, a necessity.

"All right," he said, "we'll tremble together."

"I'm shaken," she said, "did you do it each way?"

He shook his head.

Somebody saw them down there on the rails, oblivious of the rain beating in their faces. Consuelo was so tall she could lean over comfortably, resting her chest on the top. Hercules had to stand up on the bottom board and cling like a little monkey to obtain the same view. "Bless them," said the friend, "I hope they're on to a winner."

They were on to a winner. After the race, as the numbers went up their eyes shining met. Tears were not far off. The benison of success wrapped them in its certainty along with the thrill of victory. Wordless, they walked together through the crowd to the bar and presently sat with a gold-necked bottle and a plate of chicken sandwiches between them, pledging one another in their bliss and hopefulness.

* * * * *

"But why, why, why?" said Veronica, fretfully, "must I come in. Can't I sit in the car? I feel such a fool, everyone will be laughing at me. I can't face it."

Eustace said: "This isn't dressing up. The thing has to be genuine. If you suffer embarrassment and confusion, all the better, my dear. The clothes will be part of you. The situation comes to life."

"I'm going to suffer all right," Veronica said grimly, "What do I look like, Bridgid?"

"Better than I ever saw you in your life, if you don't mind. 'Tis a lovely fit on you, down to the little boots even; isn't that so, Mrs. Guidera?"

Mrs. Guidera, safe in navy blue, nodded agreeably: "It doesn't look one bit out of the way, miss," she said, "and if it's able to do all Mr. Mills thinks, if I was you I'd be said by him and chance it."

"Well, let's scuttle across to the bar during the next race." Veronica made the suggestion more calmly.

Bridgid and Mrs. Guidera stirred uneasily in their seats: "We have a little tip for the first race, sir, so we'd better hurry and get the money on." They stepped blithely out into the rain and Eustace and Veronica faced each other alone in the car.

"Brave child," he applauded her. "And pretty child," he added gently.

Her hands, in their little gloves of finest leather, were in her lap; her lap was rose-coloured facecloth; the skirt swept in heavy grace from her waist to her feet; her little jacket was nipped at the waist and braided heavily, her hat was pink velvet, mercifully simple and without the decoration of flowers or feathers one might have expected from its date and occasion. Veronica was wearing the clothes in which Aunt Anna Rose had left Vienna for her honeymoon.

"Come along, my dear," he opened the door of the car into the rain. The first race had started. She hung back miserably in her corner: "But I'll get everything soaking wet," she protested.

" I expect," Eustace said soberly, " that last time she saw them they were wet—wet with melting snow——"

" Why are you so certain this will make her remember? "

" When such a feeble suggestion as my sister in her chair brought back so much that has been buried in her mind for fifty years, how do you think she'll react when she sees the very clothes she wore when she did the thing? "

" Oh, stop saying she did the thing."

" Whodunnit I don't know. ' The Thing ' happened. Every reminder has been hidden from her in mausoleums like that basket trunk for years—hidden from her like bodies. Remember what that trunk was like? You were crying, weren't you? So was Bridgid."

" So were you," said Veronica crossly. She did not care to think back to that strangely opened grave in the dusk of the boot room with Bridgid genuflecting and crossing herself (how rightly) as the trunks gave up their ghosts. Some exquisitely handed maid had packed that trousseau away—among black tissue paper and white tissue paper and sachets and mothballs; the dresses were stuffed and folded and laid by. Dozens of sets of cambric underclothes, embroidered, slotted, narrowly ribboned, had flattened to knife edges in their folds and pleats. Nothing had rotted, everything had been put away new. It was like a chest of old linen.

" You'd think we had a bride in the house," Bridgid said reverently. She helped to unpack with grace and calm. Not eager and pushing and searching and curious. They took all the clothes out and laid them on sheets till they came to the shoe bags at the bottom, linen buttoned bags bound with ribbon and monogrammed. Inside they found pointed boots and bronze and satin slippers with cut-steel buckles. They put everything back as nearly as possible as it had been: keeping out only the pink facecloth dress, the boots with Louis Quinze heels, the gloves, the hat; fastened the locks again with that cabinet-maker's master key which Eustace carried on his watch chain. It had solved many problems in many junk shops, but never had it unlocked such sad elegance.

He had thought, when Bridgid shook the pretty, ridiculous underclothes out of their folds, from the heart-broken little face she made, that Veronica was not going to go through with it, but again that tough, secret look had come from behind her eyes and he knew that for some untold reason she would go on.

He knew it again now as he opened his umbrella over her and she picked her skirts up out of the wet grass: "I'll tell you where we'll go," he said, "straight to the bar. You'll feel all right on champagne."

* * * * *

Aunt Anna Rose settled herself happily down in her seat at the cinema—Willy two places behind her. She liked to be solitary, to give herself entirely over to enjoyment. Besides, it was fitting. A great many school-children, whose parents had gone racing, came to the matinée. They screamed and scrambled among the cheaper seats. Their noise did not even vex Aunt Anna Rose. She closed her eyes to double the darkness and gave her whole mind to an assessment of the Jungle Queen's previous predicaments before she cast it forward to the difficulties of this afternoon. Danger was near. A passionate crisis was imminent. Would the passionate, beautiful girl make good use of her opportunities? Oddly enough Aunt Anna Rose hoped she would.

*   *   *   *   *

At five o'clock Yvonne faced Phillip. She was reeling with exhaustion and white with temper and soaking wet and bitterly cold. She had run one thousand messages since nine o'clock this morning, up and down the lake road between the fifteen acres and the farm yard, along the stony lake road with a wind from the mountains lashing her cheeks alternately with steel needles of rain—one cheek on the three miles home, the other on the three miles back to Phillip, once with his lunch, twice with a single screw, once with a message to the blacksmith.

Phillip was grimly satisfied. All day he had ploughed and he was not an experienced ploughman. But his team had worked for him with heavenly strength and docility. The great everlasting turn of the earth had all the help to the mind, all the meaning that the agonising mental anxiety about farming lacks. It is the difference between love and talking about love. In his concentration, in his renewed effort, every time he turned and started a fresh furrow the torture of the morning slipped a little farther back in his mind. And now, in the November evening with the rooks rising into the yellow air and the sweat from his horses close like clouds round them and himself, he felt that life was a whole thing. Not as it had been in the morning—a constant effort, disturbed and distracted. He turned to Yvonne to share the fulfilment of their day's work. Savagely as he had felt towards her when they set out, he was conscious that she had plodded about willingly enough on the errands he had invented to get her out of his way. And now, in the evening, he felt that bitterness washed out of him and he was ready to be kind, though too blessedly tired for anything beyond kindness.

He spoke to her out of his glow: "I *am* delighted with my horses. I shall really hate it when I can buy a tractor."

She faced him, reeling with exhaustion. At the close of such a day of torture and devotion, this was what she got: 'I *am* delighted with my horses.' Yvonne had reached the point of thwarted stimulation when every word spoken is out of proportion, and the unattained love within as measurable a distance of being the hated as being the desired. She said nothing. She turned away from him and they walked home in silence, he between his horses, she behind, leading the bicycle which, to complete her exhaustion, had punctured.

As they went back into his house, Phil felt immeasurably happier than he had done. But as they crossed the hall together the fret and constriction of responsibility squeezed his satisfaction, his vision of the labour, back into their customary grooves.

The letters on the hall table were lying as they had lain when he set out in the morning; Veronica's notes were still under the brass letterweight; the basin, still below its drip, was full now. There was a light sweat on the black and white tiles; the house felt colder than the outdoor evening.

"Let's go to the fire," he spoke distantly, picking up the notes he had left for Veronica and counting them methodically before he put them in his pocket. As he did this the whole situation of the morning resumed its horrid shape. He felt his day, distorted from its importance, had brought the problems of Ballyroden no further towards solution.

" I think I'll change my clothes first."

That dreadful tension of love was in her eyes; was in the harsh spoken word: was in her avoiding of his help with her wet coat. The sense of injury that was nearly tears, that was nearly hatred, welled up in her uncontrollably. " I know it couldn't mean less to you, just please don't give it a thought," she spoke with enormous meaning, " but I'm soaking wet and tired out. It's not really my idea of fun to ride a bicycle hundreds of miles while you walk behind two stinking, sweating horses in a deluge for eight hours."

" It's not really my idea of fun either," he answered, surprised. " It's just my life."

" Well, we could quite easily have gone racing."

He let that go: " Cheer up, dear. You'll feel better when we've had a hot cup of tea.'

" Tea "—now she was hurt—" did you say tea? Have you no ideas for a wet afternoon besides ploughing up eighty acres of raw, bleeding earth and then drinking tea? "

" Well," Phillip for once looked human and forgivable, " what did you think of doing? I know you're tired," he had a faintly enjoyable feeling of contrition towards her; she was so wet, so cross, and still so pretty. " But you know you did say you wanted a real, practical farmer's day—the sort Veronica does on her head."

" I don't care what part of her she does it on."

" Don't let's be childish," Phillip said. " You look like tears before night. Shall we try and make some tea? Everybody's out."

" Tea? " She was really desperate: " A stiff drink might still pull the day together."

" You know quite well," Phillip said with miserable patience, " that I've closed down on the drink."

She faced him. Through this denial of so little a thing, so human a thing, so necessary a thing as a drink after this day of cold and exhaustion, she recognised an asceticism which was an insult to all the teeming life in her. Her honest anger was justified: " How can you be so mean and pompous? "

He did not answer but retired maddeningly, almost unconsciously into his good public school shell of embarrassment and disdain. A monstrous obstinacy forbade this drink. But the situation was as he said. There was by his order no drink in the house. It was part of the monastic rule—the great division between yesterday and today.

In his silence her temper really went: " I will say we've had quite a day together and I mean it. Up to our knees in manure and surrounded by enormous horses—not an instant's relaxation. Not a moment's respite. Not a drink. Not a word spoken except to those horses."

" Don't you like horses? " he asked with unforgivable amusement.

She stared at him. He was never to know how near she was to an outpouring of terrible tears. And she was never to know how nearly he was turning to her if her day's awkward stoicism, her silence, her obedience had held out but an hour longer. Mercifully they were delivered from each other by Dorothy who came in blindly in her great tortoiseshell reading glasses, chin down on top of the armful of books and *gros-point*. She had taken no exercise and was full of the day's acid, longing for a cup of tea and a game of bridge or bezique or backgammon, and, oh God! for warmth.

"Rang my bell twenty times. House is like the dead. I really don't think I can bear it much longer. Oh, ducks, help me, will you? *Aren't* you wet? What have you been up to all day long? Anything nice to tell me? Wet days do have their moments, I always have found."

She looked archly over the top of her glasses, but Phillip had gone. Only Yvonne stood there holding her soaking pixie in her hands: tears melting, running to nothing more quickly on her face still wet from rain. Quite suddenly Dorothy felt very angry, entirely and really angry with this boy who could dare to pass by her child with this air, this lightness, this silence, this monstrous absorption in his own background. His disregard was as animal and indifferent as that of a horse, bred to win or lose thousands, bred to be bought or sold. Two cold days ago she had looked on this indifference as valuable because of its effect on Yvonne. Now, suddenly it was the last insult—on top of yesterday's terrible scene with Aunt Anna Rose (she was still craning round to get a view of that bruise, in the mildewed cheval glass in her bedroom); on top of an extra cold night with her electric pad out of action and a day of entire boredom—Eustace gone on some extraordinary rampage, giving Veronica a treat in the rain, as far as she could gather—a day on which she had just sustained the luncheon because she understood that Yvonne was eating sandwiches in a cosy hayloft. As the climax to all this her child came back to her cold, wet, and in an hysteria of disappointed love. She looked from the unhappy child to the fire (smouldering to its usual extinction) and the executive in her snapped suddenly to life. No more of this. Why should such ridiculous suffering continue an hour longer. Others besides Aunt Anna Rose could take trains and aeroplanes at the drop of a hat. There were such things as cutting your losses; there were such pleasures as insulting your hosts: " Don't let's discuss the thing at all, love." She put her chin down on the pile of books and tapestry and cigarette boxes and turned from the door. " Let's get out. They're all *monstrous*——"

As Yvonne crossed over to the fire, her sorrow blurred by the thought of action, Hercules and Consuelo came into the room, dripping like sad sea monsters and looking anxiously over their wet shoulders at the kind taxi driver who followed them solicitously, carrying race glasses and shooting sticks. He looked anxious, too, and knew only too well that his place was not exactly the drawing-room. He hesitated with beautiful manners and patience on the edge of whatever he meant to do.

" Thank you, thank you," there was a despairing note in the rich pitch of Consuelo's voice, " put everything down there, please, and don't let us delay you."

" Here you are, my boy, I know you're in a hurry," Hercules pressed half a crown into his hand, " don't delay a moment."

The taxi driver stood firm: " Thank you, sir," he put the matter of the tip politely aside, " you'll excuse me and beg pardon, but my fare is thirty shillings."

" Yes, yes," Consuelo agreed largely, " send the account on as usual."

" Well, I could of course, but "—he paused and found the exquisite reason for holding out on them: " I'm about buying a ferret tonight and I'd need a little help."

" Oh, *never* buy a ferret at this time of year, fatal—

fatal." Hercules was enchanted to proffer this genuine piece of free advice. " Here, look here, I say, tell you wot, have a cigarette and pop off quick."

" Well, sir," this was considered at length, " I'm gassed up with smoking. It makes me very bronchial and it plays hell with my tubes, still "—he would never be ungracious—" I'll have one—dat's definite—I'll chance one."

Hercules opened his case sadly: " Haven't a match, I'm afraid." He got his man turned round towards the door. Another pause while Consuelo's blood raced dangerously and the driver went through his pockets: " I haven't one, either, and I generally always have them threw loose in my pocket isn't dat a funny thing? " he appealed to them gently.

" Very, very, do hurry "—Consuelo's panic was perceptible to Dorothy. She approached the driver, looking blindly up at him through her reading glasses. " Try my lighter." There was some delay in finding this, too. " Oh," she rasped the wheel backwards and forwards with her excessively manicured thumb, " it won't work either."

She was a gift to the dear chap as she stood gazing blindly from the lighter to him. All his charm and tender care for ladies was uppermost as he took it from her, and his gratitude. For she had given him another reason to delay. " I'll fix it for you, ma'am. Have y'a pin? "

" Now, please don't delay him, please, please." Hercules was getting frantic.

" No hurry. No hurry at all—not the least in the world. Sure time—time is for slaves. Is this the pin? " He pondered over the lighter. He poked it. He whirred the wheel with his thumb. He brooded. " Ah, we have it." The air held an ambience of relief and victory. "We haven't." The ambience fell from the air—"we have—we haven't. Never mind. We're not beat yet. Have y'a hair-pin?"

"Only a grip."

They were as one: "Is it a curly grip?"

"It is."

He accepted it with reservation: "Well, it is and it isn't. But it's a poor workman complains." His head was down and he was picking up the whole machine, slowly, delightedly.

"Mrs. Thomas, Mrs. Cleghorne-Thomas," it was the boom of sorrow, of water in a sea cave—"You can't realise that this poor man is in a great hurry to be off and we are paying for his time."

"No," Dorothy was going to hold her moment now that she knew she could make trouble for these horrid old people, "I can't." It was insulting and included the idea of their paying for anything.

"Excuse and pardon the liberty"—the taxi driver looked up from his delicate pick-axeing of the lighter—"but I can't go till I get my thirty bob. Sir Phillip gave orders there was to be no accounts run in the garage under no circumstances from no one. Such an awkward class of an order, but I'll have to see himself about it."

"Very, very tiresome," Consuelo raised her jaw and swayed her neck, "because Sir Phillip's away."

"Oo, wot a whopper. He's been tearing up the ground all day long with a plough." Yvonne was into the trouble at once.

"Righto! Oh, righto; oh, I'll be without in the car, so. Oh—I'll take the little yoke, ma'am"—he bowed—"to amuse myself—no charge—no." He got himself out of the room and the situation with quite extraordinary charm.

Dorothy gazed happily at Consuelo and Hercules: " And how did your day go? Out in the rain, I see. Backing all the winners, I suppose? "

" Well, you suppose wrong." Consuelo was almost biting her fingers off at the awkward turn of events.

" And my feet are soaking." Hercules tried to get as near the fire as Yvonne, who was crouched miserably inside the grate. " Please may I——"

" I'm wet too "—Yvonne did not yield an inch.

" The child's shivering. And we're paying a great deal for smoke without fire in this house."

" Then my advice to you would be leave this house tonight. There's always room for two more passengers on the mail boat." Consuelo was angrier than usual.

" Mrs. Howard, I've often wondered since I came here how the myth of Irish hospitality started."

" Oh, my poor feet," Hercules bellowed suddenly, " I don't know if I've got any. Why couldn't Bridgid find my gummers today of all days. Where is she now? " He crouched himself together and shouted " Bridgid! I can feel pneumonia settin' in—LOOK OUT "—he sneezed so suddenly and terribly that Yvonne jumped out of the grate and out of his way. " Ah, that's better." He was a little comforted and considered the wet girl more happily: " You look a miserable object. Had a serious day's farming? "

" Farming's over," Yvonne said quite politely.

They could really have left it at that.

" You're very wet," Consuelo looked her over, too. " Why didn't you sit indoors with the gestation tables? " The implication was crystal clear.

" The answer to that one is that I'm *sick* of the gestation tables." Yvonne spoke bravely enough but turned her head to Dorothy. " Mummy? "

" Yes, darling, I know—our packing. Let's get at it and we'll wire Harry to meet us at Claridges tomorrow, what do you think? Mightn't it be fun? He may not be in the Stud book but he's a sweet, cosy chap. . . ." It was the abandon of mother love talking, protective, suggestive, promising comfort to the hurt child. Be a brave girl and don't cry about your cut knee: well, before you're twice married. This may smart a little, darling, but it's going to make you better. . . .

Hercules and Consuelo looked at them as one looking at an unknown ship putting out to sea. They looked from their own point of trouble. If the ship had been sinking, Hercules and Consuelo would hardly have been able to take in the disaster because of the discomfort the storm caused to themselves. So now they said, just before they were left alone:

" Send Bridgid along if you see her."

" Tell Mrs. Guidera we're ready for tea—*more* than ready for tea."

" You don't know where Mrs. Guidera and Bridgid are? " Dorothy felt she deserved this treat. She had been waiting for it.

" No."

" Gone racing——" Dorothy sailed out.

"——With Uncle Eustace——" Yvonne followed her.

Hercules and Consuelo stared at one another, really devastated. Consuelo dropped her head and shook it once: " I can believe it of Bridgid, Tots."

" I was always afraid Mrs. Guidera would hot you one day."

" You're jealous."

" No. You're jealous."

" Oh," Consuelo's voice reared itself up above trivialities, " don't let's start quarrelling about Bridgid and Mrs. Guidera. Aren't we properly souped today, without that? "

" Oh, crumbs. If only we hadn't. We are in a jam now. We're in a *dreadful* pickle."

" Well, the bookmakers will wait." That defeat was too immense to discuss. " If only that torture of a man would take his taxi away before Phil meets him. It's then we're for it, dear. Absolutely no question we're for it."

Hercules cocked his head like a listening bird: " Car's gone."

" *Can't* have—can't be true." Relief welled in them to sink in a salty tide as Eustace and Veronica came in.

Full of champagne and absurd confidence, Veronica swept up the room. She seemed to fill the clothes with happiness. She managed her skirts as prettily as a pigeon its feathers. The little boot heels clicked. She was like a little girl intoxicated with the Christmas tree and the music of the waltz. She was touchingly happy.

" How d'you like me, Mother? " She was saucy, too, for all her friends had laughed at the immense joke all day as she sat in the bar and had a great champagne party. It was fun. They were enchanted. They had praised her and seen her as amusing, as pretty, as important, for the first time. For after every race there was more and more wine to drink.

And now, when Consuelo answered, " Actually—not much," Veronica laughed out loud and held Eustace by the hand.

" You've been drinking, too," Consuelo sniffed.

" Yes."

" Lucky thing," Hercules pouted. " Drinkin' champagne all day long in the bar, I s'pose, while your poor old uncle was backing losers in the rain."

" Well, we backed every winner and Bridgid got the Tote Double."

" Disgraceful," Hercules almost whimpered.

" If you can take in the suggestion, my dear," Consuelo spoke from some far off disgusted place where only aristos go, " I should change out of that little musical comedy number before Aunt Anna Rose gets back. I happen to recognise it from the photograph as her going-away dress, and I think she may find this—er—prank—rather —er—poor—er—taste."

Veronica reeled prettily and gave a sharp hiccup. Consuelo, for the first time in life as she faced her daughter, faltered. For the first time her daughter just faintly resembled herself.

" Lucky me," Eustace skated by every issue, " such a day out with the Rose of Dublin—not to mention Bridgid."

" How dare you mention Bridgid? " Hercules was really in a state.

" Very well, I won't mention Bridgid." Eustace had never quite got himself into a blessed condition of patience and enjoyment about Hercules. For instance, at the moment he did not see why his own numbed feet should not have a little warm up at the fire. " I won't say another word about our day," he promised, " if I may just get my poor old feet near the fire. . . ."

Then it happened. Hercules saw his gumboots on

the stranger's feet. The implication, though dreadful, was not complete.

" Feet? " he said, " feet? By God, sir, it's you, sir." He was so shocked as to be delighted at the felony. " How did you get them? Bridgid keeps them for me herself in the bottom shelf of the hot-air cupboard with me hotsy totsy socksies. Pinch another man's only gummers on a wet day, too. It's a cad's trick—I wouldn't do a thing like that myself, sir, really I wouldn't. Whippin' off to the races in my boots. It's what I said—there won't be a biscuit or a pheasant left in the place soon."

Eustace was slightly exasperated by such nonsense. " I haven't as it happens held a gun or a bag of biscuits in my hand since I came here. As for the boots, I really couldn't know they were your property—Bridgid very kindly lent them to me. She said wet feet would be bad for my ears."

As disaster sometimes goes like clockwork, Bridgid at this moment came in with the tea things.

" Didn't you say wet feet would be bad for my ears, Bridgid? "

" You never lent him my gummers, did you, Beebee? " Hercules swallowed before and after he spoke and Bridgid's heart really felt torn across. What had she done?

" Oh, holy mother, guide me between ye." She put down the tray and stood appalled before her favourites.

" Oh, Beebee, I believe you did—and you gave me so many rows for splashin' in the puddles too. I can't have any fun any more and it's not fair."

Eustace said inexcusably because the drama fascinated him: " You were thinking of my ears."

" Mend you for a fool "—Hercules flew at Bridgid then

like a dog: " What do you want meddlin' his ears, you old fairy? Why d'you let her, anyway? " he whirled on Eustace, " you'll only end up stone deaf."

" Stone deaf? How dare you, Master Hercules? " All Bridgid's natural courage came back at this attack on her healing powers. " Me that walked five miles for a herbal blister at the right turn of the moon, I don't want my work spoiled by a chill on his liver, do I? "

But Hercules was outside reason: " What's his liver got to do with his ears? Haven't you enough to do to look after *my* health? "

" I have you only too well. I can't knock any little thrill out of curing you of anything at all." She was finding a way out. They would not have it.

" I'm not a *bit* well," Hercules objected, " I'm sneezin' —sent off racing without my gummers."

" But I've had no ear trouble for three whole days." Eustace bunched his fingers and kissed them in Bridgid's direction: " And you made novenas for my ear, too. You spoil me. You spoil me."

" I thought you only made novenas for my gout." Hercules' voice had grown very small. " Nothing's the same. Second best is good enough for me. Boots snatched off me feet—biscuit supply halved, and "—he snatched a breath of real pain—" *now* I know where my own little woolly bedshawl's gone too——"

"——It's gone to the wash," she cried in vain.

" *Did* you give it to him, Beebee? "

" I never liked you in it, Master Hercules." There were tears in her eyes now. " It made you look so babyish."

It was then that Phillip came in with a basket of eggs in his hand and rather a desperate look in his eyes. He hated hens; he was still wet and very tired. "I've done the trap-nests," he said drearily. Then he saw Veronica: "My dear—are you all right?"

"Oh," Veronica's lovely confidence went down into the heels of her silly boots, "I *know*—don't say it—you needn't."

He looked at her—even the wilting of shyness which changed her prettiness as a child's can fade and glow from moment to moment, could not change her back into the one he knew. She had become a character—a character of which he could not guess the word or the letter. What was it all about? He felt heavy and sad and very far away from his friend. He had heard she was back and hurried in to ask her about the newly-calved cow which had a funny look, didn't look too good, he didn't think, and now he stood before her and could not ask her about the cow. It was his first step away from her in strangeness. For the first time and so entirely she had stepped apart from his life and up into a little life of her own, to which an approach must be made. This morning it had angered him. Tonight he felt afraid. The thing was too fantastic. She saw that he did not understand, and for the first time did not take her for granted.

With the sudden realisation that the power was hers, a quickening ran through her, a physical current of glory that carried her up and out of the power of love, that terrible destructor of the personality. It was as though she breathed in another air. She took a breath of this different air and looking at him out of her new face, her new eyes, she asked: "How's our cow?"

He told her: went on and on telling her, so that he could feel the relief of her presence, make it tangible to himself again through all the strangeness, reassure himself of her. He could feel there was trouble all round him in the room. He suspected everyone. But he only wanted to feel sure of himself and Veronica. He ignored them and through the mask of the cow's condition he said to her apart: "You must never ever behave like today again."

"You mean——?"

"Don't leave me to battle it out."

Her heart was seized and lifted up in the words, and yet she would not let herself take a wrong meaning. Never believe it, she said to herself, don't fool yourself, stay where you are. It was partly champagne, of course, and the echo of her afternoon's success, but she found she could say out loud to them all in answer to her darling's confidence:

"I must go—I must take my chance—I've been offered a very, very good job. Eustace wants me for his secretary."

"You *can't* do this——" Phillip said. They were the focus now for all in the room—breath was drawn in sharply to attend.

Eustace spoke very softly: "My dear boy—think of her first. Try putting her a long way first. . . ."

Consuelo sailed with majestical foolishness into the silence: "Now, Phillip, perhaps you see what happens when you let in the gipsies."

Eustace who had shot his arrow in the air was the first to seize on this relief.

"Be fair now," he glinted at her, "we don't exactly pinch the spoons."

"You've pinched my Beebee," Hercules reminded him. "That's a good start."

" 'Tis a lie." Bridgid denied the thing.

" Yes," Hercules pressed on, " and my own little bed-shawl too."

" 'Tis a nasty lie—oh, such rude, dirty talk." She bent in despair over the arrangement of her tea things.

Hercules turned from her, bunched in sad resignation: " Don't care if I never see me boots or me biscuits or me little shawl again—I'm feelin' very dicky—very dicky, yes, I'm . . ." He produced another terrible sneezing fit.

Against the barrage, Phillip said: " So you're leaving me, Veronica? "

" You won't be alone, will you? "

He stared at her. Her meaning was quite clear to him. Before he could answer, Consuelo, with her talent for overhearing all conversations and a sure touch on the wrong note, said: " You'll have me, my darling boy. Toujours là—toujours——" She was stopped by a cry from Hercules:

" Oh, I do feel dicky, I do feel dicky now. The heart —the old heart——"

Like a great cat she was up and across the room to him. Together she and Bridgid caught him as he swayed. When the taxi driver, who had hovered embarrassedly in the doorway, advanced towards Phillip, Hercules fainted dead away.

" Thanks be to God," Bridgid laid him quietly down, " he's ill at last. Would it be a tiny stroke, I wonder? "

Everybody, including the taxi driver, crowded round Hercules. It was a street accident, a drama. They loosened his tie; they put a cushion under his head; they listened to his murmured breath; they heard him whisper, " Brandy, brandy." And as they flew off to procure it, Phillip, Eustace and Veronica, he rolled his head and moaned a little.

" What's that he says? " The taxi driver put his hands on his knees and bent down towards him, again helpfully in the picture. Hercules sat up as straight as a tin soldier. " Have they gone? "

" Lie down, darling," Consuelo implored him.

" I'm all right, Pets. Beebee, is it true you had the double? "

" Oh, I did, I did. I don't rightly understand it, but I had the two legs and twenty pounds."

" Lend us thirty shillings till tomorrow, old gal."

" Thank God—you're yourself again." With tears she produced the notes from some mysterious cleavage in her dress.

" Make it two pounds," Consuelo had the true instinct for the moment, " it's easier to remember." Nobody questioned the perfect reasoning of this suggestion.

" Here you are now "—Hercules paid over thirty shillings to the taxi driver. " Off you hop. You'll miss your ferret."

" I'll not. I'll not." He was entranced, he could not go. " Is that a fact you had the double? " he asked Bridgid.

" *Will* you go," Hercules implored him.

" Well, to get the double beats the devil." The taxi driver still hovered, pondering on this miracle. " Doesn't that beat the devil? " He wandered out of the room.

" Lie down, darling," Consuelo patted the cushions of the sofa, " we may as well have this nip of brandy. Personally, I think pneumonia's settin' in."

" You had the heart across me," Bridgid assured her rogue. " Well, for cleverality and cuteology—and look at the age of it—God bless it." This piece of fooling had reinstated him always first in her affections. She was with him in the deception. She was all his again.

He pooh-poohed their praise and laughter: "Oh, it's nothing—old brain still tickin' over. . . . Just catch 'em napping . . . get up on the inside. . . ." He snuggled down as Eustace came in with his flask, but sat up as he saw that great innocent again behind: "My God—my God——"

"I nearly forgot de little job for de lady." The taxi driver put the cigarette lighter down on a table. "It turned out a nice little job too, dat's definite. Wait now till I show you de trick of it—it's simple."

"For heaven's sake, my dear man——" Hercules turned quite a colour and the taxi driver peered at him distressfully:

"Don't excite yourself, sir, don't excite yourself. I had a cousin once got a little strokey ting, a nasty sort of a tiny ting and de doctors could do nutting for him. Nutting—nutting. Only 'no excitement,' 'keep cool,' 'take it easy.' "

Dorothy came pouncing in dressed in her beautiful coat, jewel case in hand. "Ah," she grabbed the taxi driver as one might the only taxi with a flag up on a wet day in Regent Street, "still here—thank God. You can take us to the station."

"Well, isn't dat a funny ting, and I only came back to leave de little yoke. Fate now, you may say Fate is great, you can't cod Fate."

"That's right, you can't cod Fate." Hercules swung with the tide of happenings. "You're their taxi, remember. Nothing to do with me. Have a sip, Pets—do you good. . . ." Together they relaxed in the arms of fate, fortified on Eustace's brandy.

Dorothy, assured of her transport, turned to Eustace. "You're coming too," she said, "the child's packing for you now."

"No, no," he shook his head. "I'm not—I'm staying here."

"My dear," Dorothy touched his arm with her gloved hand, "you're bewitched."

"Yes." He put her hand in his arm; he was very fond of her. "Enchanted and possessed—two curious states at my age."

"I'm afraid for you. Why must you stay?"

"There's a kind of a magic. That's the only way I can put it. You brought me here, dear, and here you'll leave me, thank you very much—I know when to settle for happiness—ah"—he turned round, feeling that stir of life, that drama, that fullness of the air which filled the moment like a breeze behind a sail—Miss Anna Rose was returning. Willy attended her. Bridgid ran forward to greet her: "Look who's home again! Miss Anna Rose, are you perished? And did you enjoy the Jungle Queen?"

"No, dear," Aunt Anna Rose stood rather crossly in the room, "I didn't—most disappointing afternoon. That Jungle Queen's a terrible prude. *Enfin, c'est possible qu'elle est vierge.* I'll keep me hat on, Willy—just take Tito's veil off and we'll pop into our nest. We weren't amused were we, Tito? and we're rarver cold."

Eustace stepped across the room to stand between Aunt Anna Rose and the door of her chair. She was not going to escape to nowhere and back. Now or nevermore he'd put this idea of his to the test. He had the feeling that all the stars and cards and omens in the gamble and chance of life were for him now.

" My sister is leaving us, Miss Anna Rose," he said, " can you wait a moment while she says good-bye, and my niece, too, will want to say good-bye. Because they're never coming back."

" Ah "—she lit up. " I'm afraid you'll have a choppy crossing tonight er—Mrs.—er. The wind's gettin' up nicely." She dwelt on the thought with pleasure. Actual journeying gave her great pleasure, especially if it was likely to be difficult. " Mark all your reservations, you'll need them—mention my name to the steward at Waterford and ask for Cabin twenty-four, it's the stateroom. He always gives it to me. Just slip him ten shillings and he'll look after you—such a nice man. And when you get to the other side tell the guard you've been staying at Ballyroden, he'll remember me."

" Really, how interesting. Remarkable man he must be. I always understood you hadn't left Ballyroden for fifty years." Inexcusable to the last, Dorothy stood there in her smart, expensive clothes and said that to the old lady. But she was frightened at Eustace's bewitchment and defection and all patience with these mad Irish had suddenly fled.

It was as the people in the room sucked in together a whispering breath of dismay on this announcement and before Aunt Anna Rose could reply, that Veronica came whistling into the room, flushed with excitement and wearing the very dress and hat which Aunt Anna Rose had worn on her last actual earthly journey.

But Aunt Anna Rose gave a great cry when she saw her: " What are you doing in my dress, little What's your name? Take it off, do you hear. Put it away.

How dare you? Do you want to remind people? Do you want them to know? Oh——" Suddenly, like a child, a child afraid in the dark, deeply afraid, she turned —not to her own family but to Eustace. "I couldn't help it," she lifted up her lovely face, "it was an accident. You believe me?"

"Look at her, Miss Anna Rose," Eustace took her hands in their pretty gloves in his and turned her towards Veronica again. He was inexorable.

"Look at your lovely youth," he insisted quietly. "Shut out fear. There is nothing to be afraid of—only remember if you can the day you wore this dress, and you will remember, I promise you, you will remember what you did with your rubies that day."

"I can't." She turned from the room, her face towards his shoulder. "Don't make me."

"You can," he insisted and such strength was in his conviction that they all stood round spellbound, impillared in the tension of the moment. "Look—look at your lovely youth."

"Oh." She stared at Veronica, at Phillip, who was behind Veronica now. She held Eustace's hand, swinging it quietly like a child does who is given a grown-up's hand, and she looked through and past them all before she said in rather a lost, hopeless little voice: "They are somewhere in this room—that's all I know. Somewhere in this room with me—I'm sure."

"Oh, but where"—Eustace pressed her—"where in this room?"

Suddenly she was a little fierce at all the annoyance. A cold tired old lady again, or as near to it as she would ever be. She made a movement away from him, dropping his hand: " I don't know. Find 'em yourselves. Don't worry me. Let me get into my nest."

The moment was going, the moment was passing. Magic fell from the air. No one could save the moment that held all hope—held it as a sieve holds bright water. Eustace had put out all his strength. It was not enough.

Veronica, gentle, cosy, loving, inspired, stopped the passing magic: " Phil," she said modestly, not sure if she was being very clever or very silly—" d'you remember how we found the lost bottle of champagne? "

" Yes "—he saw the incredible possibility, the chance in a million. " Aunt Anna Rose—darling—stay with us a minute. Shall we play hunt the thimble for the rubies? "

It was the silliness and warmth of the idea, the escape from those lost lands and dreadful places that flooded Aunt Anna Rose's mind with peace like light in a nursery: " Yes, yes. That might be nice. That might be very nice. That might warm me up." She sat down, squeezing up her eyes as if she were an honest child at a party.

The immense charade started, whirling round her like figures in a carnival. No one questioned the importance of the mad idea. It was too immense in its lunacy. They all took part. Dorothy, the taxi driver, Eustace, Hercules, Consuelo, Bridgid, Phillip and Veronica swept about the room; shouting, suggesting, abandoning hope; all going faster, wilder, as she cried: " Cold. *Cold.* And colder still."

" God Almighty, wot a gamble," Hercules gave best to nobody, " are they in the Chinese po? "

" Cold."

" Holy Saint Antony," Bridgid invoked the great finder of lost things—" would they be in the chimney? "

" Cold."

" I'm silly, I know," Dorothy stopped before a suit of Japanese armour, " just an idea. I've got a hunch—could they be inside this ghastly man? "

" Warmer, warmer," Aunt Anna Rose cried unexpectedly, " they're inside something."

" What about the elephant's thingummy? " Dorothy was really roused by her successful shot over the armour.

" Mother," Yvonne came in and staggered at the performance going on. " What are you doing—you'll be as potty as the rest of them. Come on driver—the luggage is all ready."

" Wait now one minute," he implored her, " I *love* hunt de timble. I have it, I have it—couldn't it be in de instrument? " He picked up the telephone which rang and rang and rang across the tumult.

" Mum, come on—we'll miss this train. Please, Mum, be sane," Yvonne was really anxious.

" All right, darling." Dorothy had been raised out of all bad temper. " Oh, but it's agony to stop. Good-bye Miss Anna Rose, Good-bye Phillip, Good-bye little Deirdre of the Sorrows "—as Dorothy took Veronica's hand in hers, Aunt Anna Rose gave a great shout—" She's hot! " It was so true that it was rather frightening.

" My God! " Dorothy dropped the hand. " You're as hot as fire."

" Am I hot now? Tell me, Aunt Anna Rose," Phillip took both Veronica's hands in his.

" Oo, burnin', burnin', don't touch her. Now I remember. We sewed them in—that was it—we sewed them in."

" Where? " Their voices lifted together. They were like hounds on a breast-high scent.

" I don't remember."

" *Mum* . . ." It was a most tiresome whine from Yvonne.

" Darling, don't be such a *bore*," Dorothy was inspired, " I know! Start at her feet and work up."

" Yes, yes." Hercules smacked his lips. " That's the riding of it."

Phillip knelt and took Veronica's foot in his hand.

" Oh, my tiny feet "—Aunt Anna Rose saw them again, those pretty little boots, after all the years. " Never——"

" Rolled in your stocking tops? " Dorothy insisted.

" Oh, what pretty legs I had."

" Hadn't you? " Phil said thoughtfully, " Angel legs and I never noticed them before."

" But is he warm? That's the thing," Consuelo boomed.

Aunt Anna Rose shook her head. " Luke. Only luke."

" I know. I know," Consuelo pressed on, " slung on a tape in a leather purse."

" No, no," Aunt Anna Rose denied: " pas bien," she added.

" The muff, Aunt Anna Rose," Phillip put his hand inside the little barrel of sable where Veronica's hands were clenched together.

" Come out, come out," she was wild with excitement. " I'm startin' to tingle."

" So am I, actually." Phillip threw the idea away.

" So am I," they cried, answering one another like hounds' voices getting to cry, " so am I . . . so am I . . ."

" Where next, Miss Anna Rose? " Eustace had his arm in hers. " Where shall I try next? "

Phillip had his hands on Veronica's shoulders: " Let me take off this hat, I can't see you properly."

" In my hat, of course," Aunt Anna Rose said in a

cool, triumphant little voice. " All this fuss about nothing: it was in my hat, I remember quite, quite distinctly—distinctly . . ." Her voice faltered in the second distinctly: " But it's gone," she said miserably, " I'm cold again. The bird has flown."

" My God, I've seen it." Eustace dropped her arm, he could not help himself, and sat down as in Hunt the Thimble one must.

" Where? " cried all the voices.

" In your own hat, Miss Anna Rose—one moment—may Willy give it to me? Look, it's Tito—look. . . . Yes, I'm terribly right. His crop is bulging with them."

" Ah," she breathed, " that was it. Good idea. Good for fifty years. *Very* bien. Gently with my boy," she implored her friend.

They all bent, clustered, gathered like a cloud round her.

Hercules finally said: " Like a pigeon off stubbles. Golly, golly, riches."

Willy said with regretful respect: " Thousands of pounds passing through my hands from hat to hat, day after day. . . ."

Consuelo finished with an air of faint condemnation: " Ah," she breathed, " if darling Roddy had only known——"

Bridgid, pinching too, said: " There wouldn't be one left tonight."

" Pardon me," the taxi driver put forth the gentlest thumb and finger. " Oh, dere's de price of a lot of ferrets in dem—dat's definite."

" May we see them, Aunt Anna Rose? " Veronica asked.

" Yes, darling, of course. They're for you, aren't

they? I remember now. I'm not afraid, am I, Eustace? —help me, there's a little fastening . . ."

From wing to under-wing, little hooks beneath the close grebe held the birdskin together. From the crop and poked up under the bone structure of the wings poured out rubies with diamond daisies set between; reluctantly, catching in their bird, they poured on—more of them and more of them, from small to great and from great central stone to small—finally the clasp, of such beauty as to kill belief.

Dorothy spoke for their worldly value. Rocking on her feet, she knew and spoke:

"Am I seeing things?" she asked. "There's the whole of Cartier's in there."

* * * * *

So she had it. She had her twenty-thousand pounds' worth of independence. It lay cold in the safe, alone in the dark, far from Tito's keeping. They had folded the rubies up in tissue paper—pieces that Bridgid had collected from the Cleghorne-Thomas packing. Phillip and Veronica had locked them away, the long paper parcel awkward and heavy in their hands. It was as if a cold third person had been added to their lives.

The safe was in the pantry. The pantry was icy damp with its clean, wet sinks and draining boards and flagged floor. Its window, of the same height and careful construction as the drawing-room windows, let in the opal winter light; the light seemed to draw itself back into the closing day, its tide leaving unregretfully the high dark cupboards of glass; the old knife cleaning machines; the stacks of empty bottles and tidy little trays set with cups or glasses for milk, and the low dark labyrinths of water-pipes where frogs might breed—the toad, ugly and venomous, bears yet a precious jewel in his head.

Veronica, holding her skirts with both hands just off the floor, felt a dismal association of ideas. The triumph had been won, the great offering was in her hands, yet she found it impossible to say to Phillip: Here they are. They are for you. Suddenly she was a moneyed woman offering him, not an unpaid lifetime of work and love, but simply twenty thousand pounds or so. This was the situation she had created by her obedience to Eustace. For this idea only she had made her fearful, laughable throw in the dark. Should she win, she would hand the rubies over to Phillip and make her little broken-hearted exit from his life, leaving him to his Yvonne and to Ballyroden. But to Ballyroden ransomed by Veronica, not by foreign money. Now, with the way changed and cleared by Yvonne's going, she had not the power or the wits to use her victory. She was entirely held in the pincers of her own success. An old-fashioned rich girl who could not follow her heart.

Phillip did not make anything easier. He talked away, covering her silence: " I'm terribly glad for you, old girl. It straightened everything out—when I think of all your Mother's money my dear old Dad spent."

" Poor Uncle Roddy," she said, " need we scold him any more? "

He suddenly felt angry at her pious little statement. Why should she, who was now secure, ignore their late familiar coalition against the Dead and the Old. Her attitude turned him into the puritan scold of the party.

" I'm more than glad you needn't," he said, " and now I feel free of a big debt towards you."

Two things stood like mountains between them; his own wanton junketing with that great idiot beauty, and Veronica's terrible new solvency. He looked from a distance at her skirts, dropped now in a ring on the floor, falling from the spry new hour-glass figure. He looked at the soft, badly cut hair in her neck, stooped in the dusk and in her silence. He felt afraid of her and beset by all his mistakes about her. Let him at least keep her property free from sentiment, deal with it as the business matter it was—sell it, tie up the proceeds, settle them on her. In this generation let everything be done that was right and strict. And all he could find to say was: I feel free of you. He had not really said that. But in his nervous defence, in that hopeless distance they had drawn away from each other, that was the meaning of what he had said. She was as far off as his own unkindness had put her. And because he had put her away from him by unkindness, he could at last see her plainly and wish for her as a lost thing is clearly perceived and desired.

When, at the end of his adventure and his day, she had come back to him, he had thought it only a matter of putting out a hand to have his friend warm beside him again. But it was not his friend who came back, it was a stranger, needed by other people, admired and petted and laughed at in her daring. He knew fully what it had cost Veronica to wear this crazy fancy dress. It was almost outside possibility that she had done so, as immeasurably unaccountable as it was that, through such bravery, the rubies had gained their reality. The thought of the rubies filled him with a hard calculating dislike—the thought of each thousand pounds they represented as a separate distance between himself and Veronica.

In the icy pantry he was cold. His wet clothes hung

on him like metal. Out of his cold and his exhaustion he had a sudden clear picture of Veronica heaping up a fire with short lengths of laurel wood that she had cut in the shrubberies—Veronica wearing a tweed skirt with a seat in it—not this elegant costume piece which, he thought angrily, she had no business to wear anyhow, the thing might have a curse on it. In cold and tiredness any fear is rational. He saw her too as she had stood an hour ago, with Aunt Anna Rose clipping the fastenings of the rubies round her neck and on her wrists. The rubies and the dress and the tragedy of the past all coloured his picture of her now, filling him with a true sense of changing years and flying happiness. Even his sense of guilt was lost in this fore-knowledge of the cold days that come when youth has finished with its mistakes.

"Veronica," he said as she stood still in her ring of pink cloth, speechlessly hurt by the words he had spoken, "Veronica, I'm so terribly cold and wet."

He had meant to say: I love you. Forgive me. You aren't to mind that I was cruel to you. What's more, I will be again. But you are that single star for me. That only one. I'll leave you and come back, my darling, and you must wait for me always because of my need for you.

The glory of that under-voice was clear to her. It was plainer than a bell. Its certainty lifted her like wings, bearing up her life in that different air which loved women breathe.

THE END

Also by Molly Keane (M. J. Farrell)

YOUNG ENTRY

New Introduction by Diana Petre

At nineteen, Prudence Lingfield-Turrett is carefree and indiscreet much to the frustration of the aged cousins who attempt to keep her unladylike behaviour in check. In two years she will inherit the family wealth and property; in the meantime, whether hunting, fishing, playing with favourite dogs or on the dance floor, Prudence is in pursuit of fun. Her great friend Peter has shared this devil-may-care attitude; since adolescence the two girls have conspired in many a regrettable episode. But with the arrival of Major Anthony Countless, the new master of hounds, Peter seems less interested in their friendship and Prudence must look elsewhere for entertainment . . .

In the delightful *Young Entry*, first published in 1928, Molly Keane shows her affinities with her fellow Irish writers, Somerville & Ross.

Also of interest

THE LAST OF SUMMER

Kate O'Brien

New introduction by Eavan Boland

"What mystifies me still is how an actress from Paris comes strolling in here, of all things, this quiet evening . . . "

It is 1939, the last summer before the outbreak of war. French actress Angèle Maury abandons a groups of friends travelling through Ireland and takes herself to picturesque Drumaninch, birthplace of her dead father. She has come to make sense of her past. Self-conscious with her pale, exotic beauty, Angèle braves the idiosyncratic world of the Kernahans: her enigmatic aunt Hannah, her ridiculous but loveable uncle Corney and her three cousins — Martin, charming, intense, Tom, devoted to his mother, and their bright sister Jo, who combines religious faith with a penchant for gambling.

But is there some mystery surrounding the past? History threatens to repeat itself as Angéle finds herself seduced by the beauty of Ireland, and by the love of two men . . . First published in 1943, *The Last of Summer* is a perfectly structured psychological love story.